BABYMOUSE AND FRIENDS*

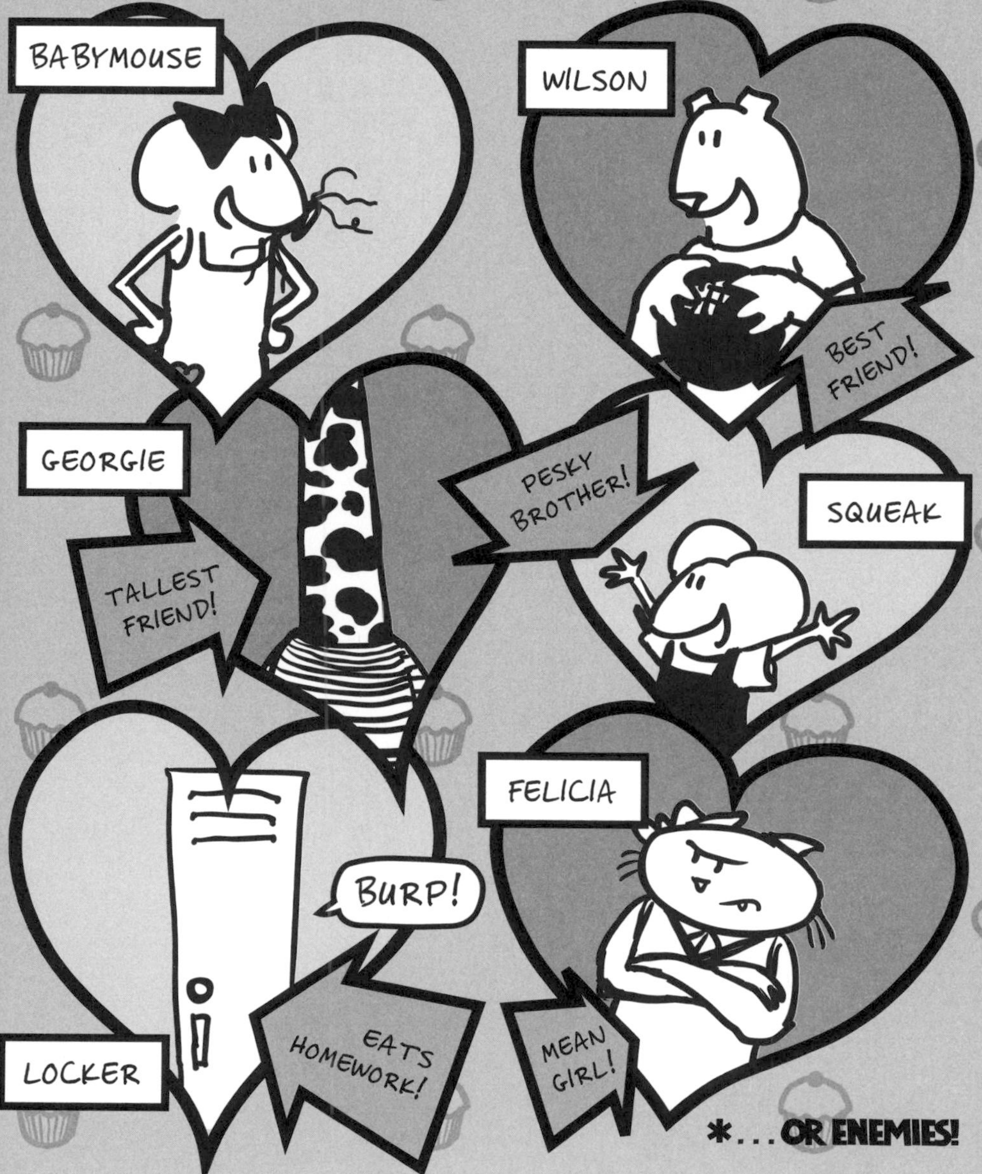
BABYMOUSE
WILSON
BEST FRIEND!
GEORGIE
PESKY BROTHER!
TALLEST FRIEND!
SQUEAK
LOCKER
BURP!
EATS HOMEWORK!
FELICIA
MEAN GIRL!

*. . . OR ENEMIES!

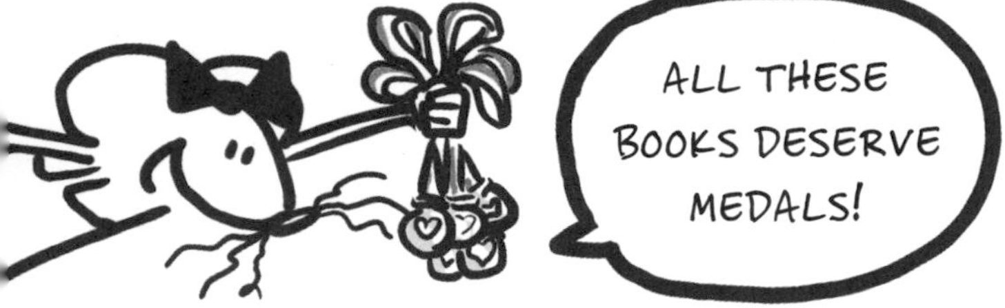
ALL THESE BOOKS DESERVE MEDALS!

BE SURE TO READ **ALL** THE **BABYMOUSE** BOOKS:

#1 BABYMOUSE: QUEEN OF THE WORLD!
#2 BABYMOUSE: OUR HERO
#3 BABYMOUSE: BEACH BABE
#4 BABYMOUSE: ROCK STAR
#5 BABYMOUSE: HEARTBREAKER
#6 CAMP BABYMOUSE
#7 BABYMOUSE: SKATER GIRL
#8 BABYMOUSE: PUPPY LOVE
#9 BABYMOUSE: MONSTER MASH
#10 BABYMOUSE: THE MUSICAL
#11 BABYMOUSE: DRAGONSLAYER
#12 BABYMOUSE: BURNS RUBBER
#13 BABYMOUSE: CUPCAKE TYCOON
#14 BABYMOUSE: MAD SCIENTIST
#15 A VERY BABYMOUSE CHRISTMAS
#16 BABYMOUSE FOR PRESIDENT
#17 EXTREME BABYMOUSE
#18 HAPPY BIRTHDAY, BABYMOUSE
#19 BABYMOUSE: BAD BABYSITTER
#20 BABYMOUSE GOES FOR THE GOLD

BABYMOUSE
GOES FOR THE GOLD

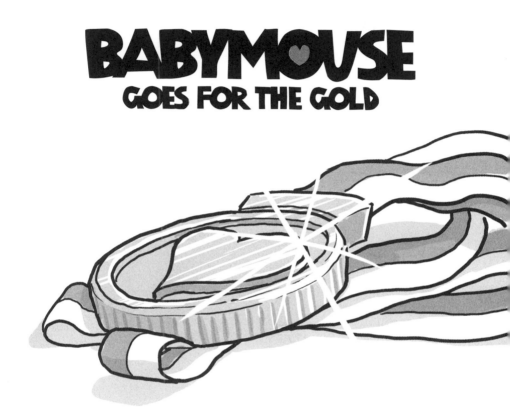

BY JENNIFER L. HOLM & MATTHEW HOLM

RANDOM HOUSE NEW YORK

LET'S DIVE IN!

SPECIAL THANKS TO
JOEY WEISER AND MICHELE CHIDESTER
FOR COLORING ASSISTANCE!

All rights reserved. Published in the United States by Random House Children's Books, a division of Penguin Random House LLC, New York.

Random House and the colophon are registered trademarks of Penguin Random House LLC.

Visit us on the Web!
randomhousekids.com
Babymouse.com

Educators and librarians, for a variety of teaching tools, visit us at
RHTeachersLibrarians.com

Library of Congress Cataloging-in-Publication Data is available upon request.

ISBN 978-0-307-93163-4 (trade) — ISBN 978-0-375-97099-3 (lib. bdg.) —
ISBN 978-0-307-97546-1 (ebook)

MANUFACTURED IN MALAYSIA   10 9 8 7 6 5 4 3   First Edition

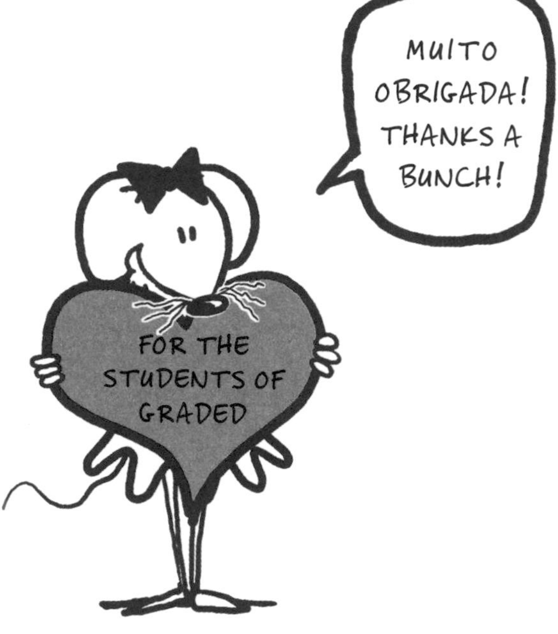
MUITO OBRIGADA! THANKS A BUNCH!
FOR THE STUDENTS OF GRADED

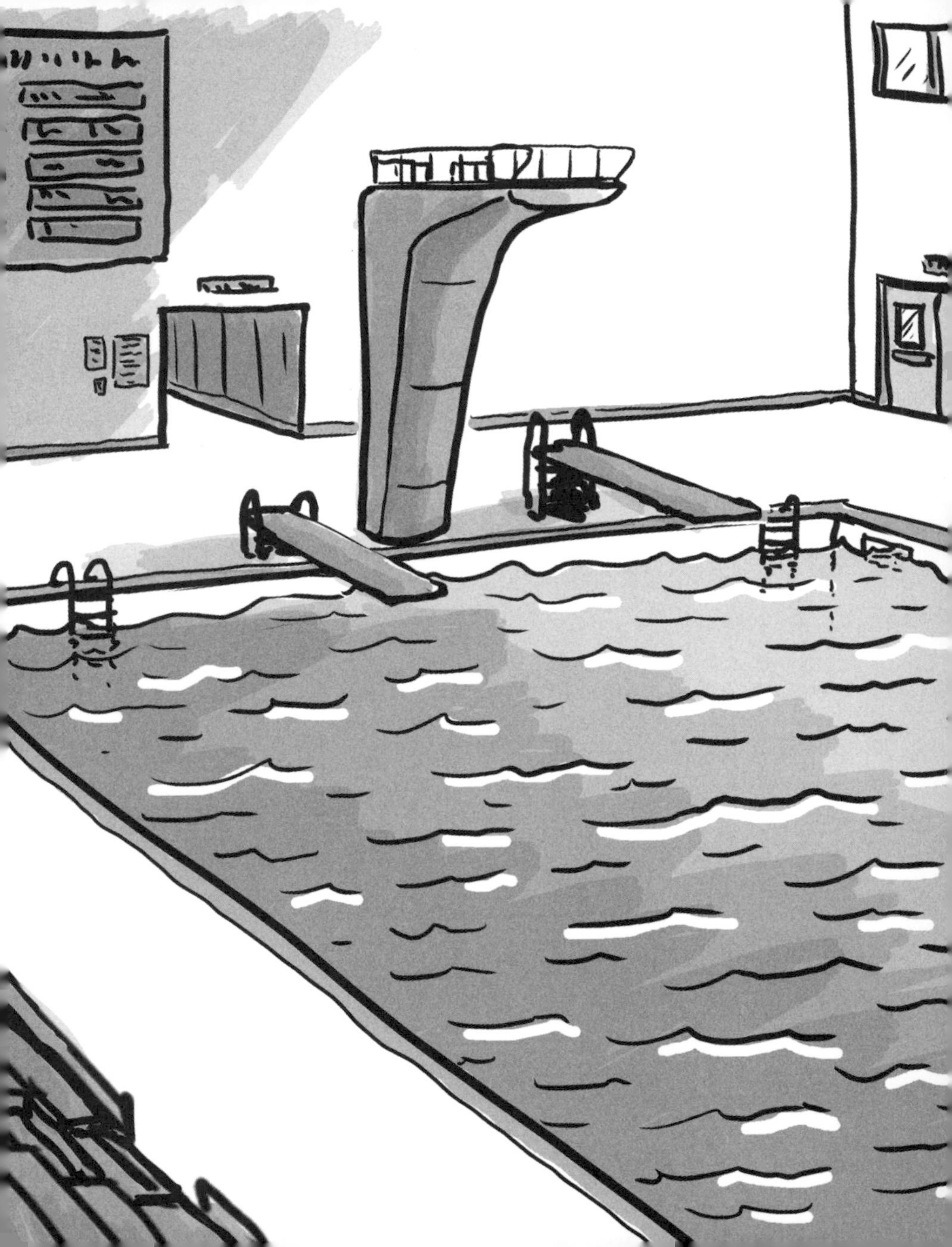

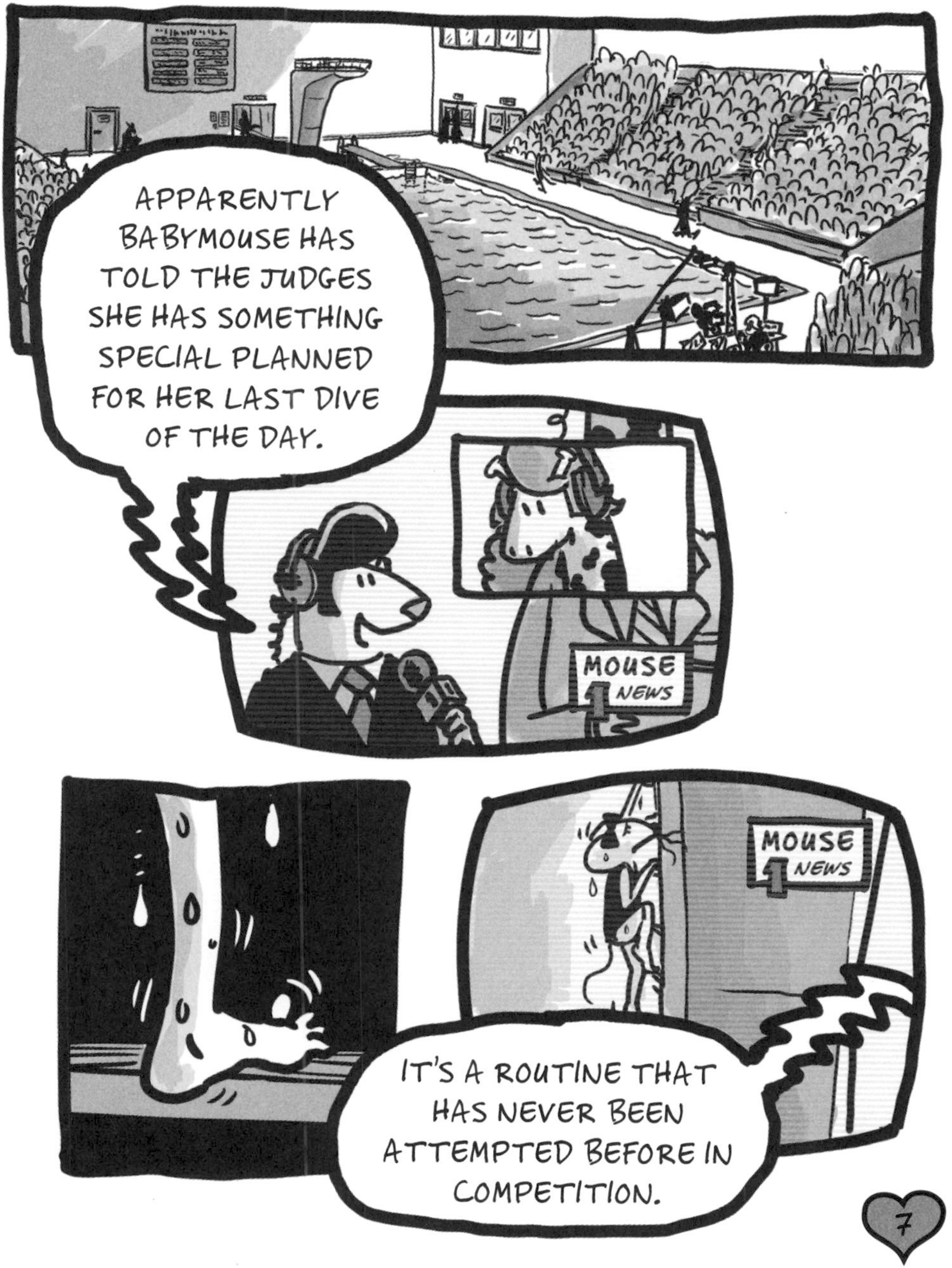
APPARENTLY BABYMOUSE HAS TOLD THE JUDGES SHE HAS SOMETHING SPECIAL PLANNED FOR HER LAST DIVE OF THE DAY.
MOUSE 1 NEWS
MOUSE 1 NEWS
IT'S A ROUTINE THAT HAS NEVER BEEN ATTEMPTED BEFORE IN COMPETITION.

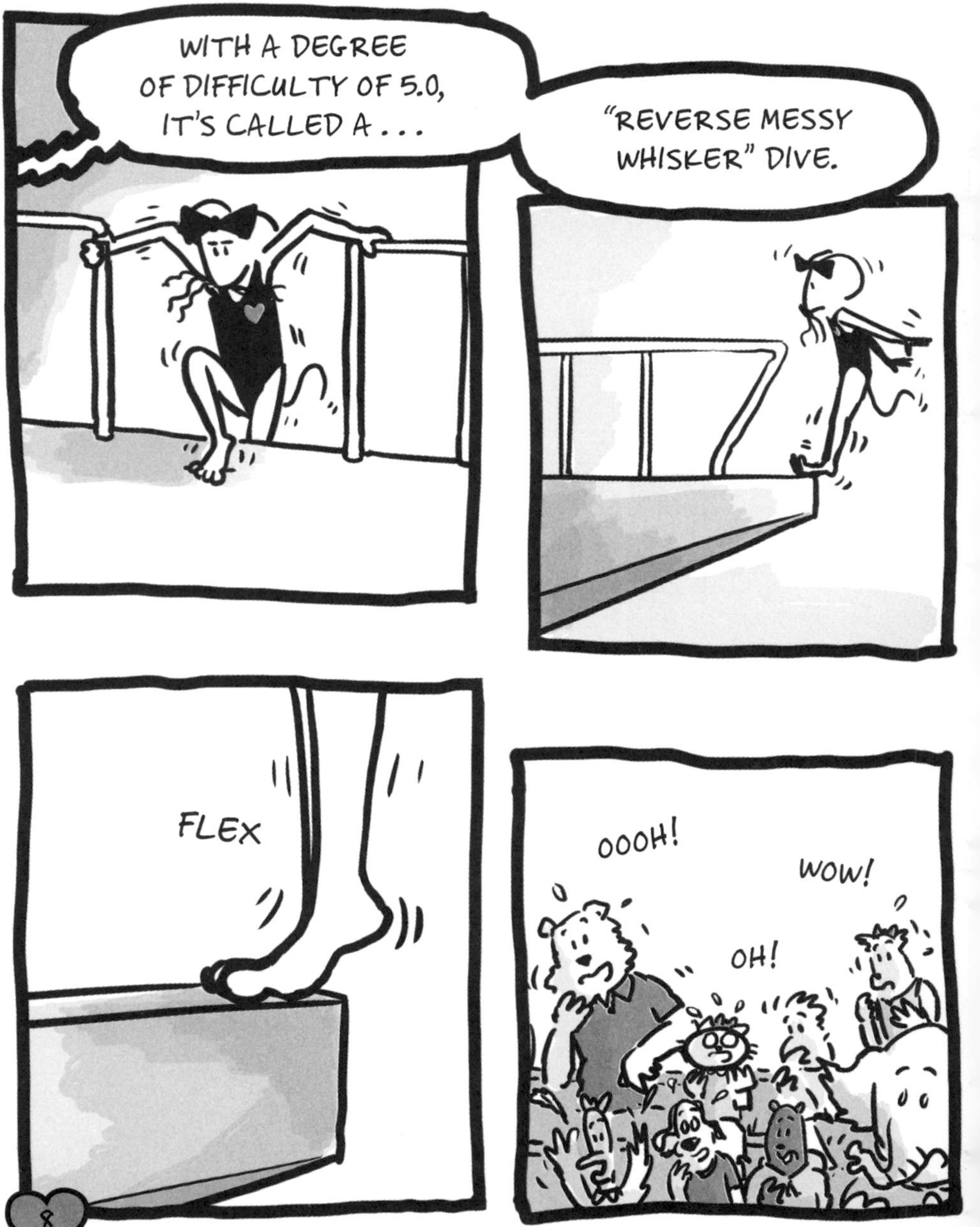
WITH A DEGREE OF DIFFICULTY OF 5.0, IT'S CALLED A . . .
"REVERSE MESSY WHISKER" DIVE.
FLEX
OOOH!
WOW!
OH!

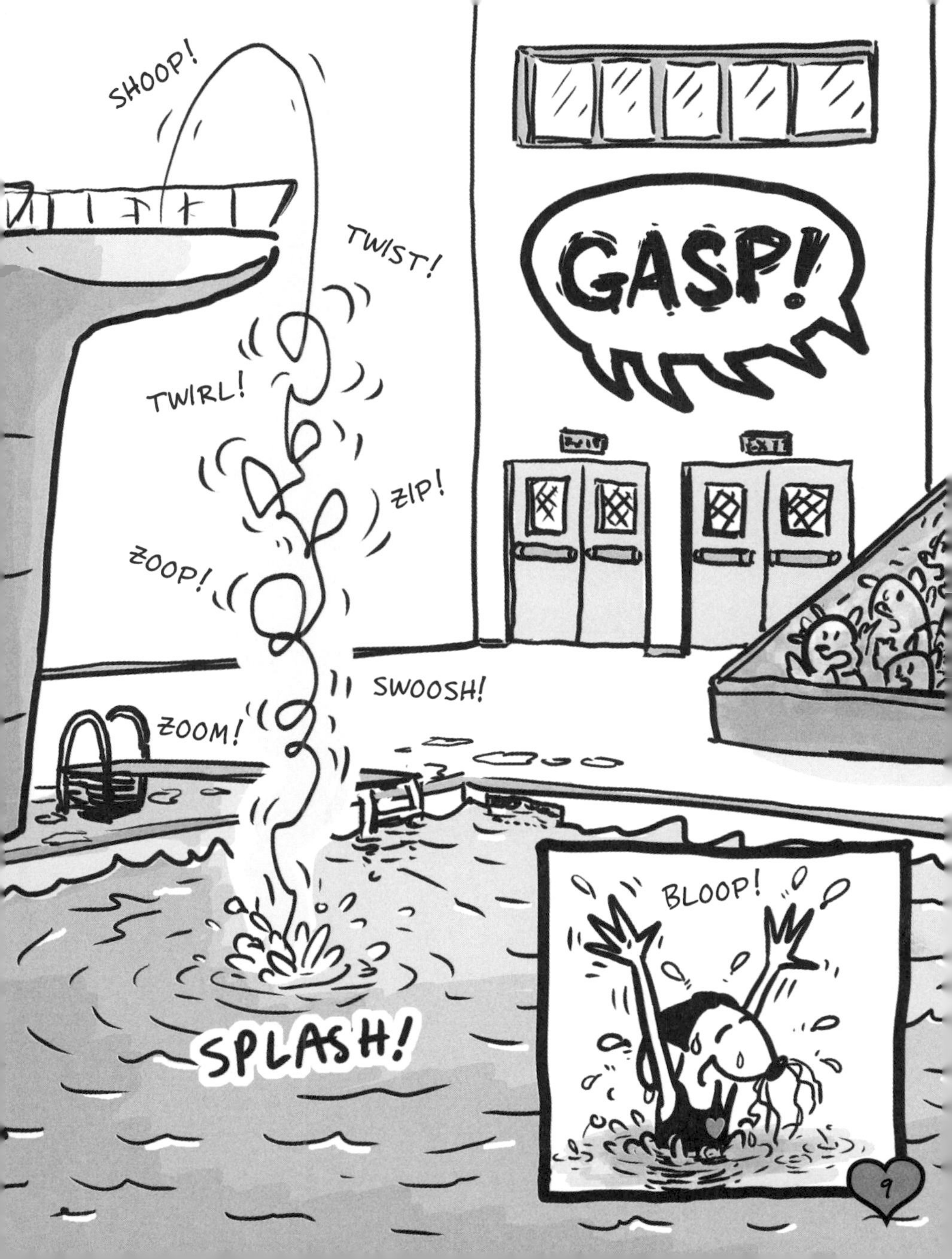
SHOOP!
TWIST!
TWIRL!
ZIP!
ZOOP!
SWOOSH!
ZOOM!
SPLASH!
GASP!
BLOOP!

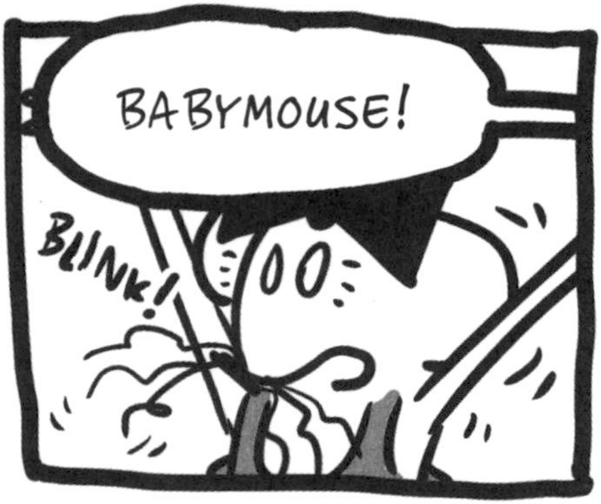
BABYMOUSE!
BLINK!

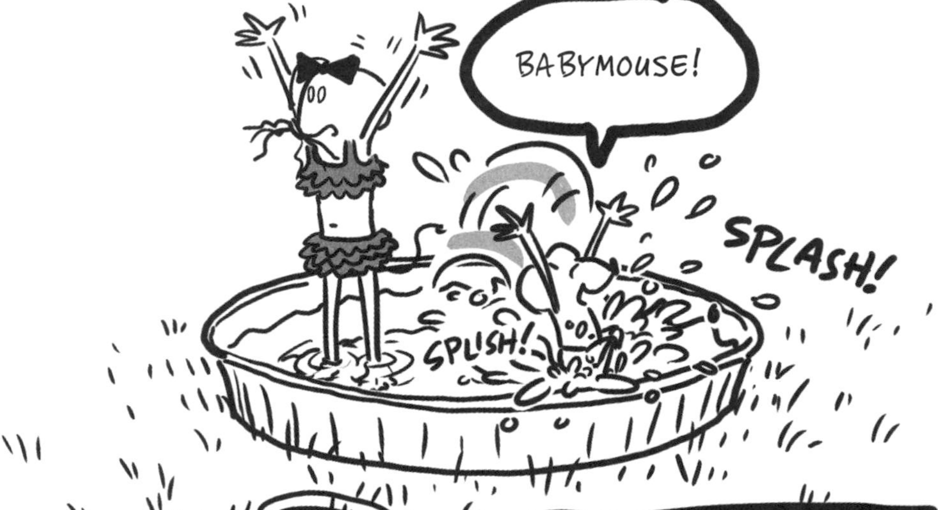
BABYMOUSE!
SPLASH!
SPLISH!

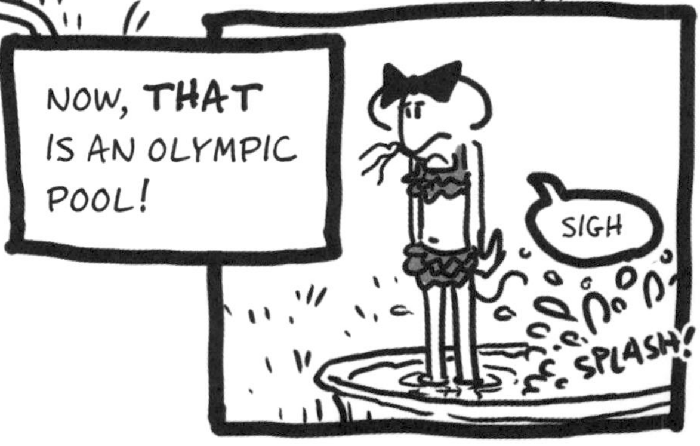
NOW, **THAT** IS AN OLYMPIC POOL!
SIGH
SPLASH!

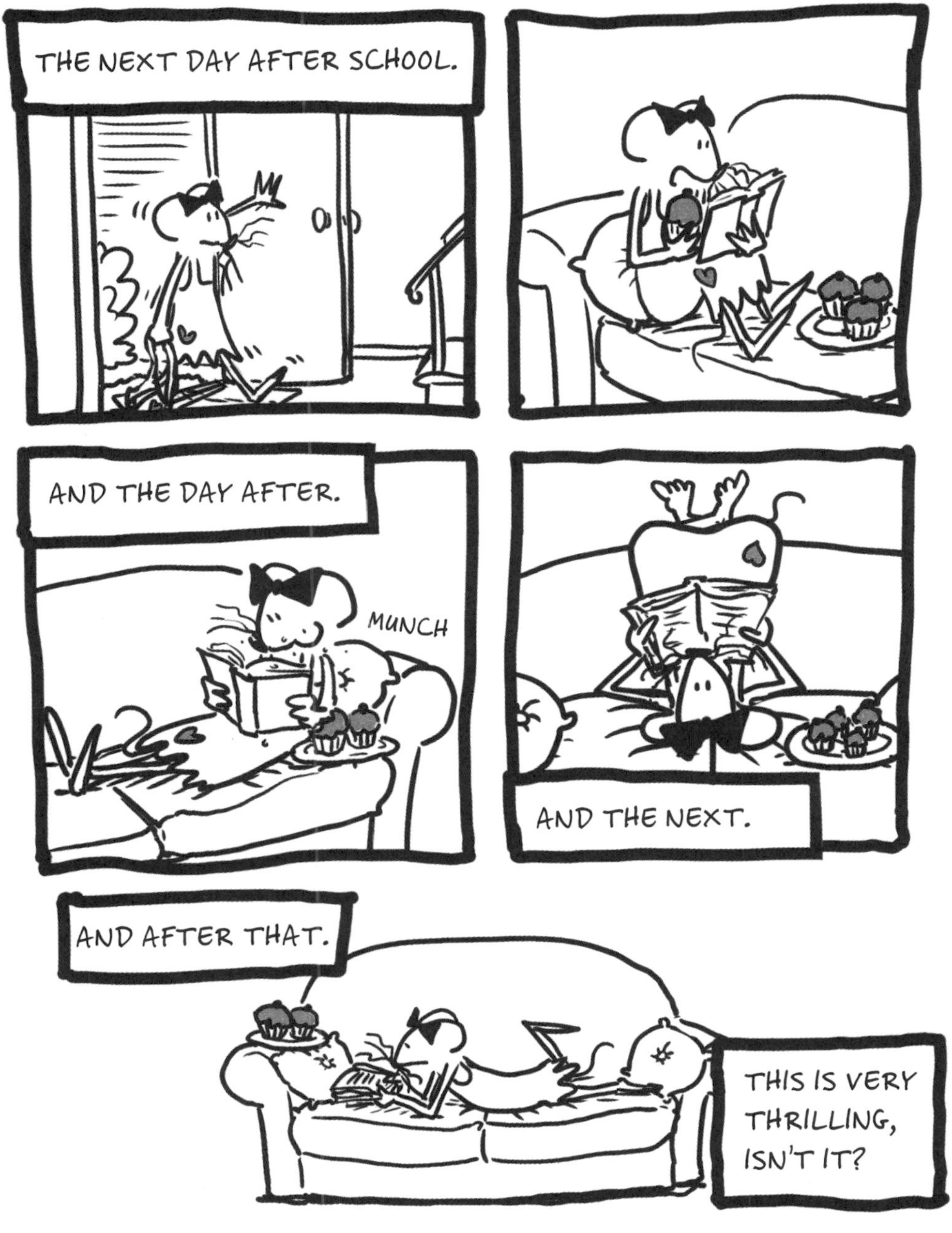
THE NEXT DAY AFTER SCHOOL.
AND THE DAY AFTER.
MUNCH
AND THE NEXT.
AND AFTER THAT.
THIS IS VERY THRILLING, ISN'T IT?

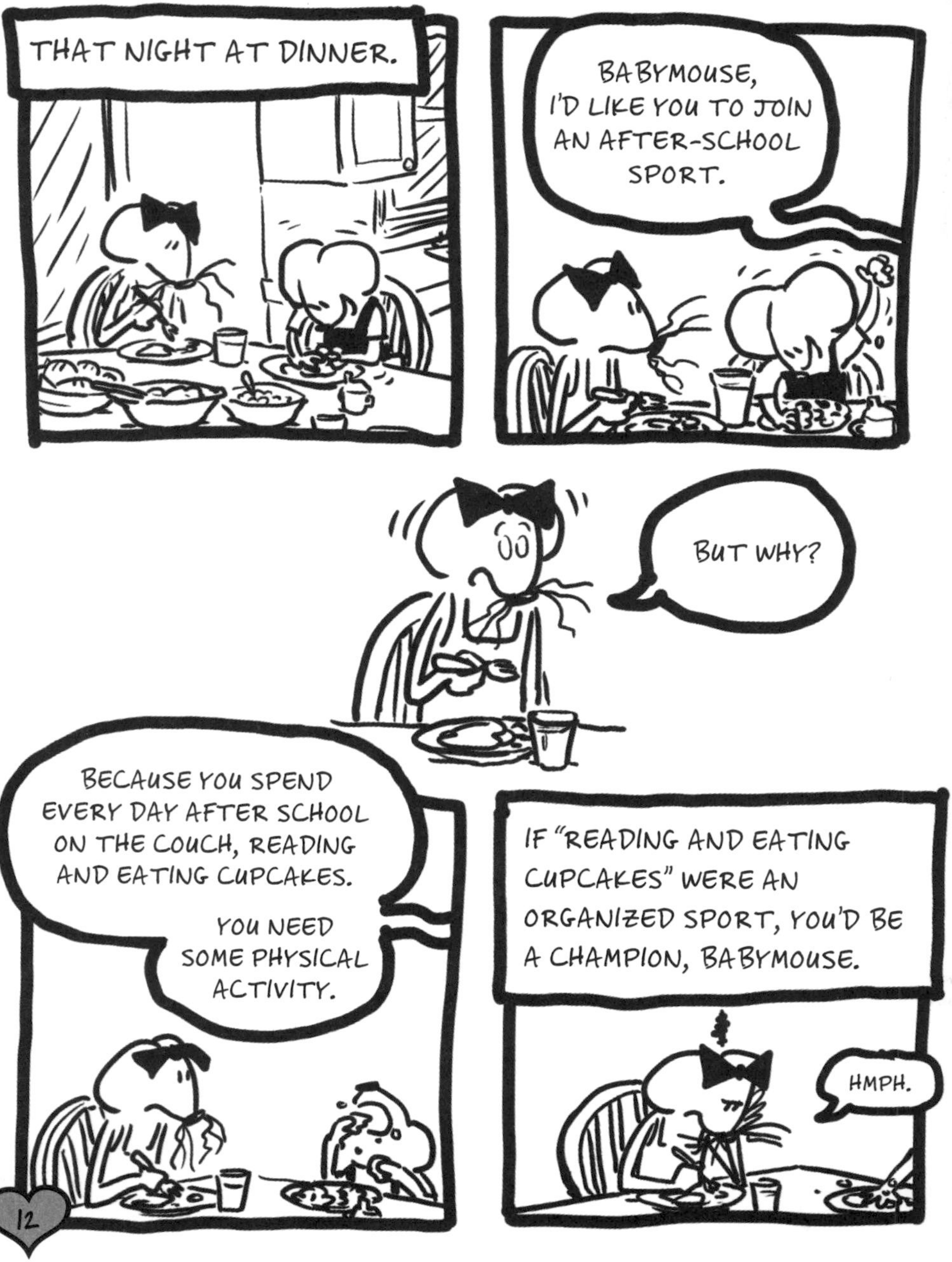
THAT NIGHT AT DINNER.
BABYMOUSE, I'D LIKE YOU TO JOIN AN AFTER-SCHOOL SPORT.
BUT WHY?
BECAUSE YOU SPEND EVERY DAY AFTER SCHOOL ON THE COUCH, READING AND EATING CUPCAKES.
YOU NEED SOME PHYSICAL ACTIVITY.
IF "READING AND EATING CUPCAKES" WERE AN ORGANIZED SPORT, YOU'D BE A CHAMPION, BABYMOUSE.
HMPH.

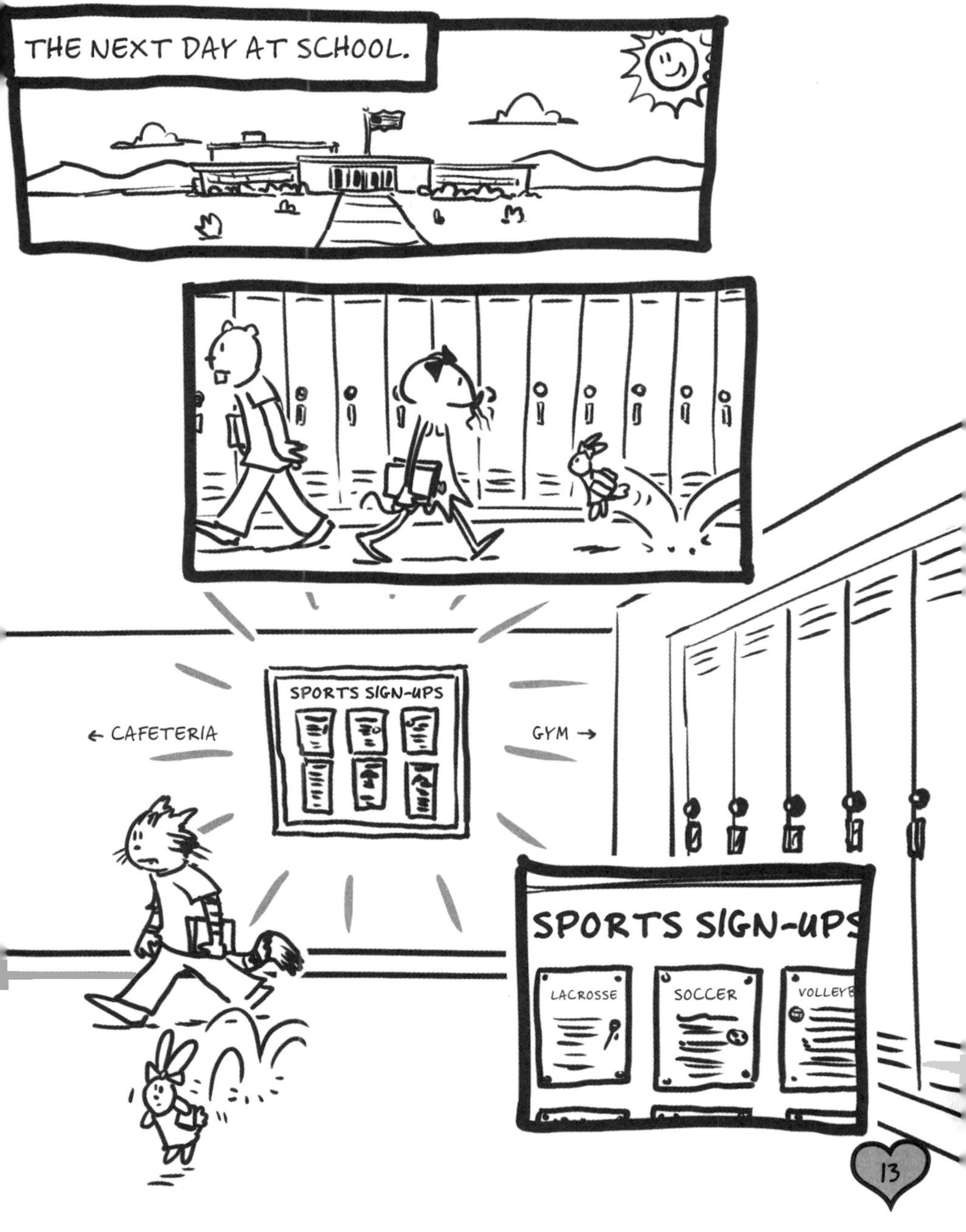
THE NEXT DAY AT SCHOOL.
SPORTS SIGN-UPS
← CAFETERIA
GYM →
SPORTS SIGN-UPS
LACROSSE
SOCCER

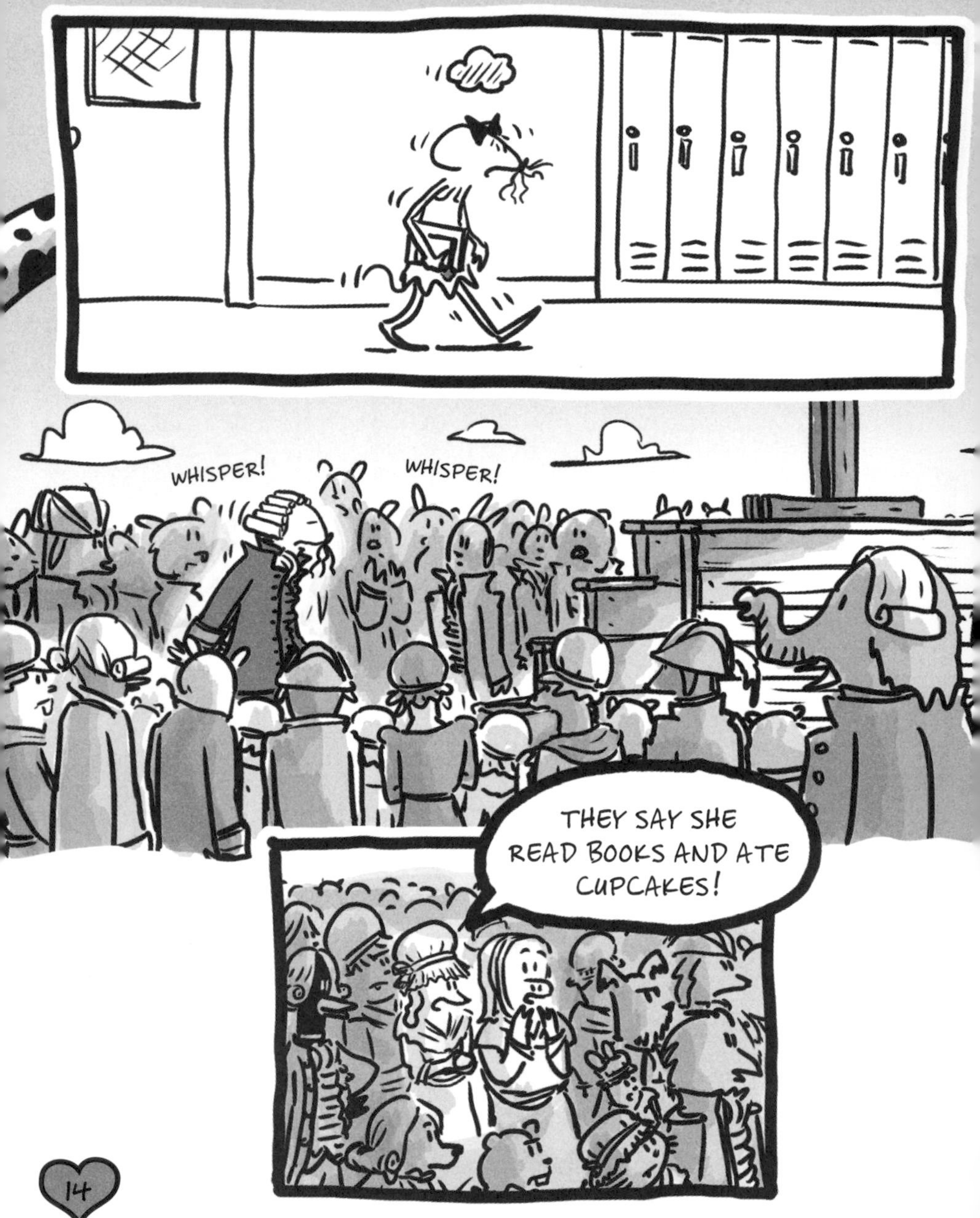
WHISPER!
WHISPER!
THEY SAY SHE READ BOOKS AND ATE CUPCAKES!

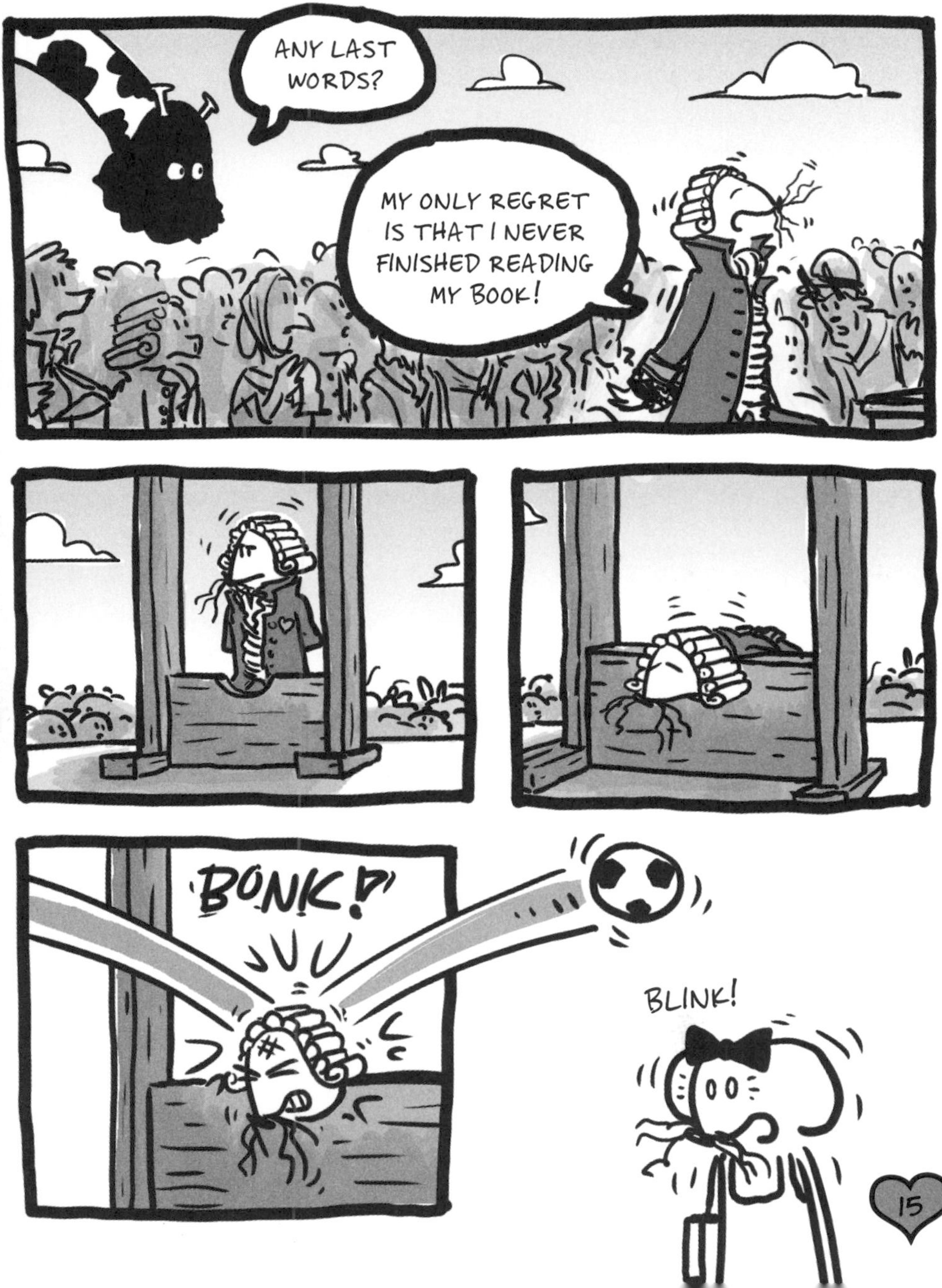
ANY LAST WORDS?
MY ONLY REGRET IS THAT I NEVER FINISHED READING MY BOOK!
BONK!?
BLINK!

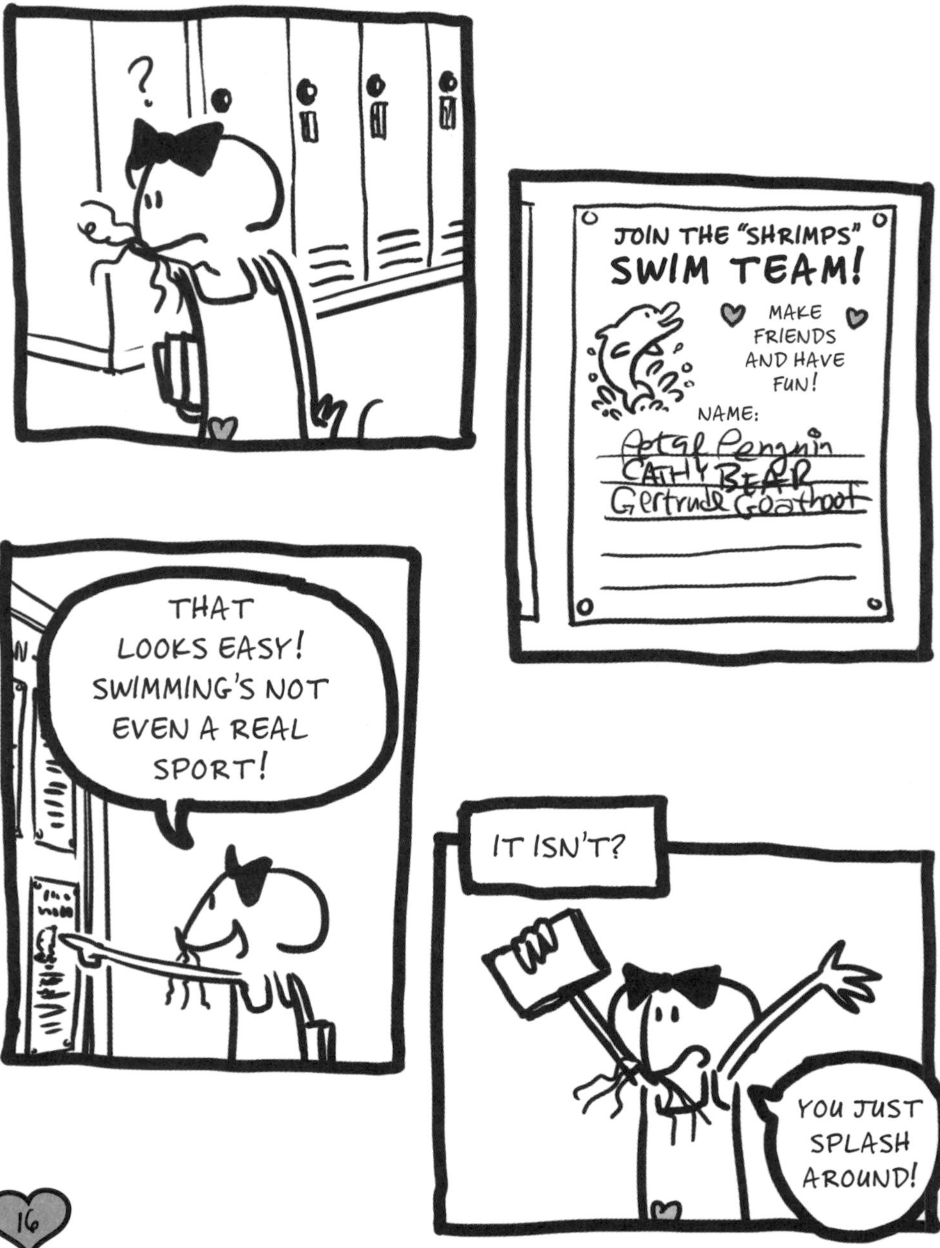
?
JOIN THE "SHRIMPS" SWIM TEAM!
MAKE FRIENDS AND HAVE FUN!
NAME:
Petal Penguin
CATHY BEAR
Gertrude Goathoof
THAT LOOKS EASY! SWIMMING'S NOT EVEN A REAL SPORT!
IT ISN'T?
YOU JUST SPLASH AROUND!

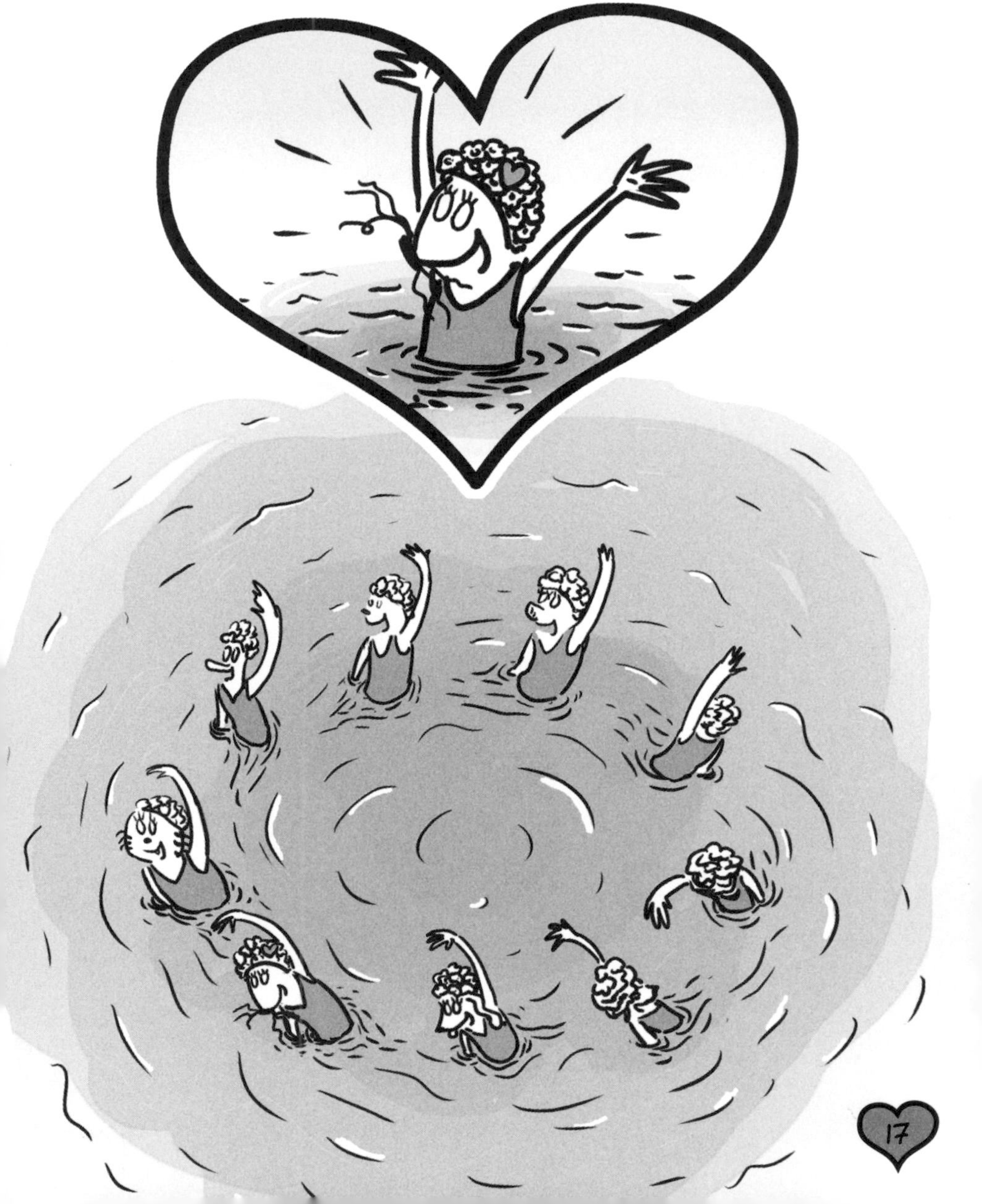

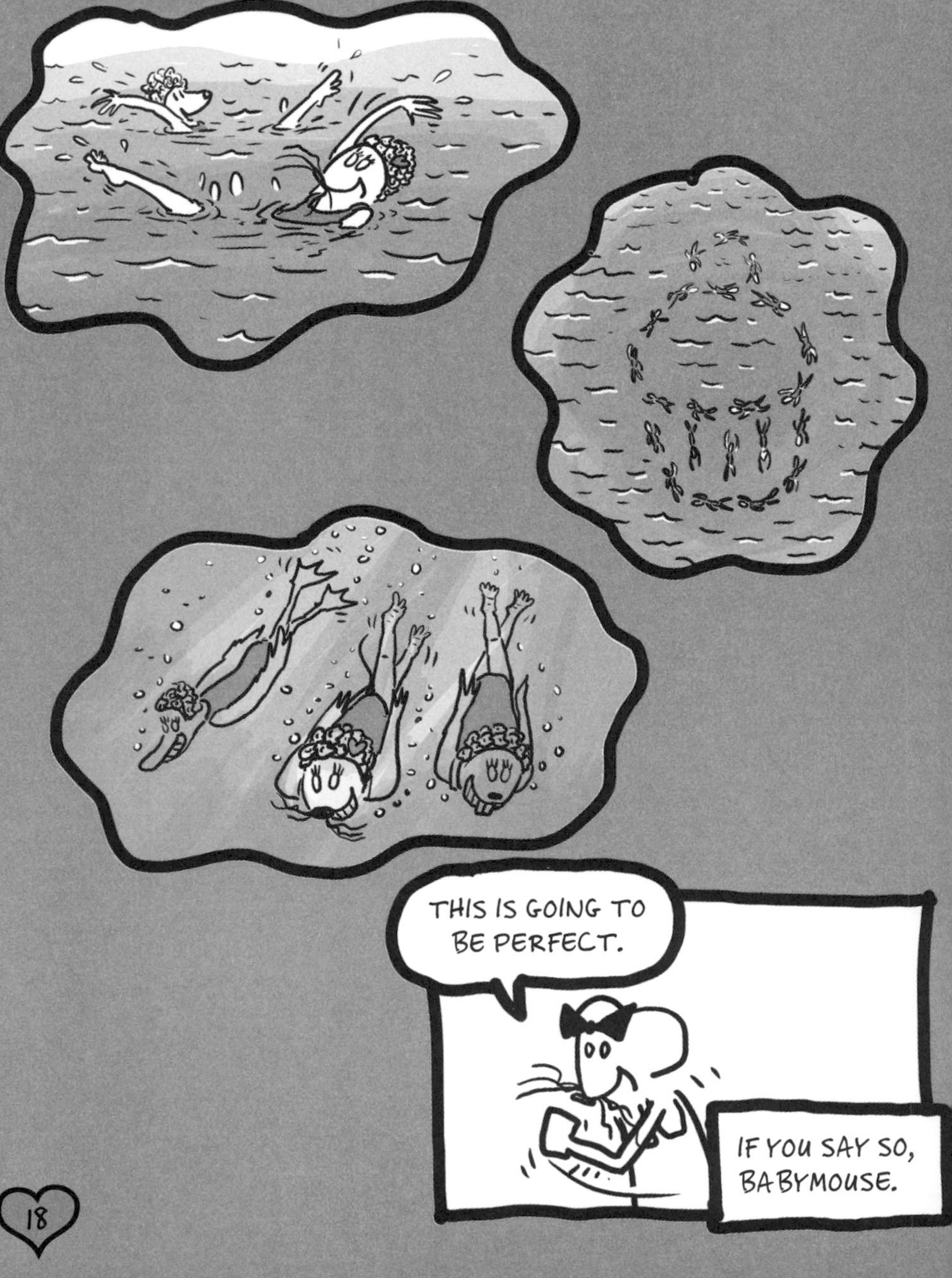
THIS IS GOING TO BE PERFECT.
IF YOU SAY SO, BABYMOUSE.

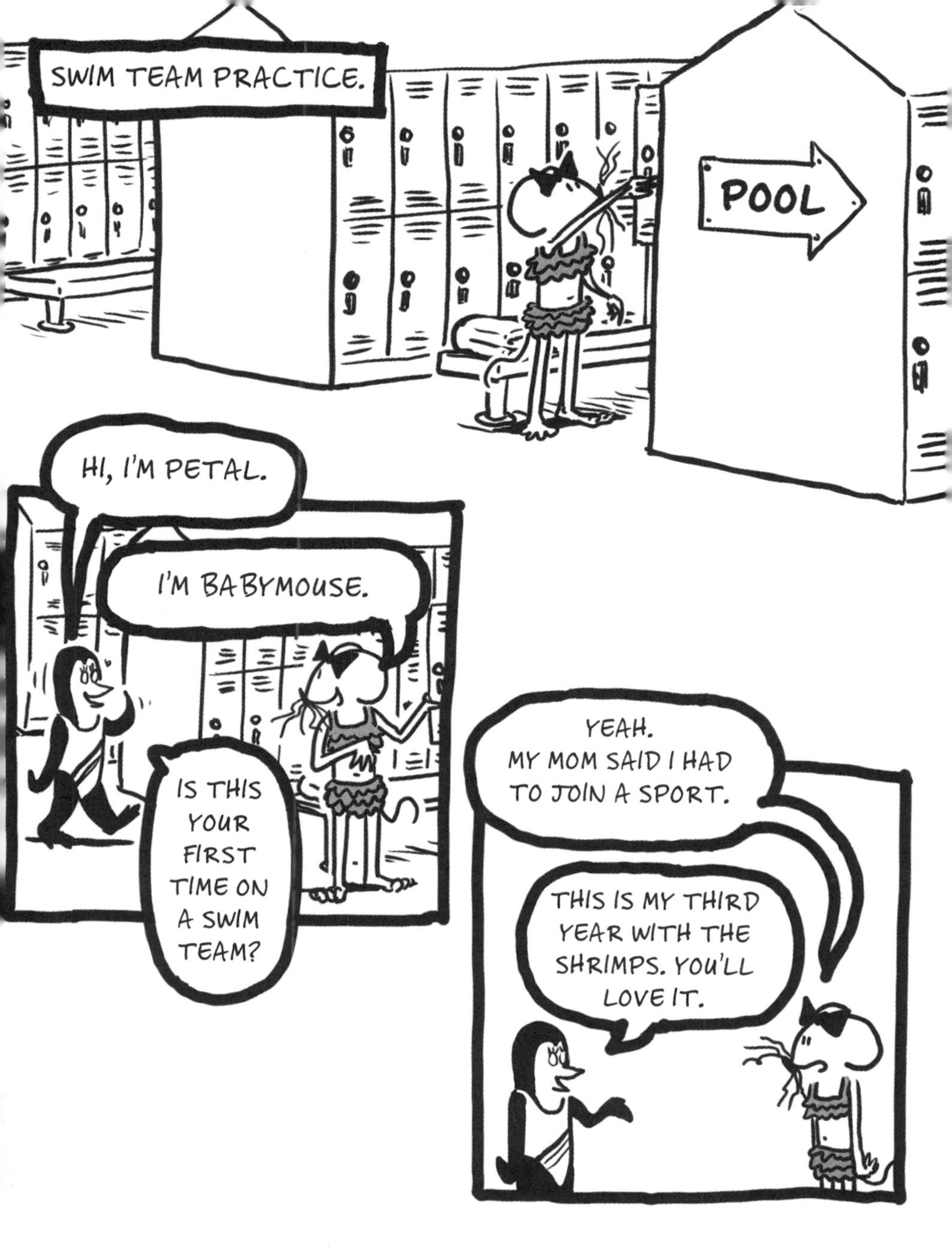
SWIM TEAM PRACTICE.
POOL
HI, I'M PETAL.
I'M BABYMOUSE.
IS THIS YOUR FIRST TIME ON A SWIM TEAM?
YEAH. MY MOM SAID I HAD TO JOIN A SPORT.
THIS IS MY THIRD YEAR WITH THE SHRIMPS. YOU'LL LOVE IT.

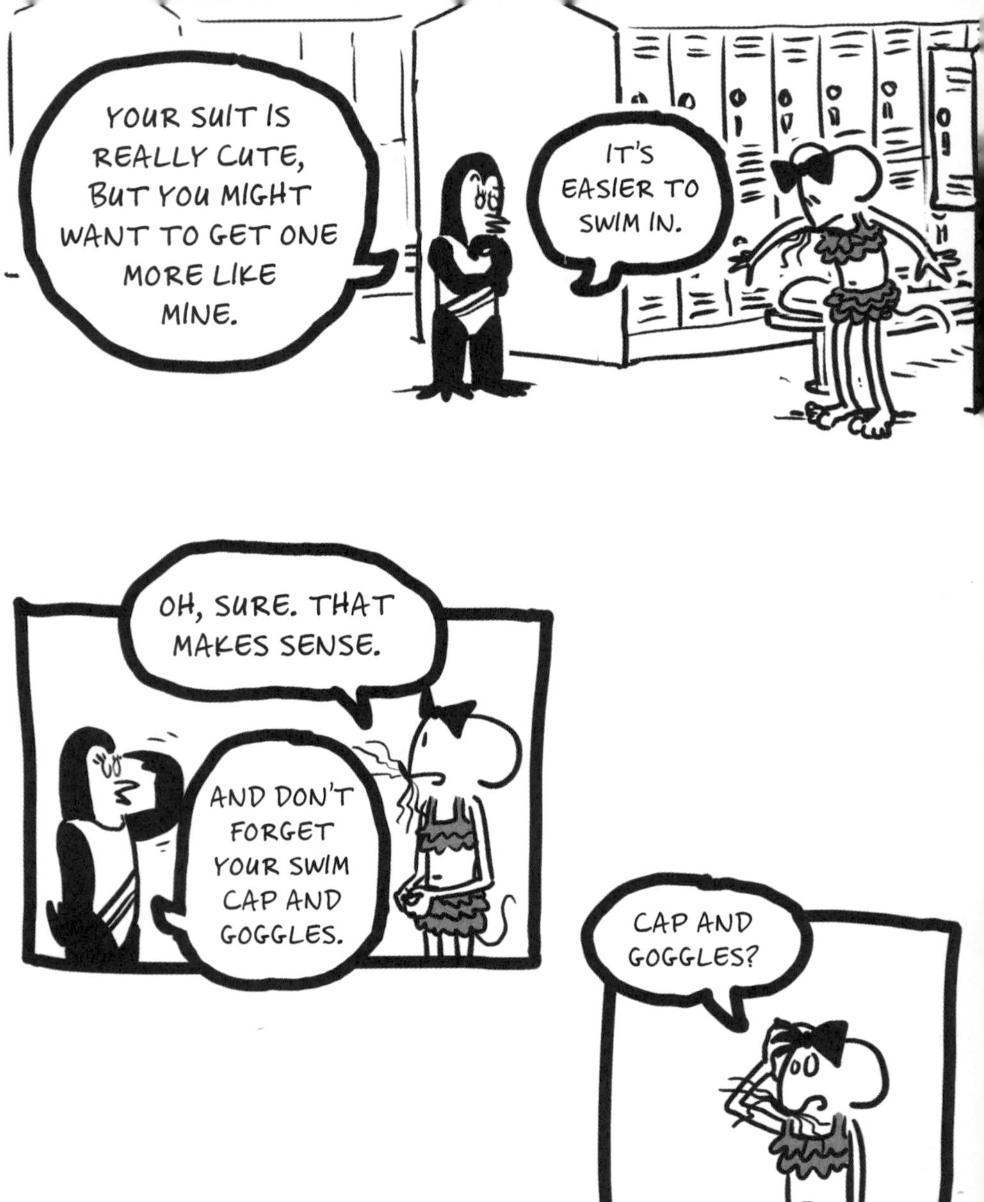
YOUR SUIT IS REALLY CUTE, BUT YOU MIGHT WANT TO GET ONE MORE LIKE MINE.
IT'S EASIER TO SWIM IN.
OH, SURE. THAT MAKES SENSE.
AND DON'T FORGET YOUR SWIM CAP AND GOGGLES.
CAP AND GOGGLES?

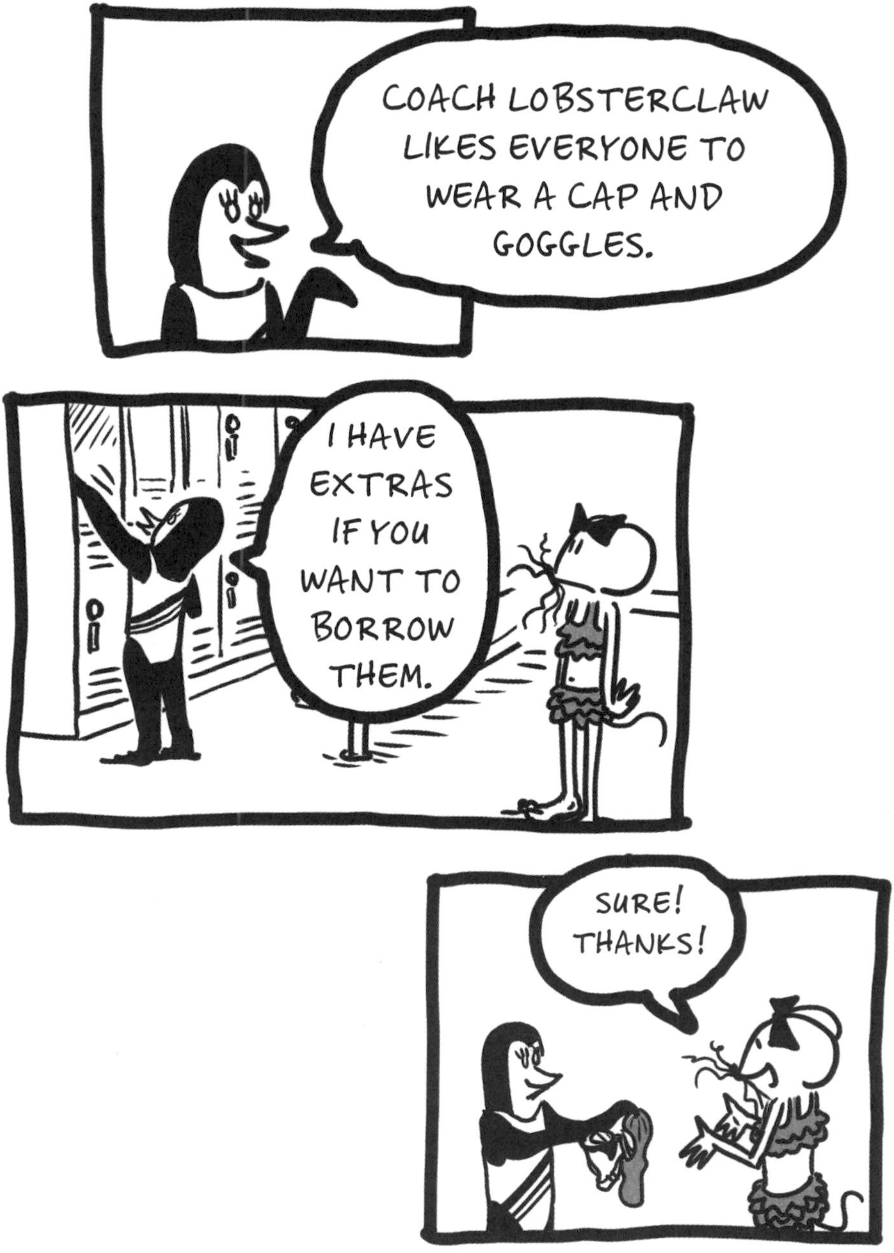
COACH LOBSTERCLAW LIKES EVERYONE TO WEAR A CAP AND GOGGLES.
I HAVE EXTRAS IF YOU WANT TO BORROW THEM.
SURE! THANKS!

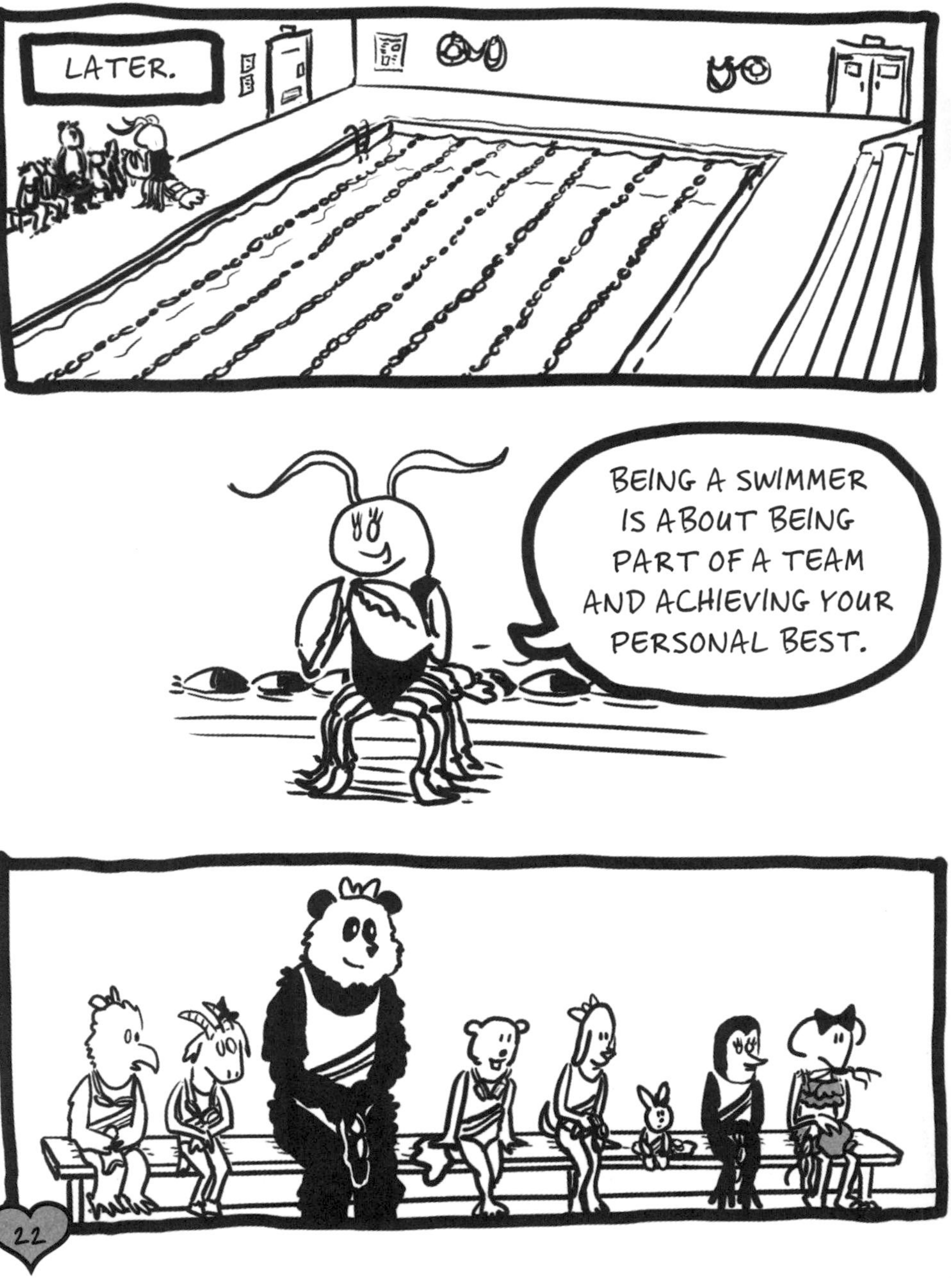
LATER.
BEING A SWIMMER IS ABOUT BEING PART OF A TEAM AND ACHIEVING YOUR PERSONAL BEST.

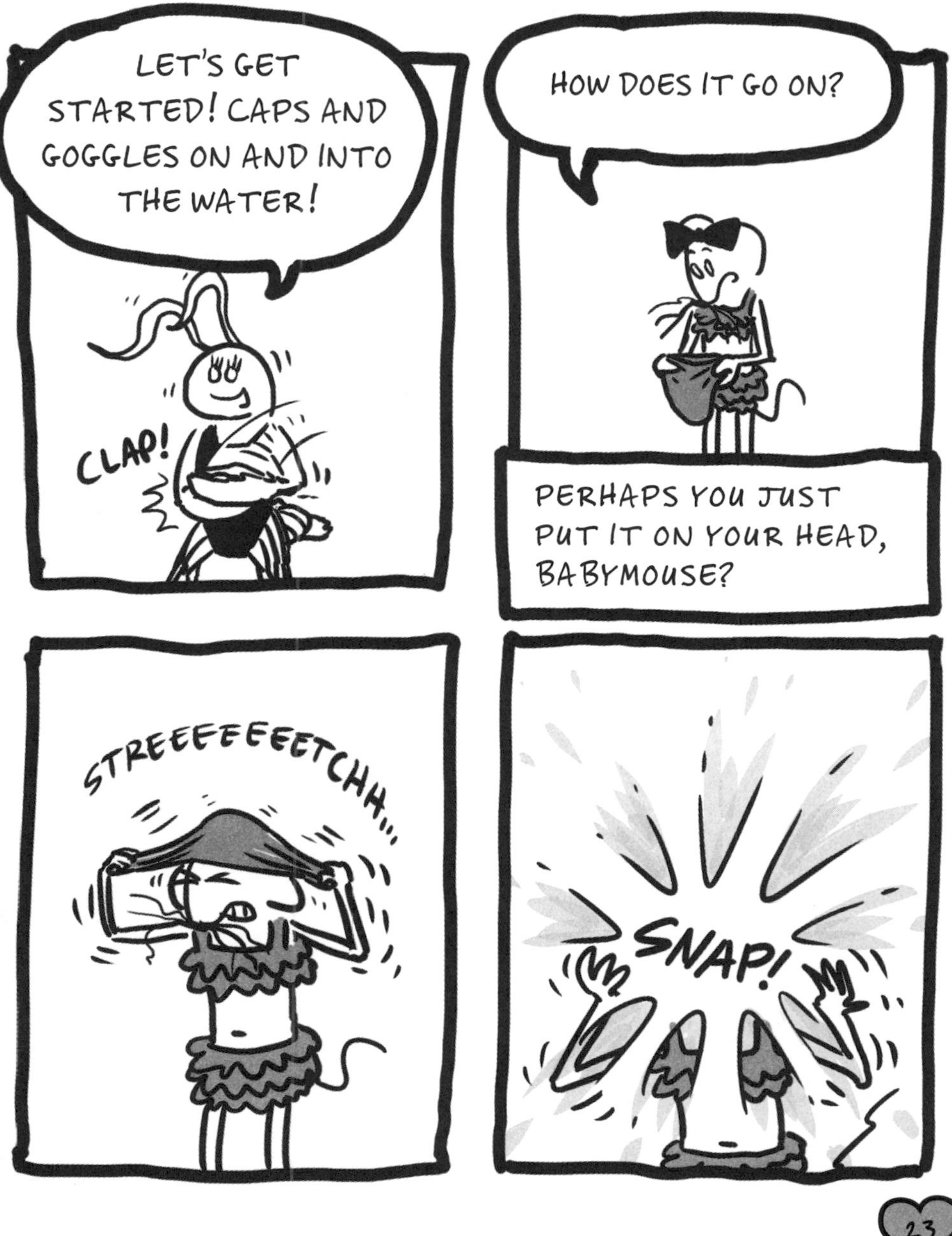
LET'S GET STARTED! CAPS AND GOGGLES ON AND INTO THE WATER!
CLAP!
HOW DOES IT GO ON?
PERHAPS YOU JUST PUT IT ON YOUR HEAD, BABYMOUSE?
STREEEEEEEETCHH...
SNAP!

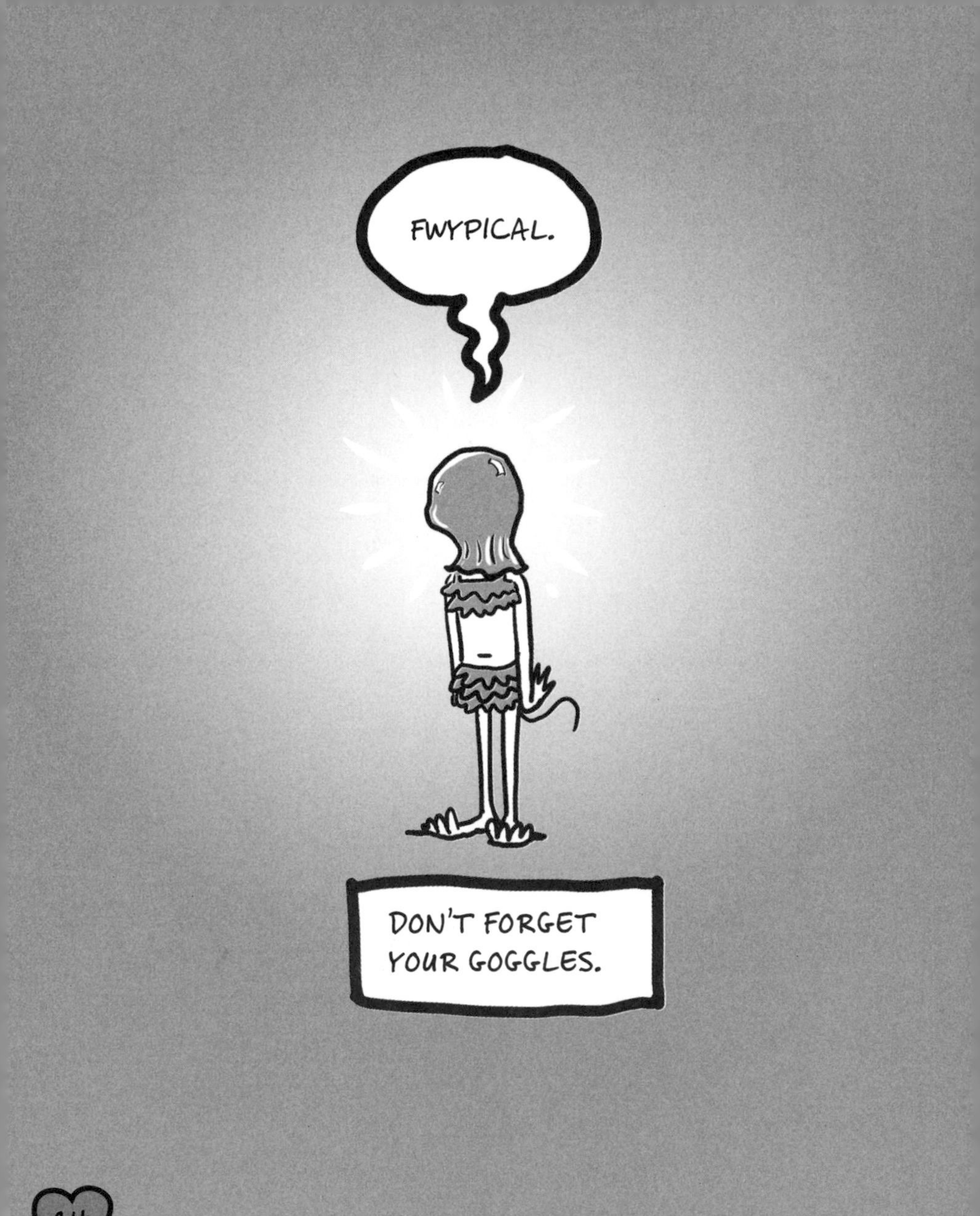
FWYPICAL.
DON'T FORGET YOUR GOGGLES.

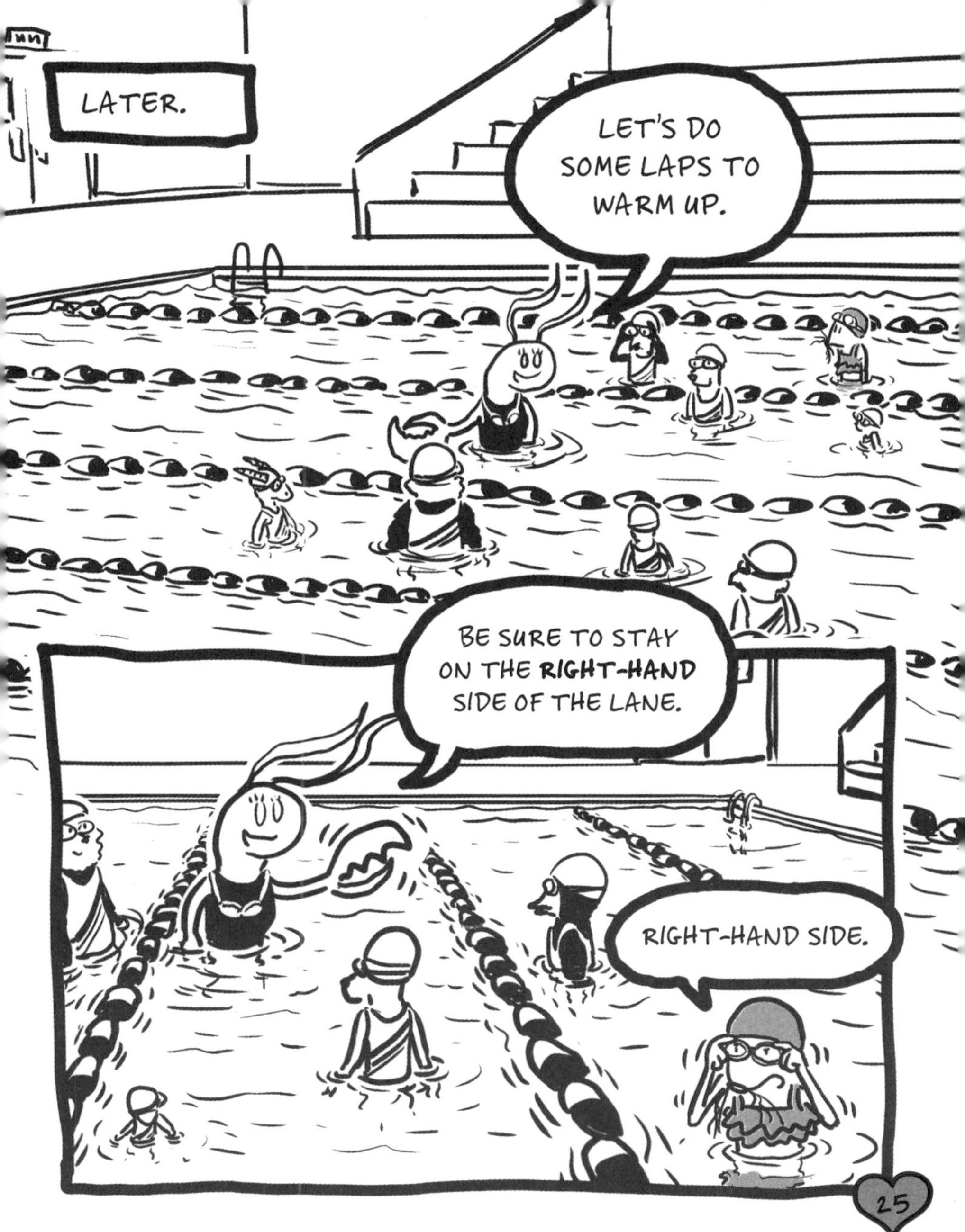
LATER.
LET'S DO SOME LAPS TO WARM UP.
BE SURE TO STAY ON THE **RIGHT-HAND** SIDE OF THE LANE.
RIGHT-HAND SIDE.

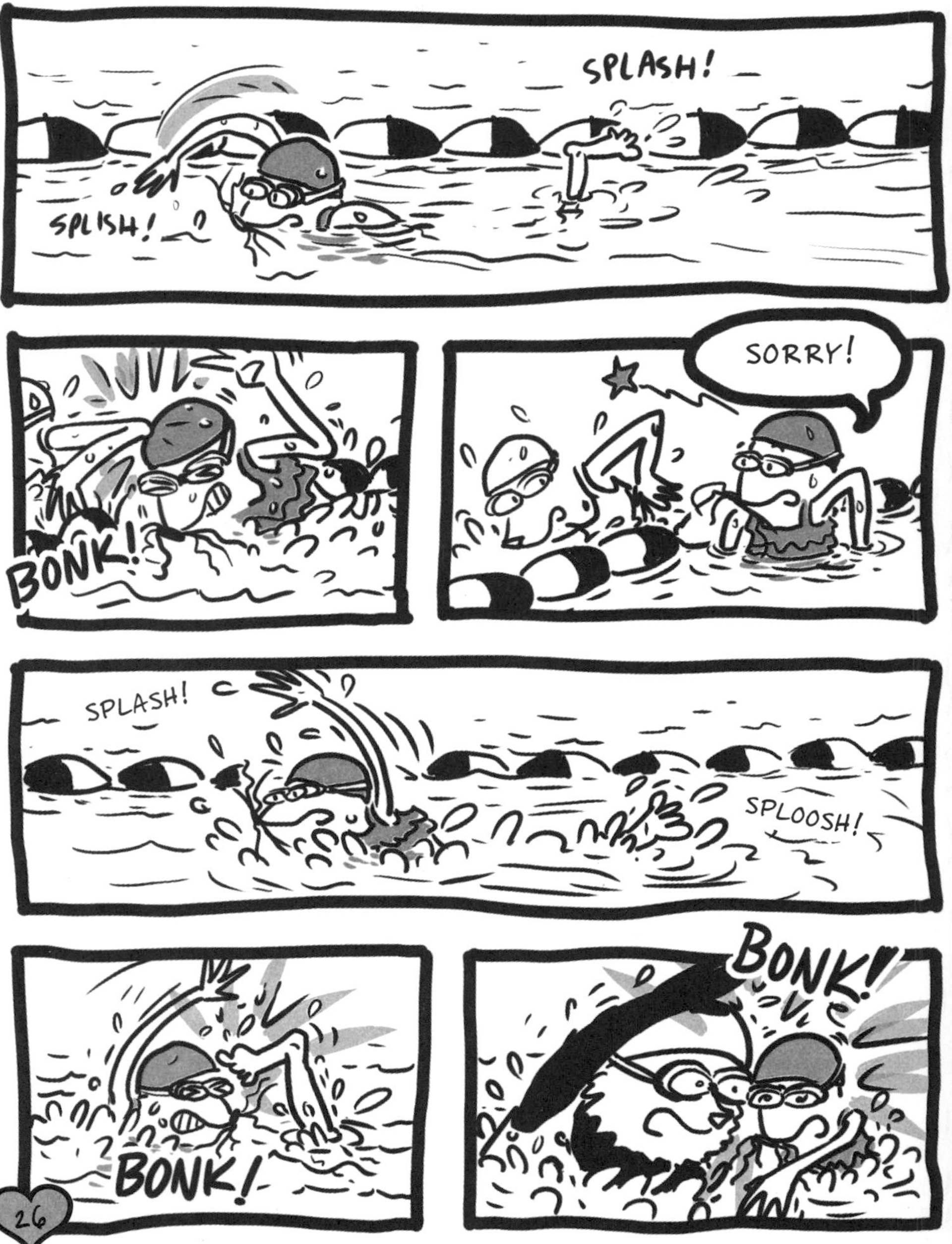
SPLASH!
SPLISH!
BONK!
SORRY!
SPLASH!
SPLOOSH!
BONK!
BONK!

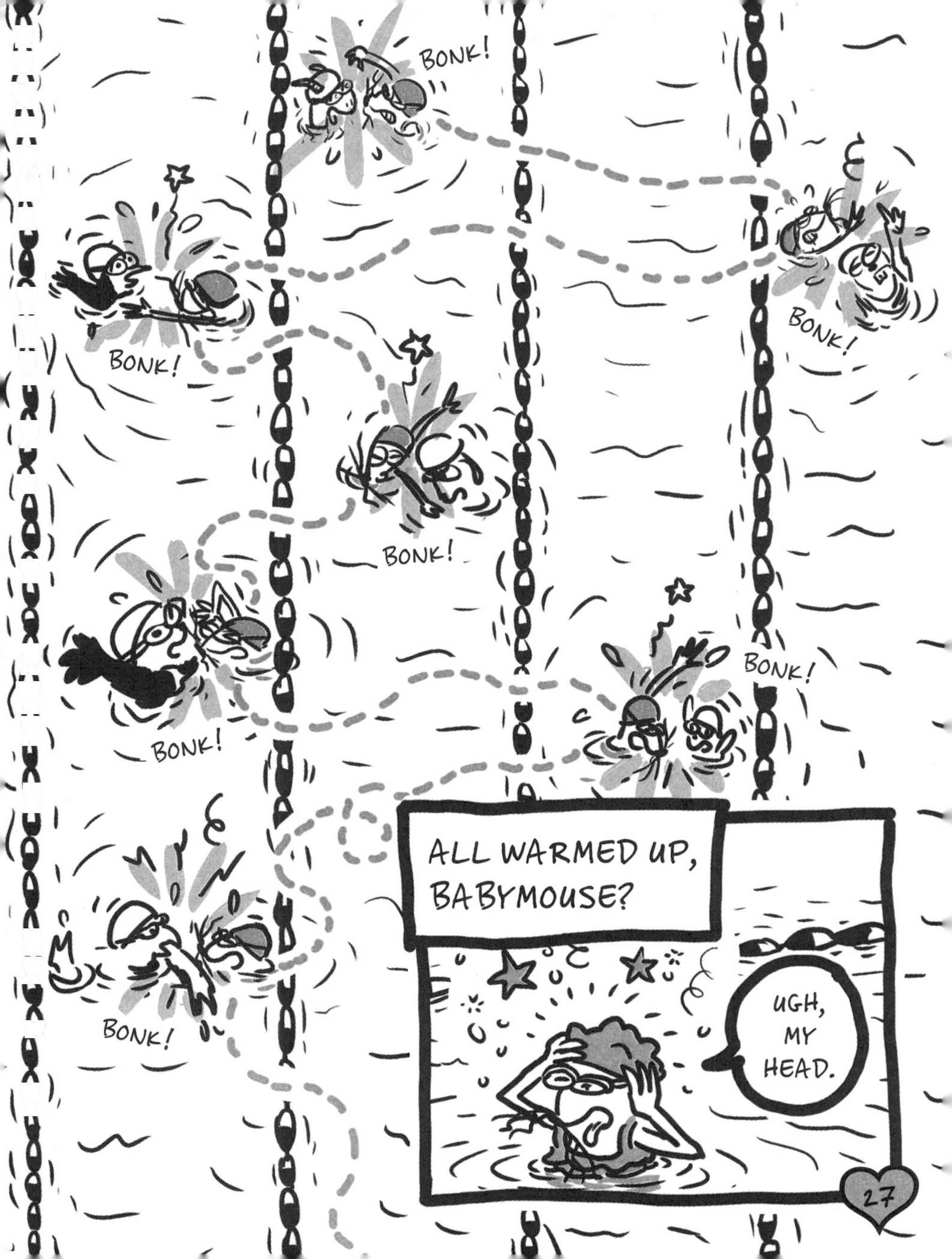
BONK!
BONK!
BONK!
BONK!
BONK!
BONK!
BONK!
ALL WARMED UP, BABYMOUSE?
UGH, MY HEAD.

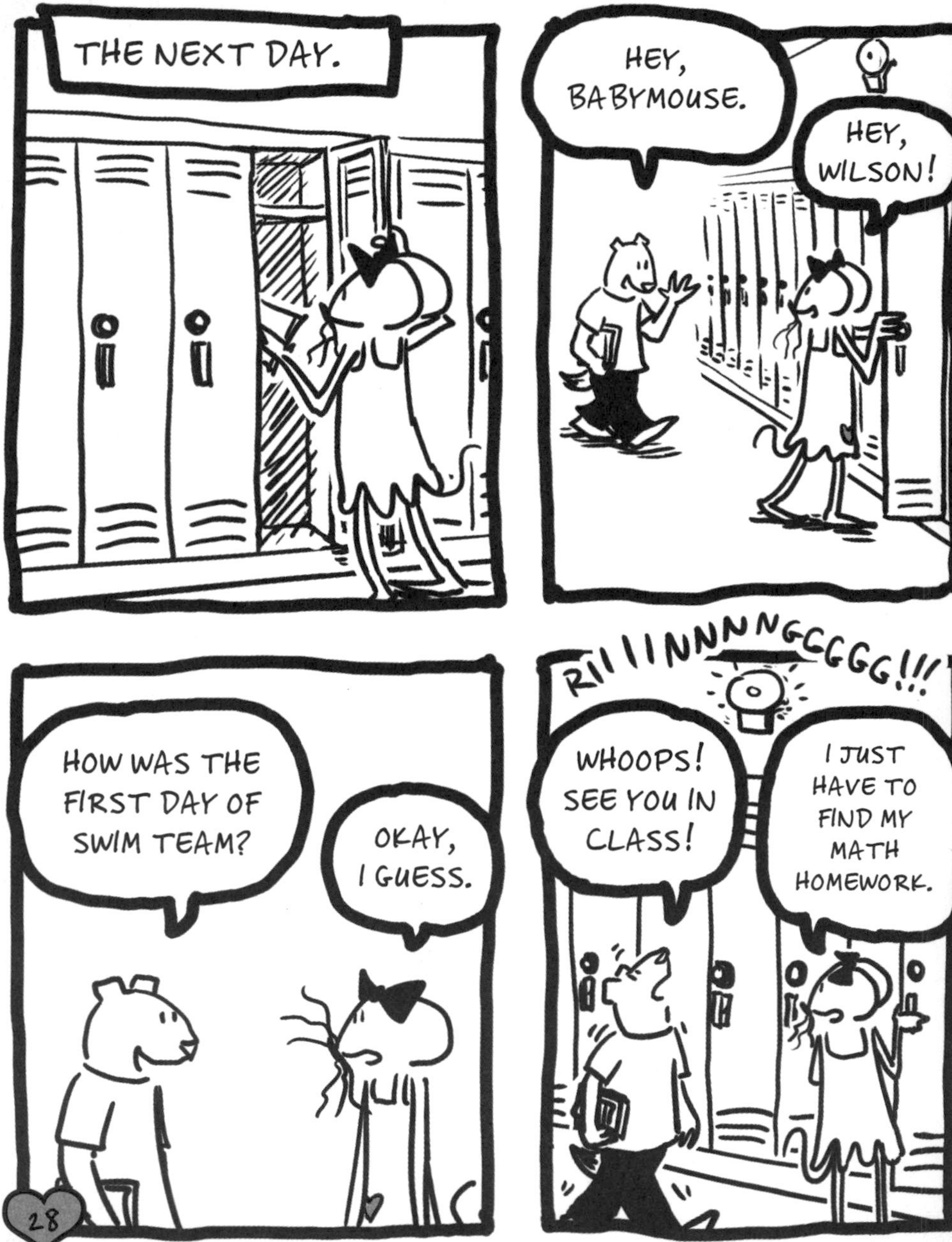
THE NEXT DAY.
HEY, BABYMOUSE.
HEY, WILSON!
HOW WAS THE FIRST DAY OF SWIM TEAM?
OKAY, I GUESS.
RIIIINNNNGGGGG!!!
WHOOPS! SEE YOU IN CLASS!
I JUST HAVE TO FIND MY MATH HOMEWORK.

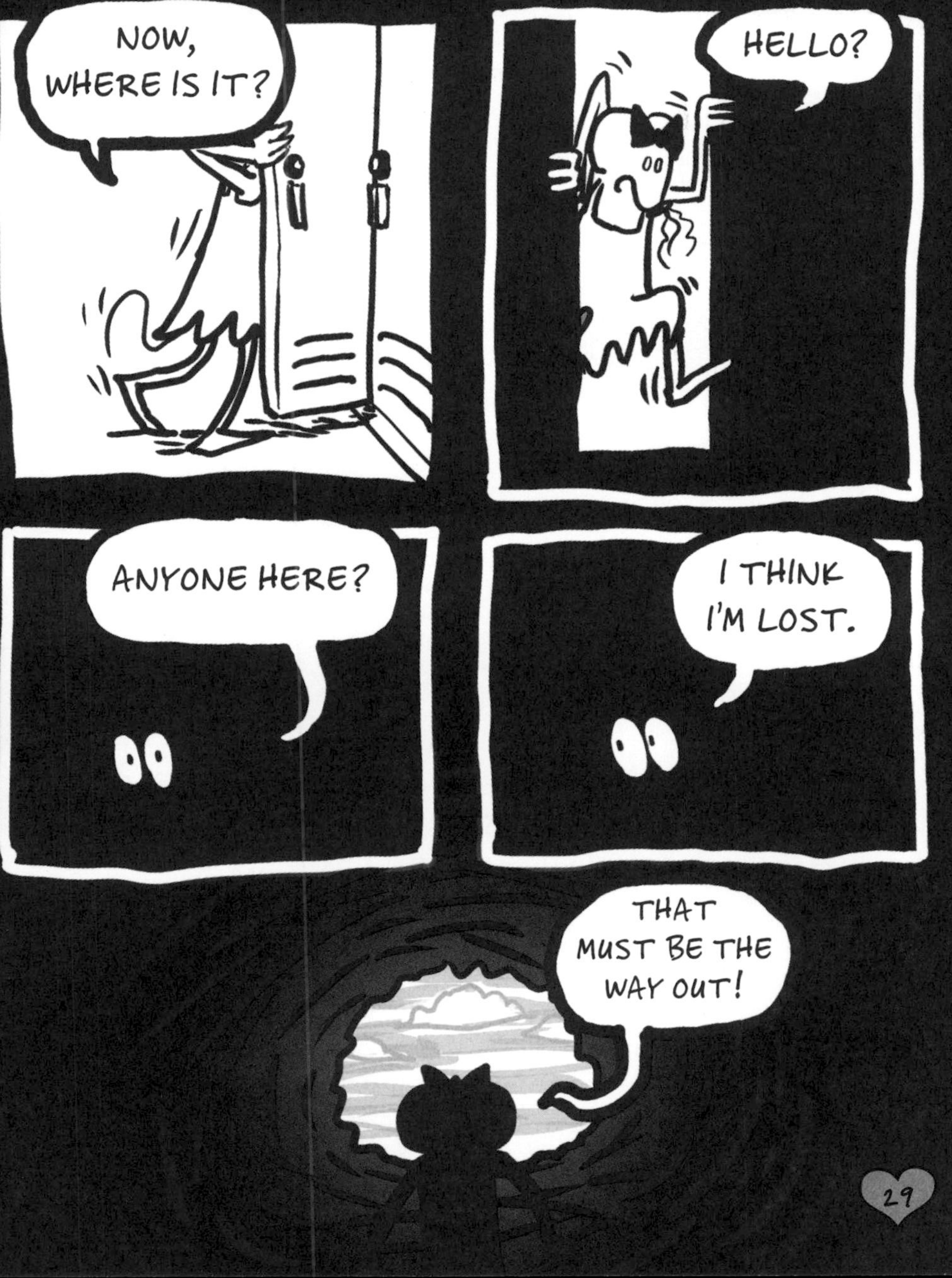
NOW, WHERE IS IT?
HELLO?
ANYONE HERE?
I THINK I'M LOST.
THAT MUST BE THE WAY OUT!

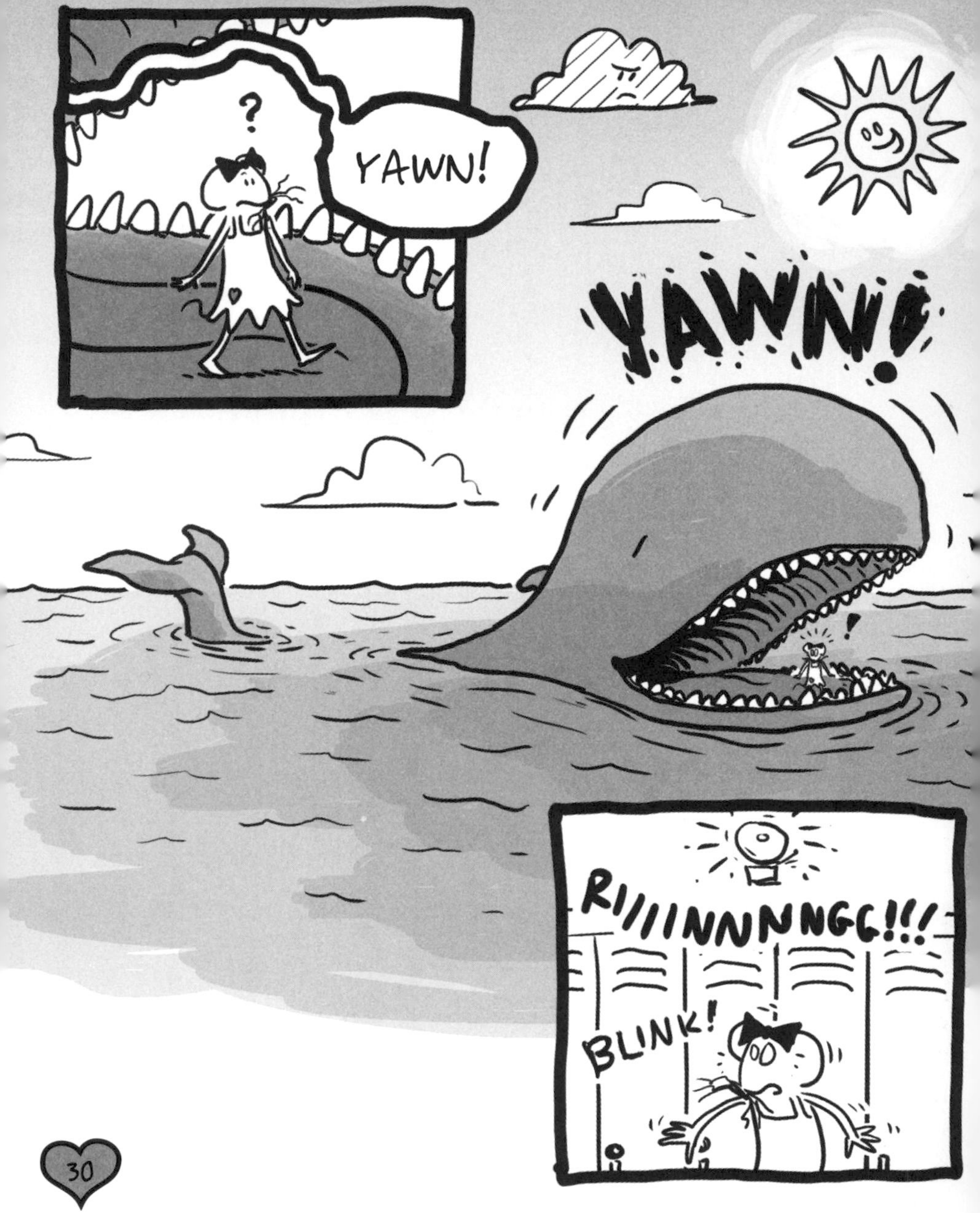
?
YAWN!
YAWN!
!
RIIIIINNNNGG!!!
BLINK!

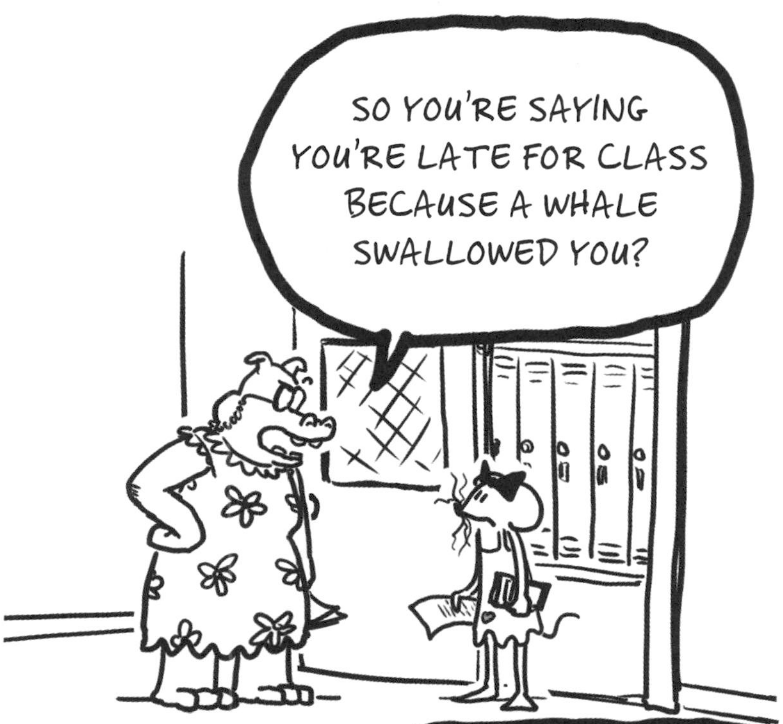
SO YOU'RE SAYING YOU'RE LATE FOR CLASS BECAUSE A WHALE SWALLOWED YOU?

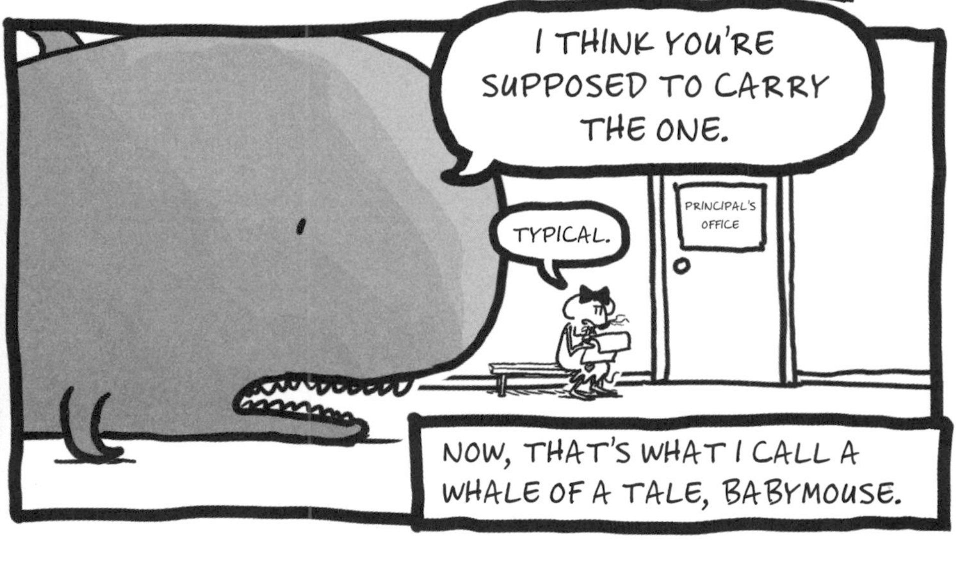
I THINK YOU'RE SUPPOSED TO CARRY THE ONE.
TYPICAL.
PRINCIPAL'S OFFICE
NOW, THAT'S WHAT I CALL A WHALE OF A TALE, BABYMOUSE.

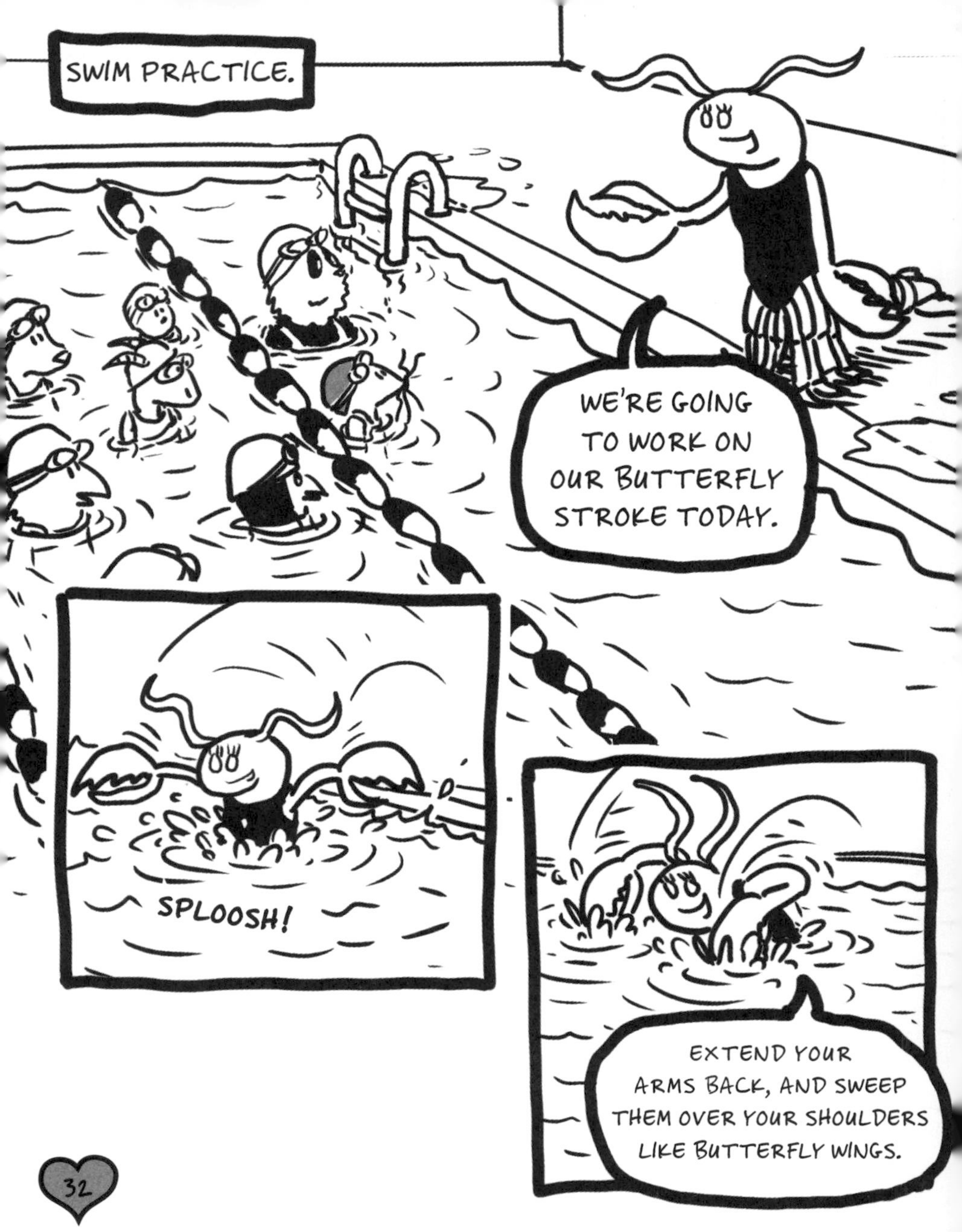
SWIM PRACTICE.
WE'RE GOING TO WORK ON OUR BUTTERFLY STROKE TODAY.
SPLOOSH!
EXTEND YOUR ARMS BACK, AND SWEEP THEM OVER YOUR SHOULDERS LIKE BUTTERFLY WINGS.

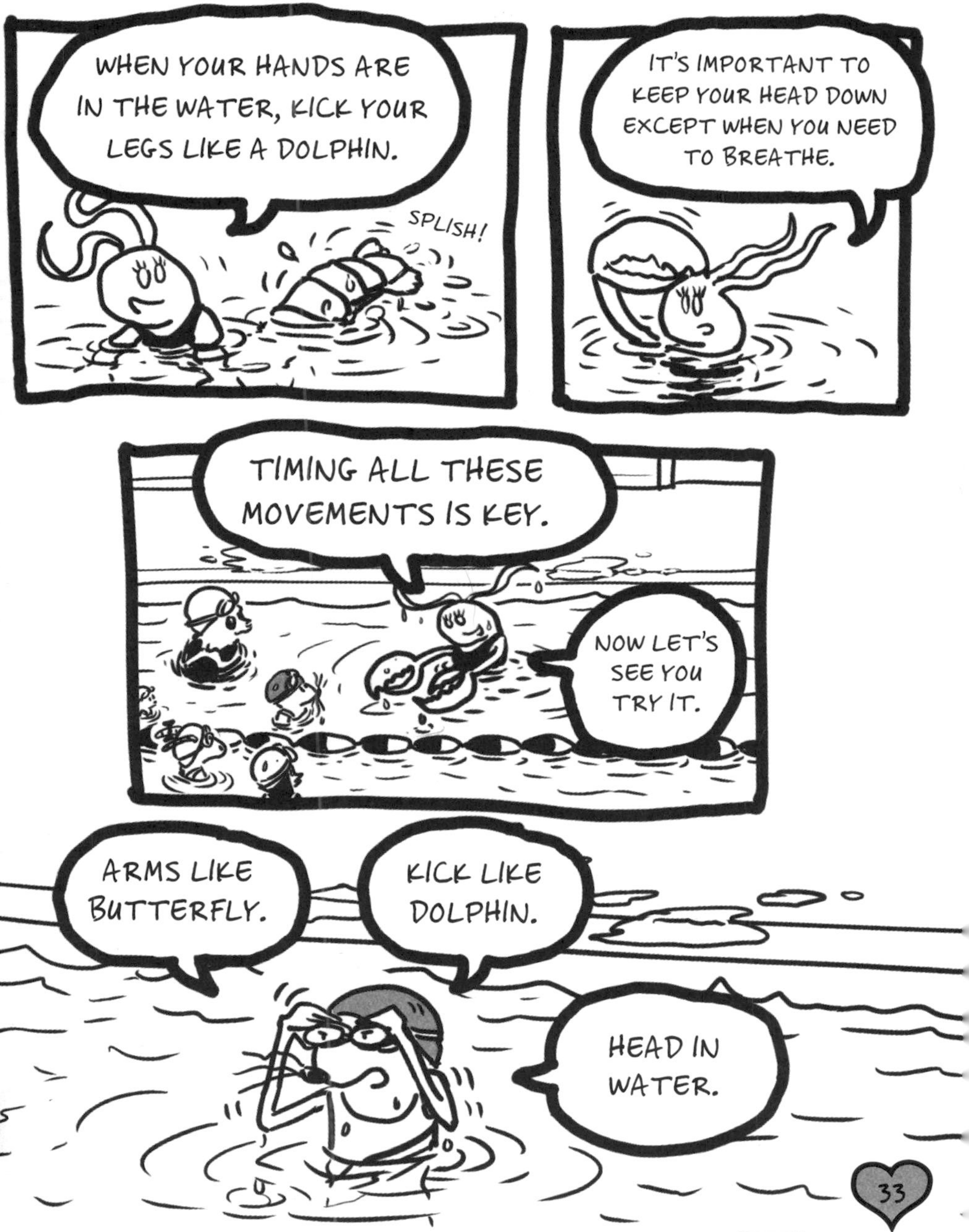
WHEN YOUR HANDS ARE IN THE WATER, KICK YOUR LEGS LIKE A DOLPHIN.
SPLISH!
IT'S IMPORTANT TO KEEP YOUR HEAD DOWN EXCEPT WHEN YOU NEED TO BREATHE.
TIMING ALL THESE MOVEMENTS IS KEY.
NOW LET'S SEE YOU TRY IT.
ARMS LIKE BUTTERFLY.
KICK LIKE DOLPHIN.
HEAD IN WATER.

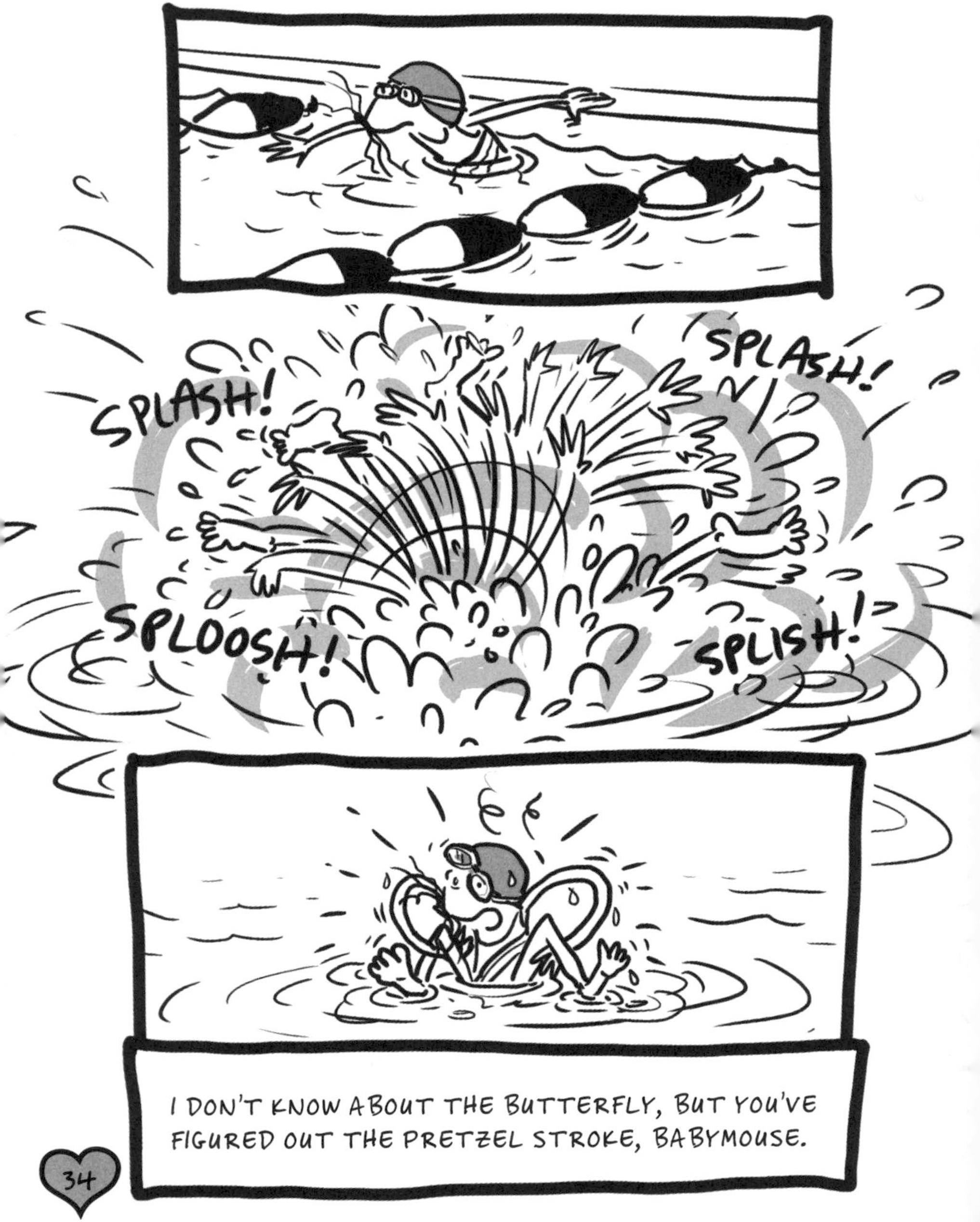
SPLASH!
SPLASH!
SPLOOSH!
SPLISH!
I DON'T KNOW ABOUT THE BUTTERFLY, BUT YOU'VE FIGURED OUT THE PRETZEL STROKE, BABYMOUSE.

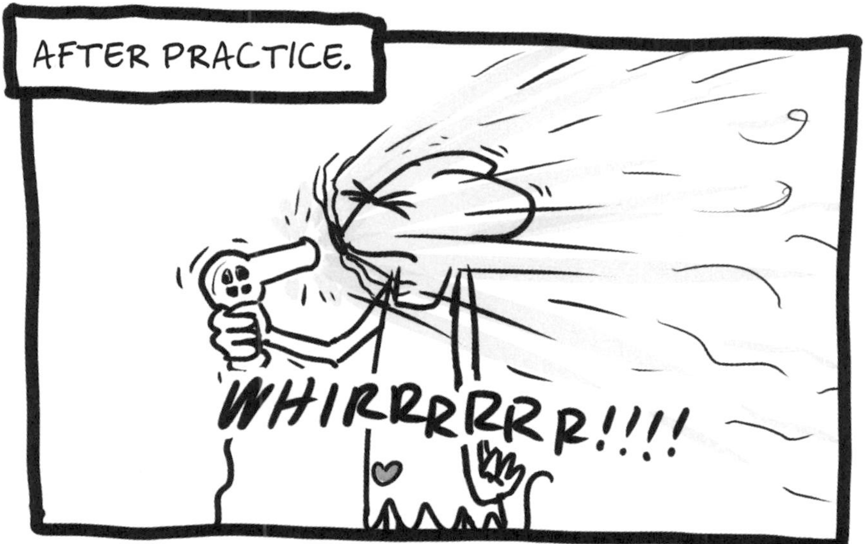
AFTER PRACTICE.
WHIRRRRRRR!!!!

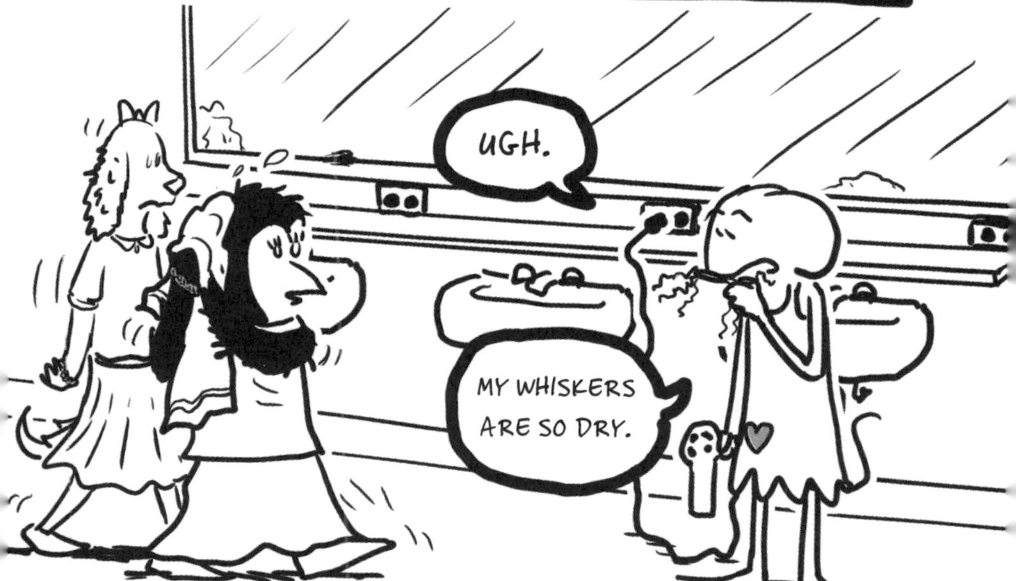
UGH.
MY WHISKERS ARE SO DRY.

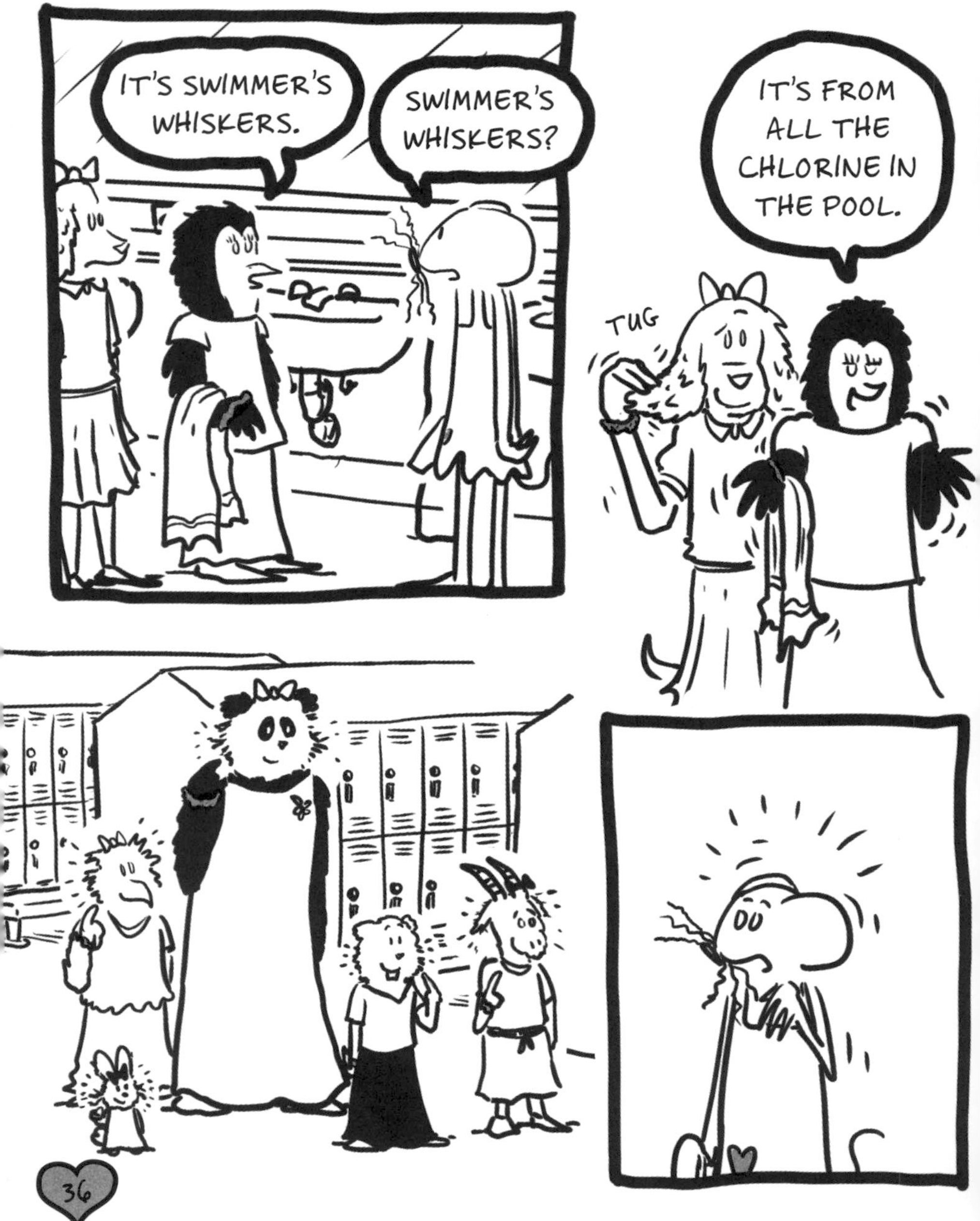
IT'S SWIMMER'S WHISKERS.
SWIMMER'S WHISKERS?
IT'S FROM ALL THE CHLORINE IN THE POOL.
TUG

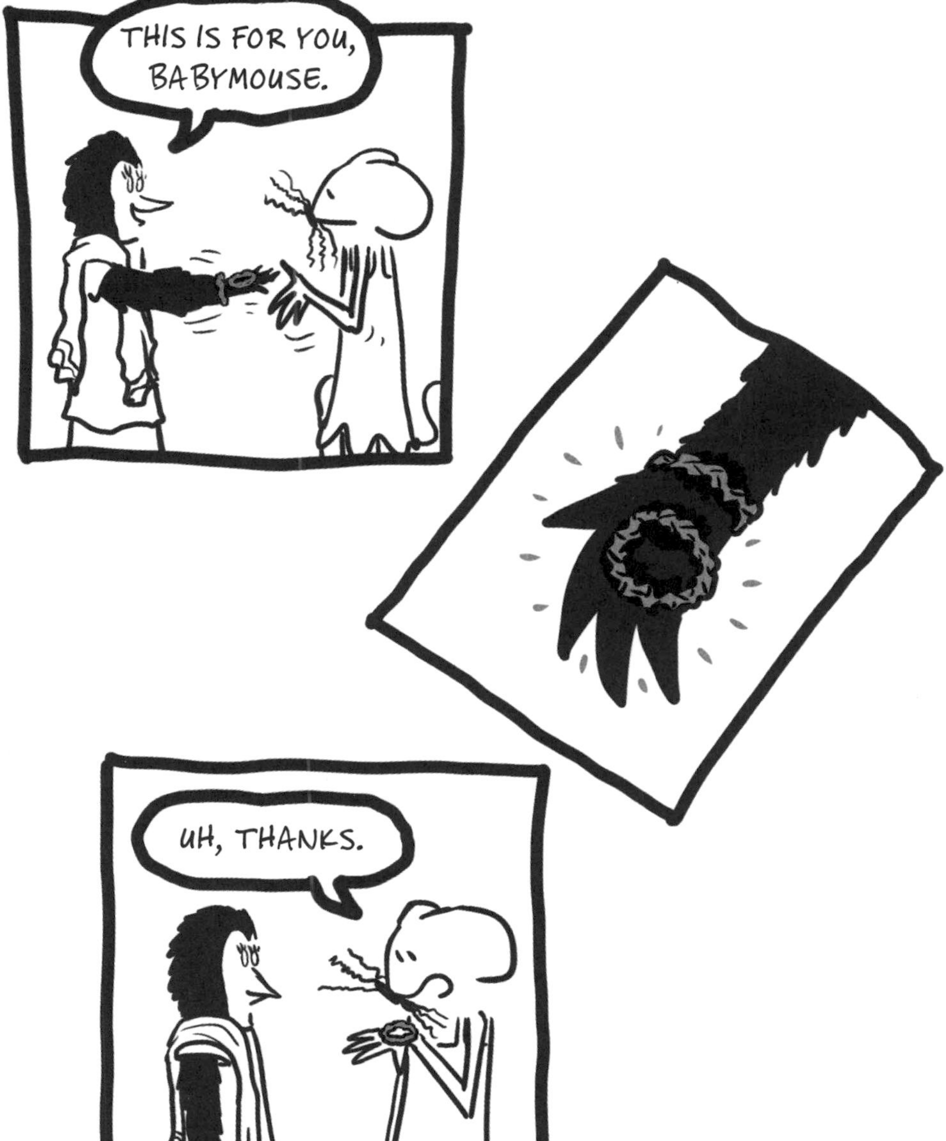
THIS IS FOR YOU, BABYMOUSE.
UH, THANKS.

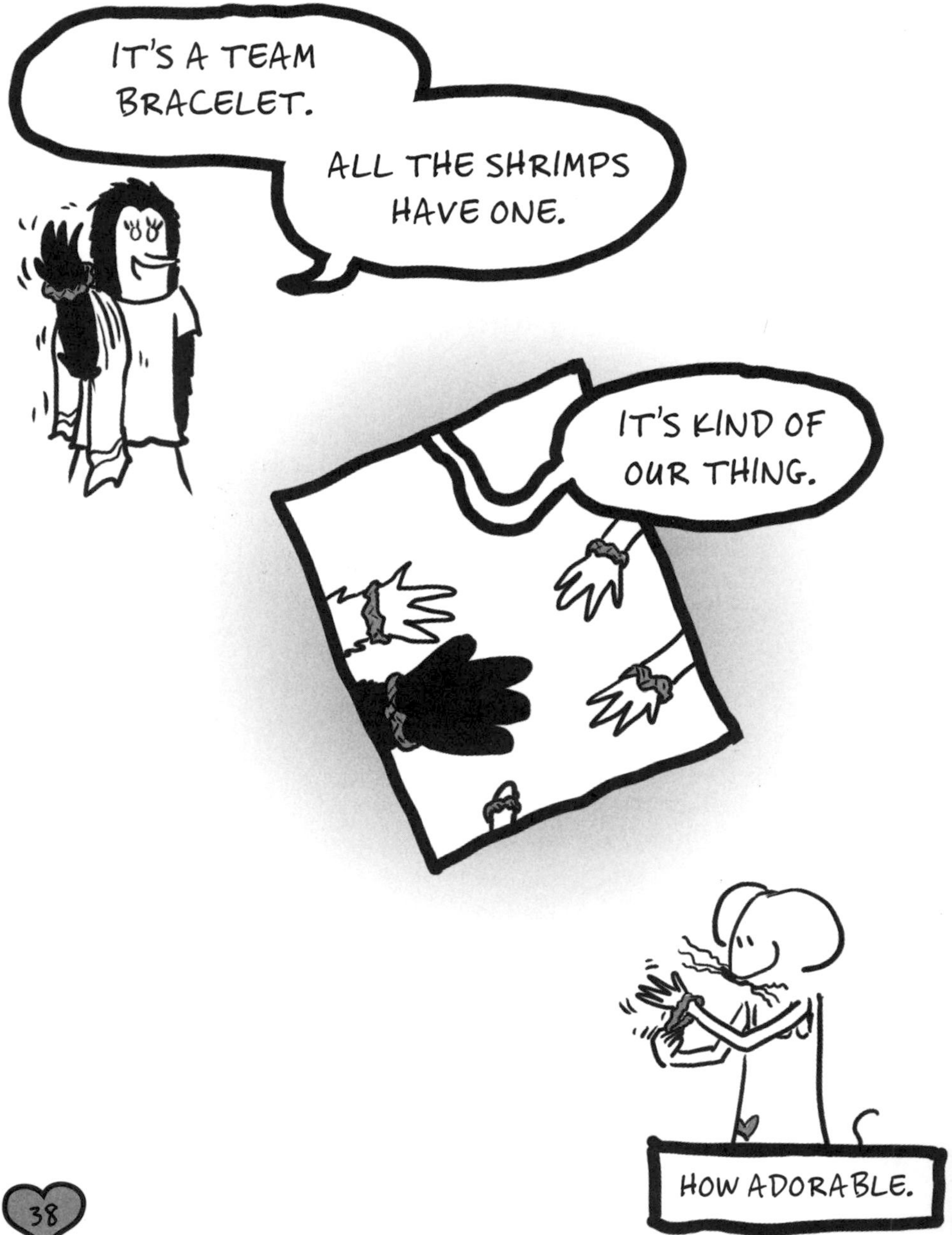
IT'S A TEAM BRACELET.
ALL THE SHRIMPS HAVE ONE.
IT'S KIND OF OUR THING.
HOW ADORABLE.

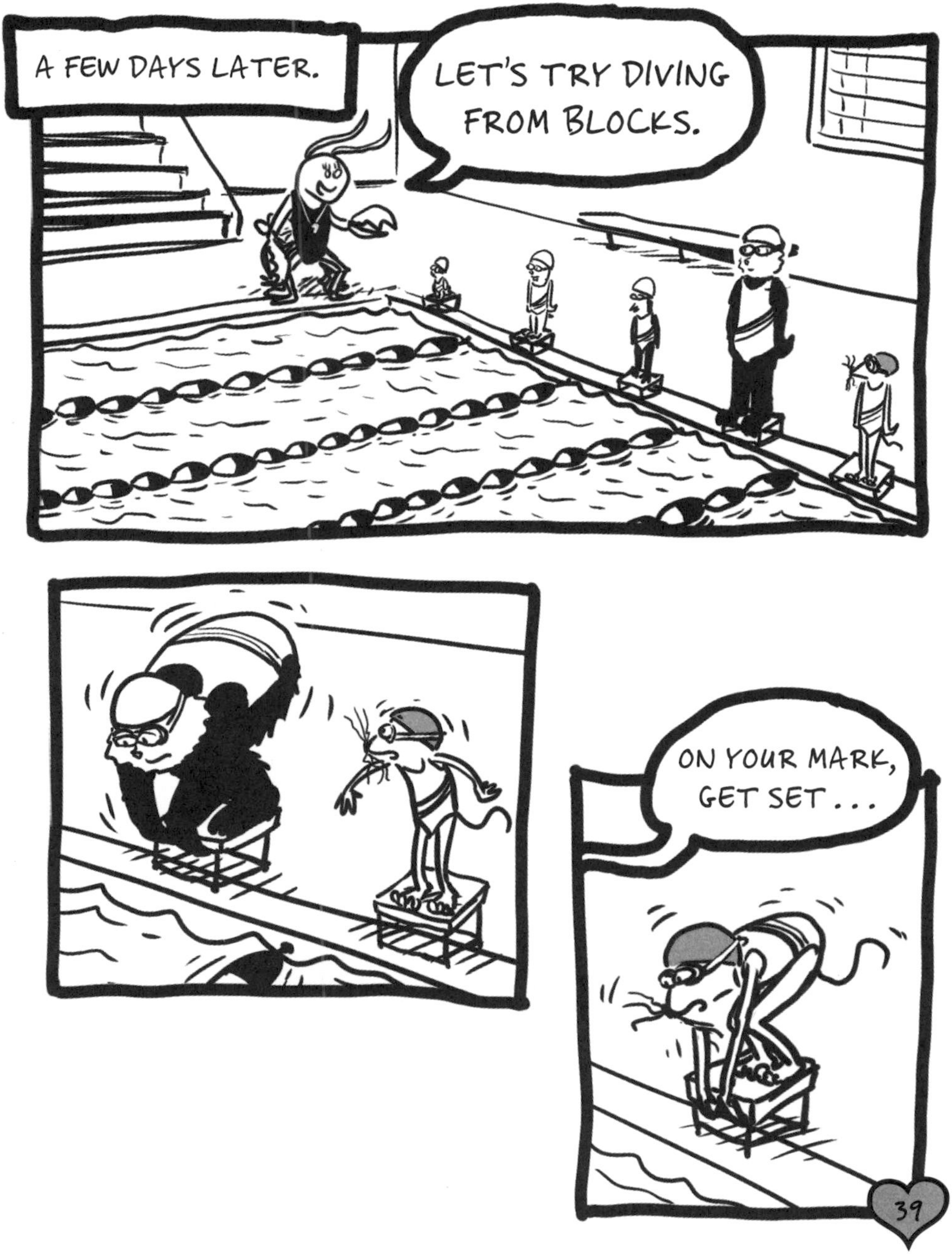
A FEW DAYS LATER.
LET'S TRY DIVING FROM BLOCKS.
ON YOUR MARK, GET SET . . .

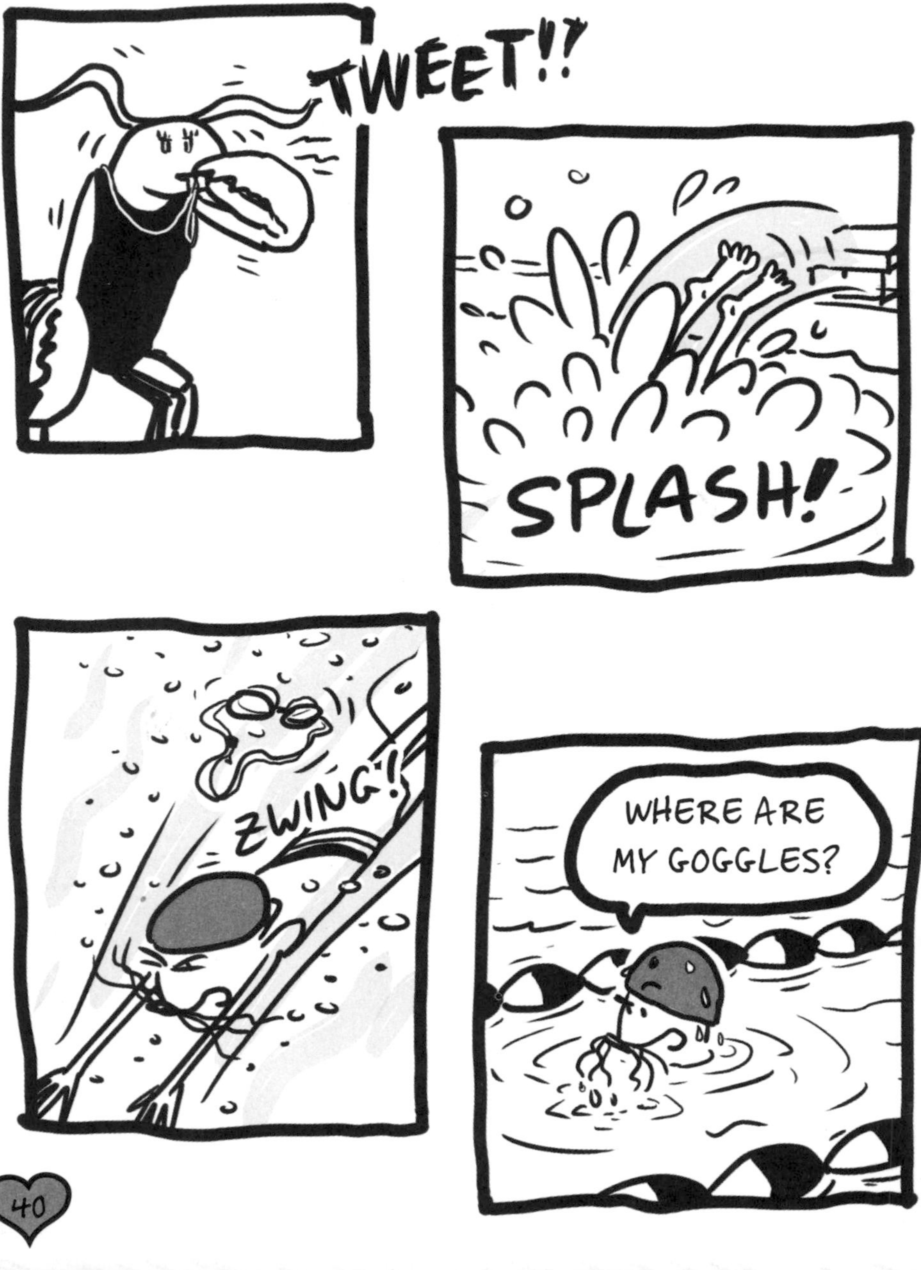
TWEET!!
SPLASH!
ZWING!
WHERE ARE MY GOGGLES?

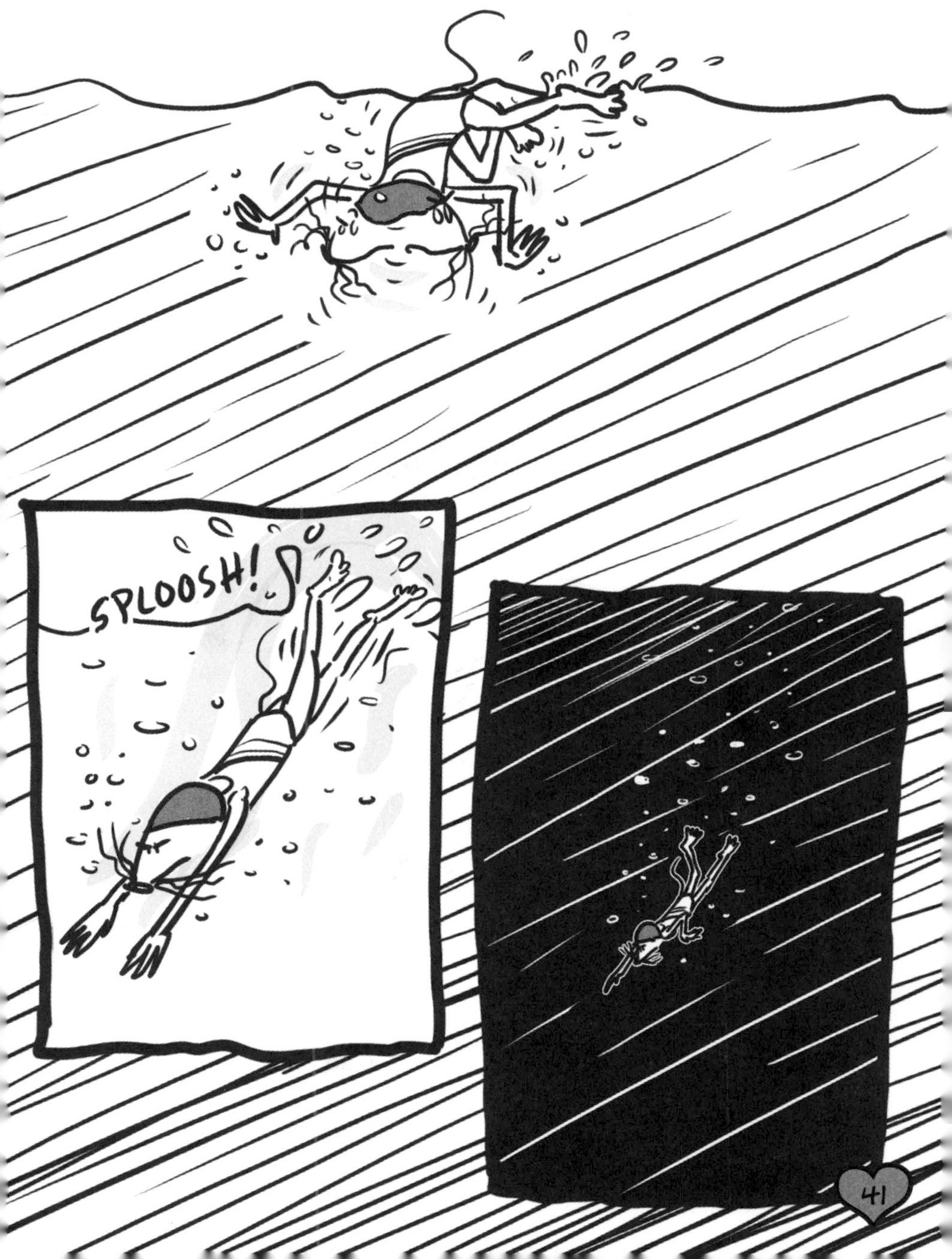
SPLOOSH!

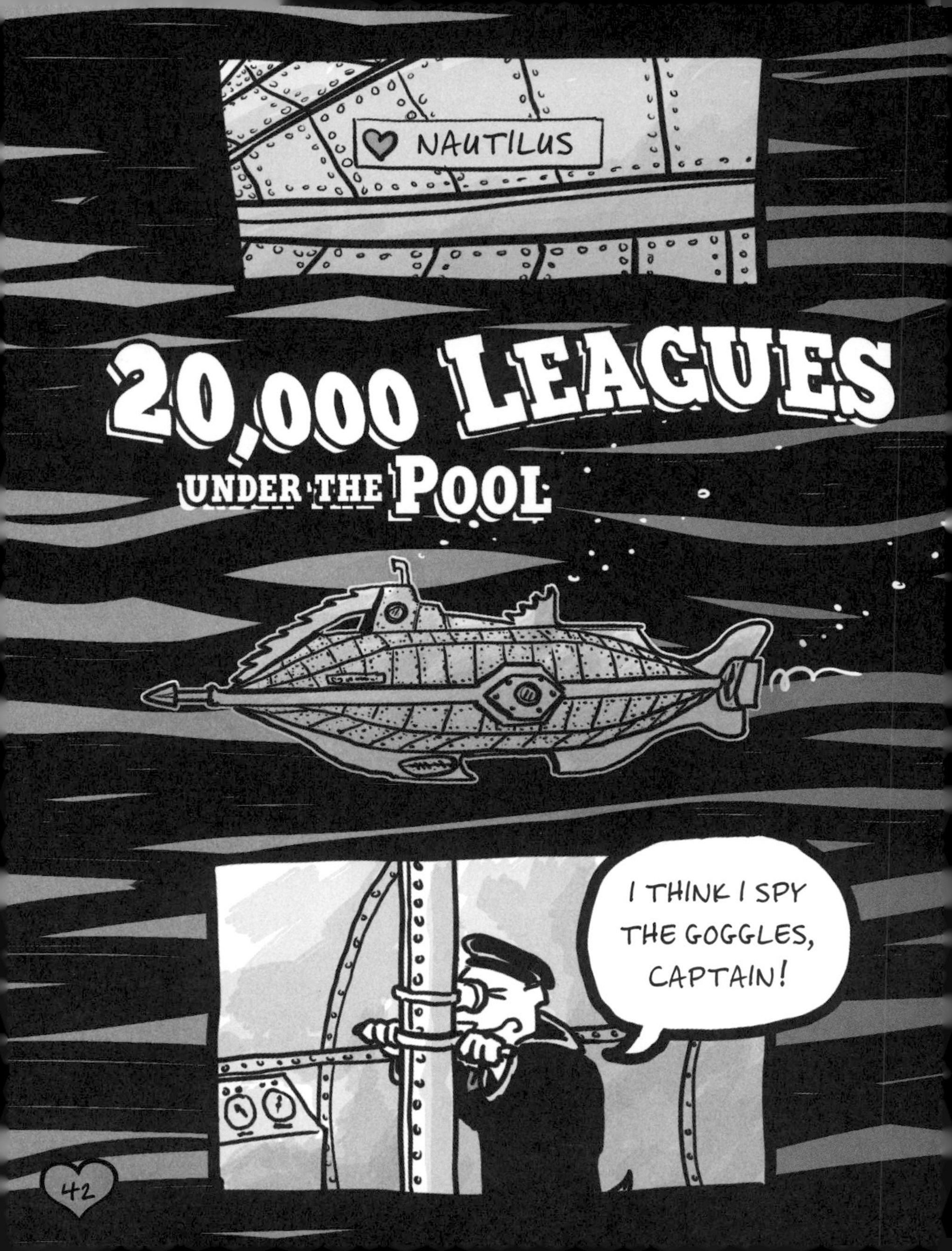
NAUTILUS
20,000 LEAGUES
UNDER THE POOL
I THINK I SPY THE GOGGLES, CAPTAIN!

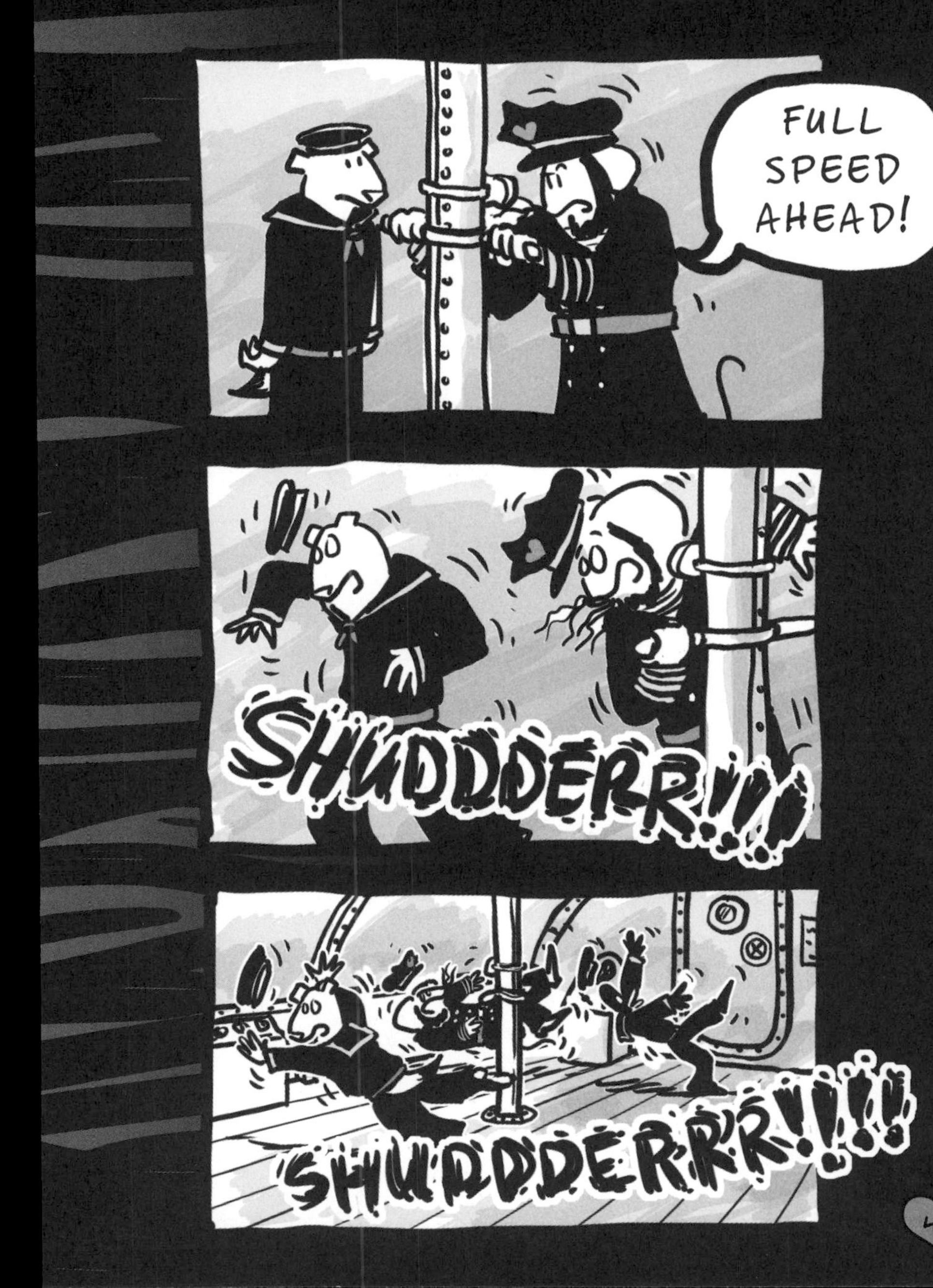
FULL SPEED AHEAD!
SHUDDDERR!!!
SHUDDDERRR!!!!

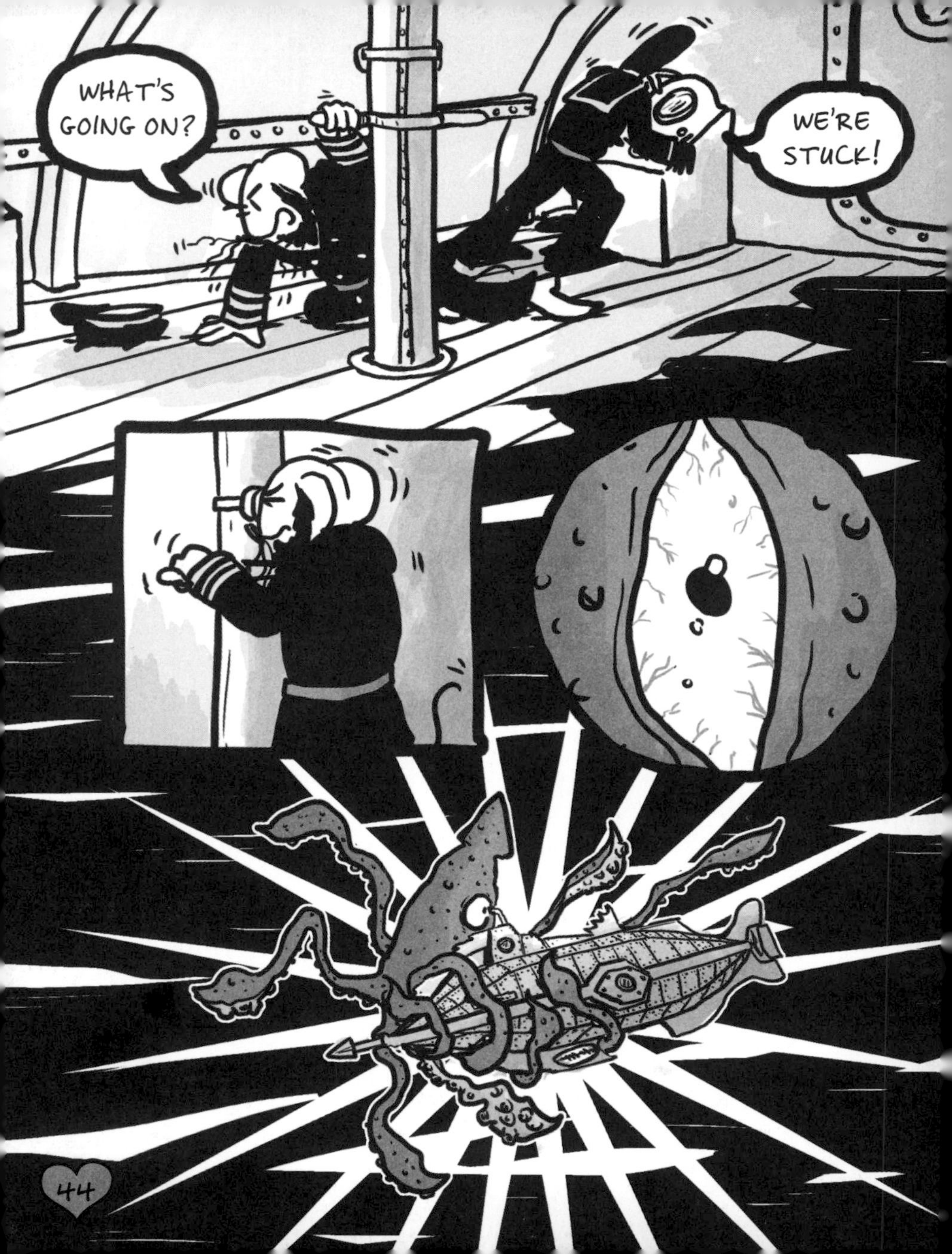
WHAT'S GOING ON?
WE'RE STUCK!

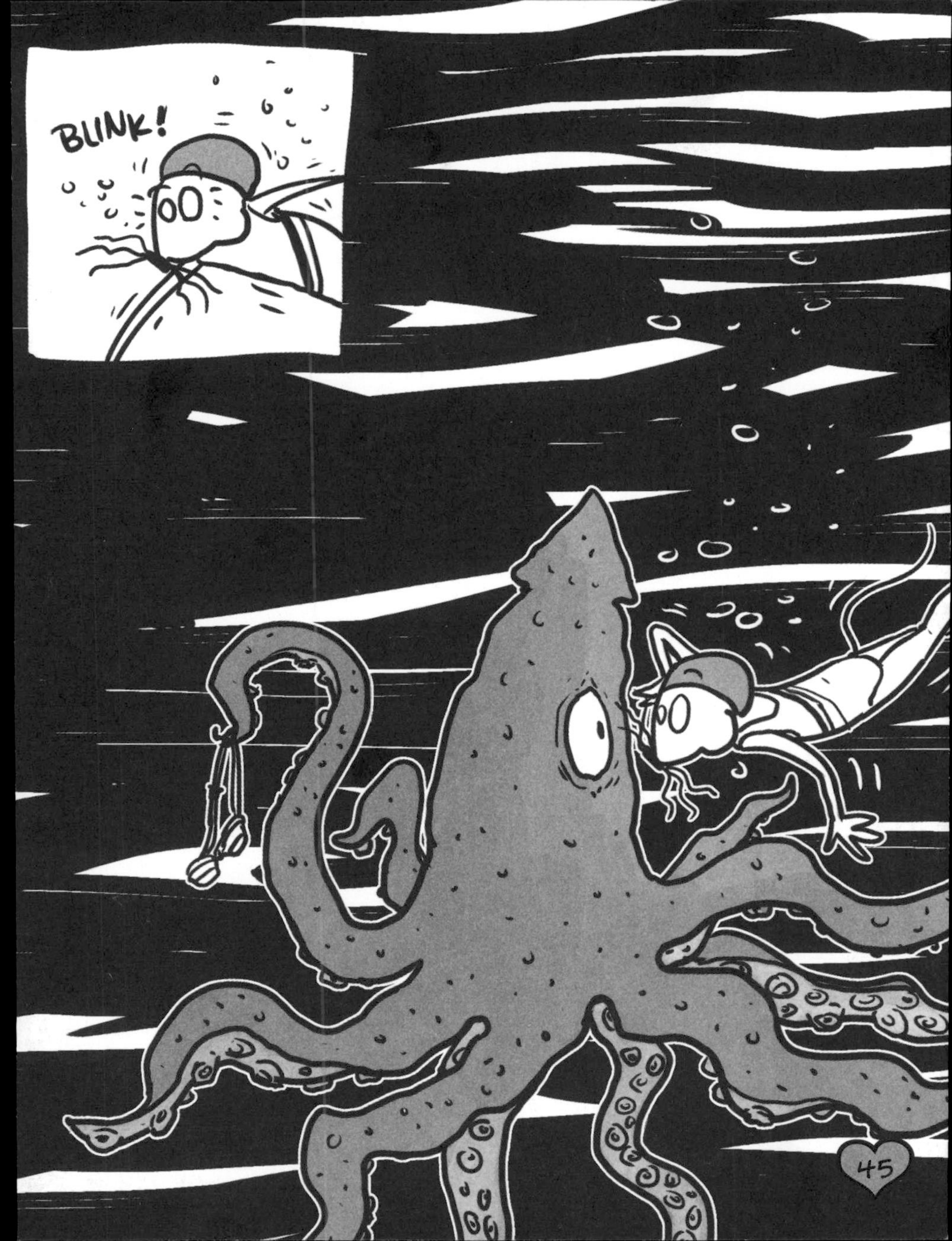
BLINK!

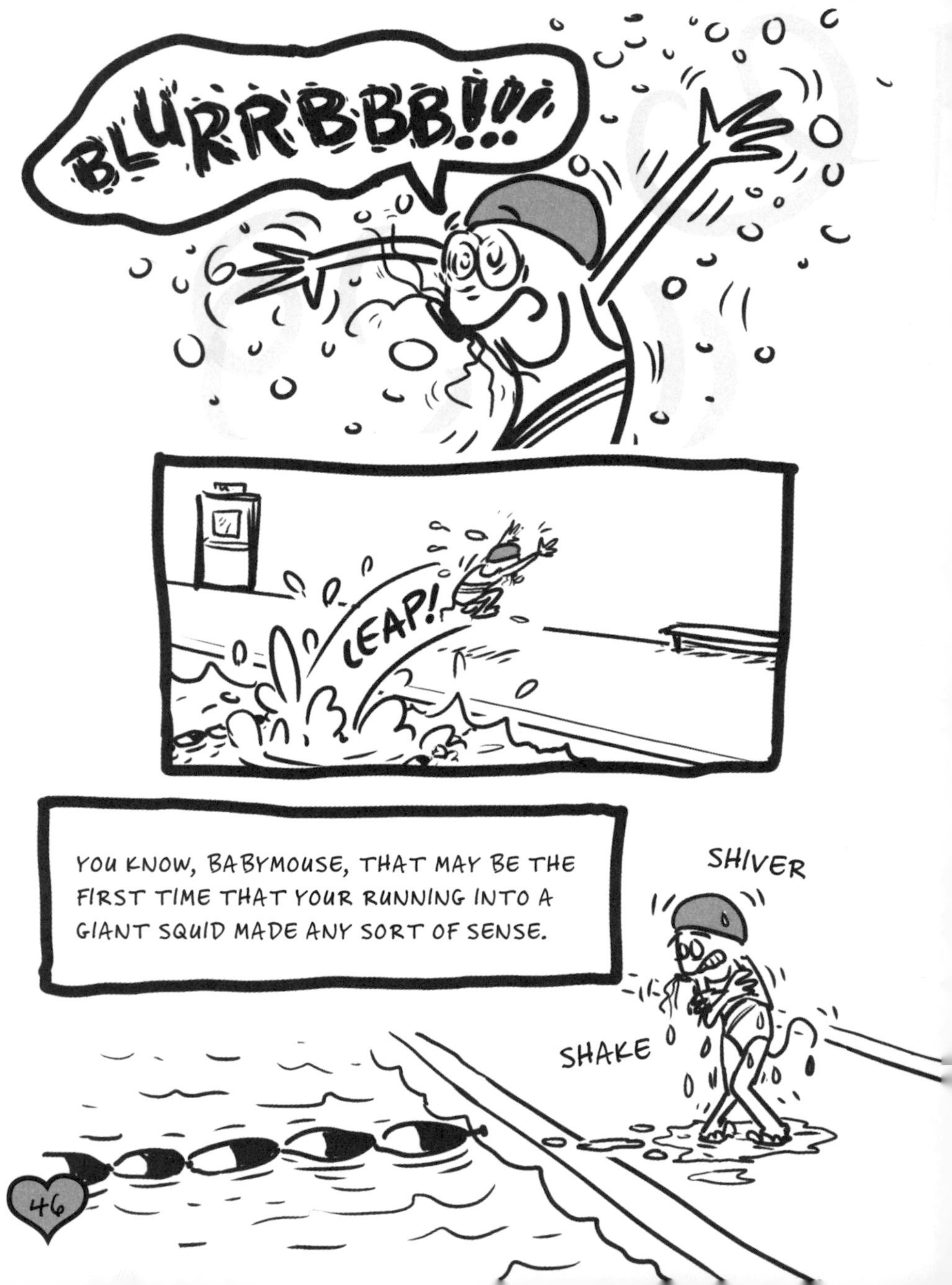
BLURRBBB!!!
LEAP!
YOU KNOW, BABYMOUSE, THAT MAY BE THE FIRST TIME THAT YOUR RUNNING INTO A GIANT SQUID MADE ANY SORT OF SENSE.
SHIVER
SHAKE

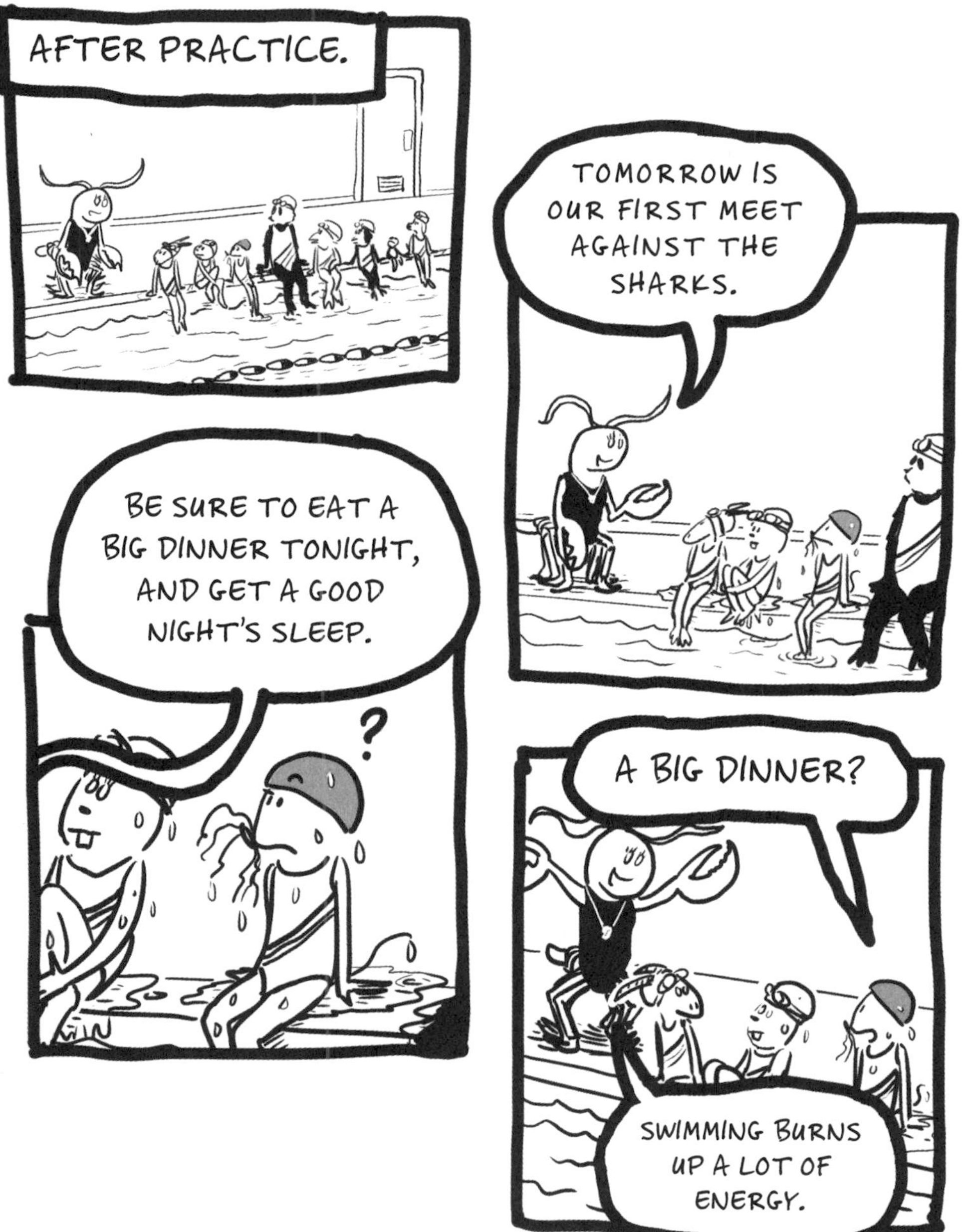
AFTER PRACTICE.
TOMORROW IS OUR FIRST MEET AGAINST THE SHARKS.
BE SURE TO EAT A BIG DINNER TONIGHT, AND GET A GOOD NIGHT'S SLEEP.
?
A BIG DINNER?
SWIMMING BURNS UP A LOT OF ENERGY.

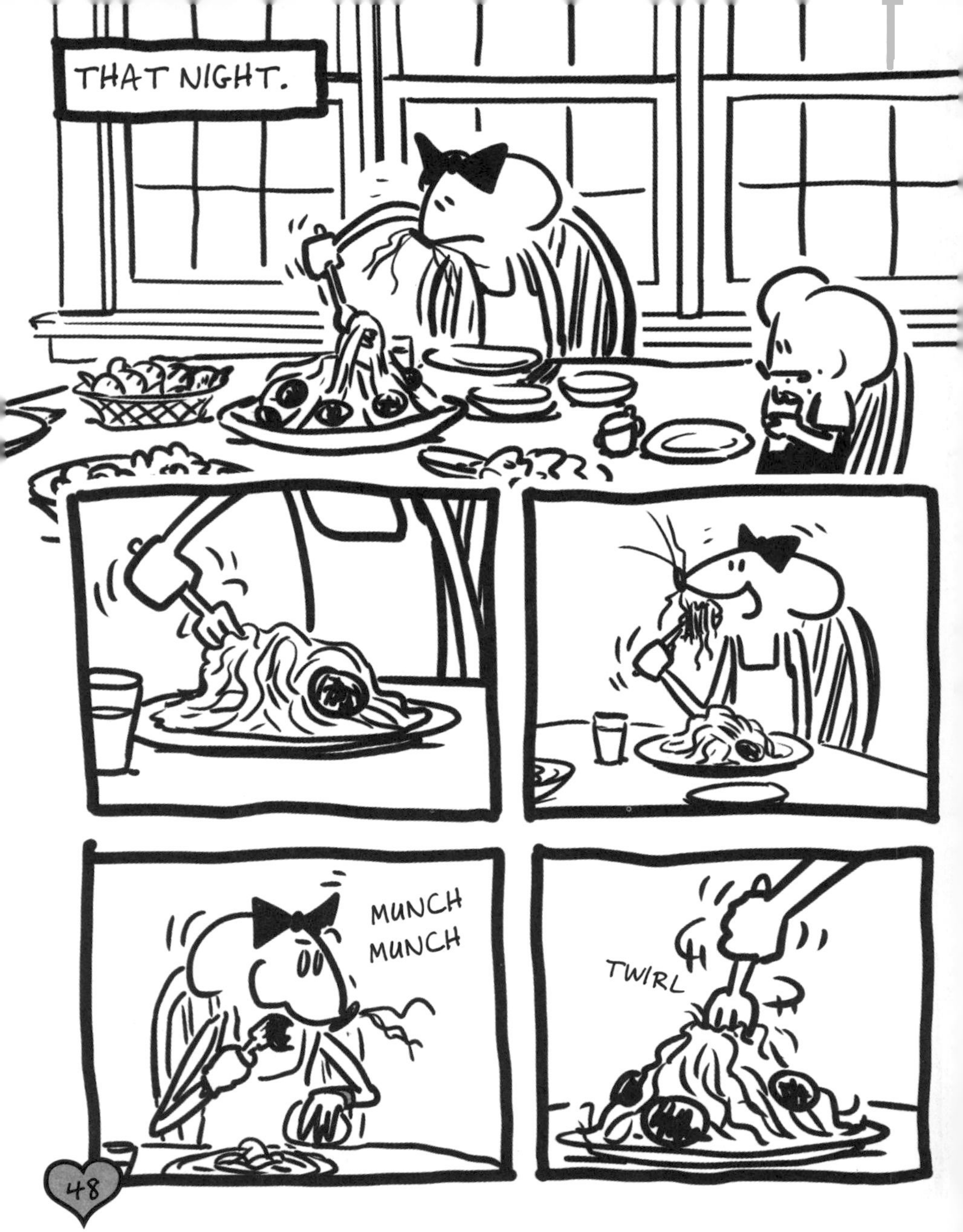
THAT NIGHT.
MUNCH
MUNCH
TWIRL

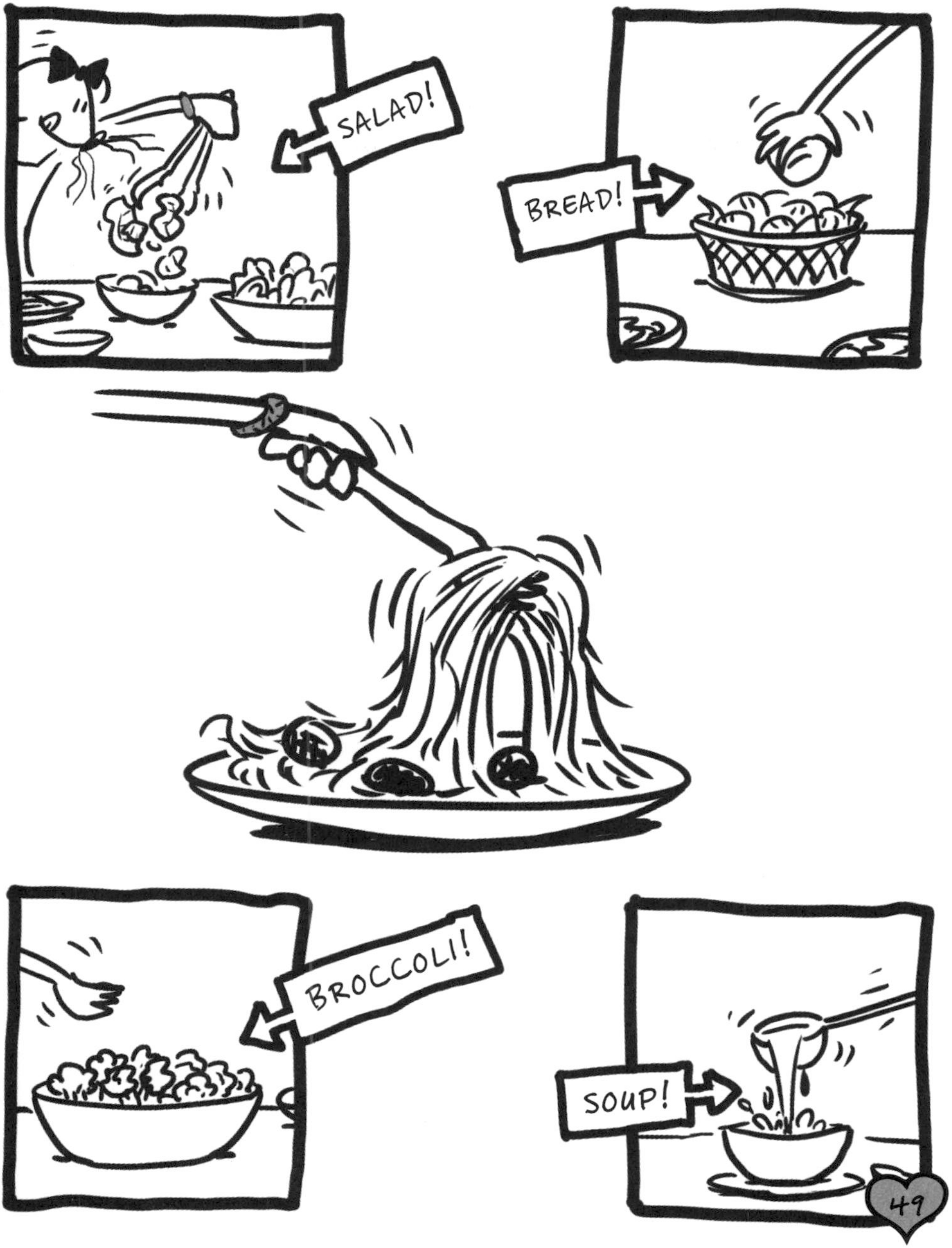
SALAD!
BREAD!
BROCCOLI!
SOUP!

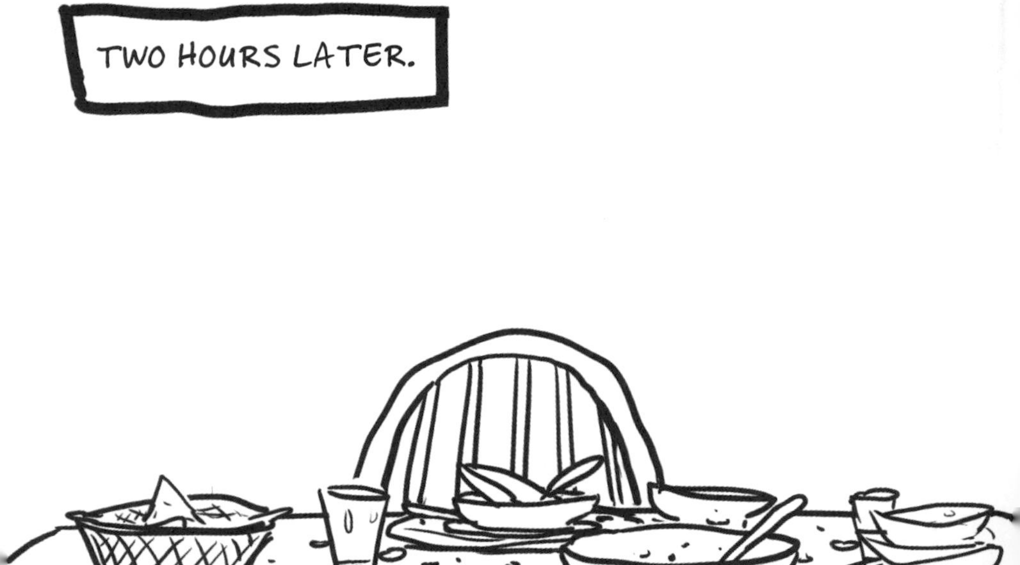
TWO HOURS LATER.

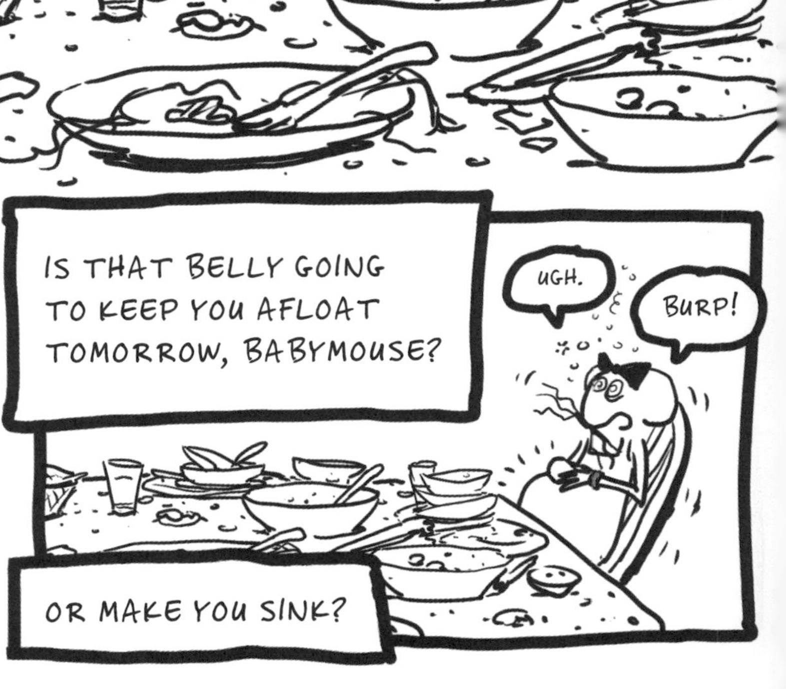
IS THAT BELLY GOING TO KEEP YOU AFLOAT TOMORROW, BABYMOUSE?
UGH.
BURP!
OR MAKE YOU SINK?

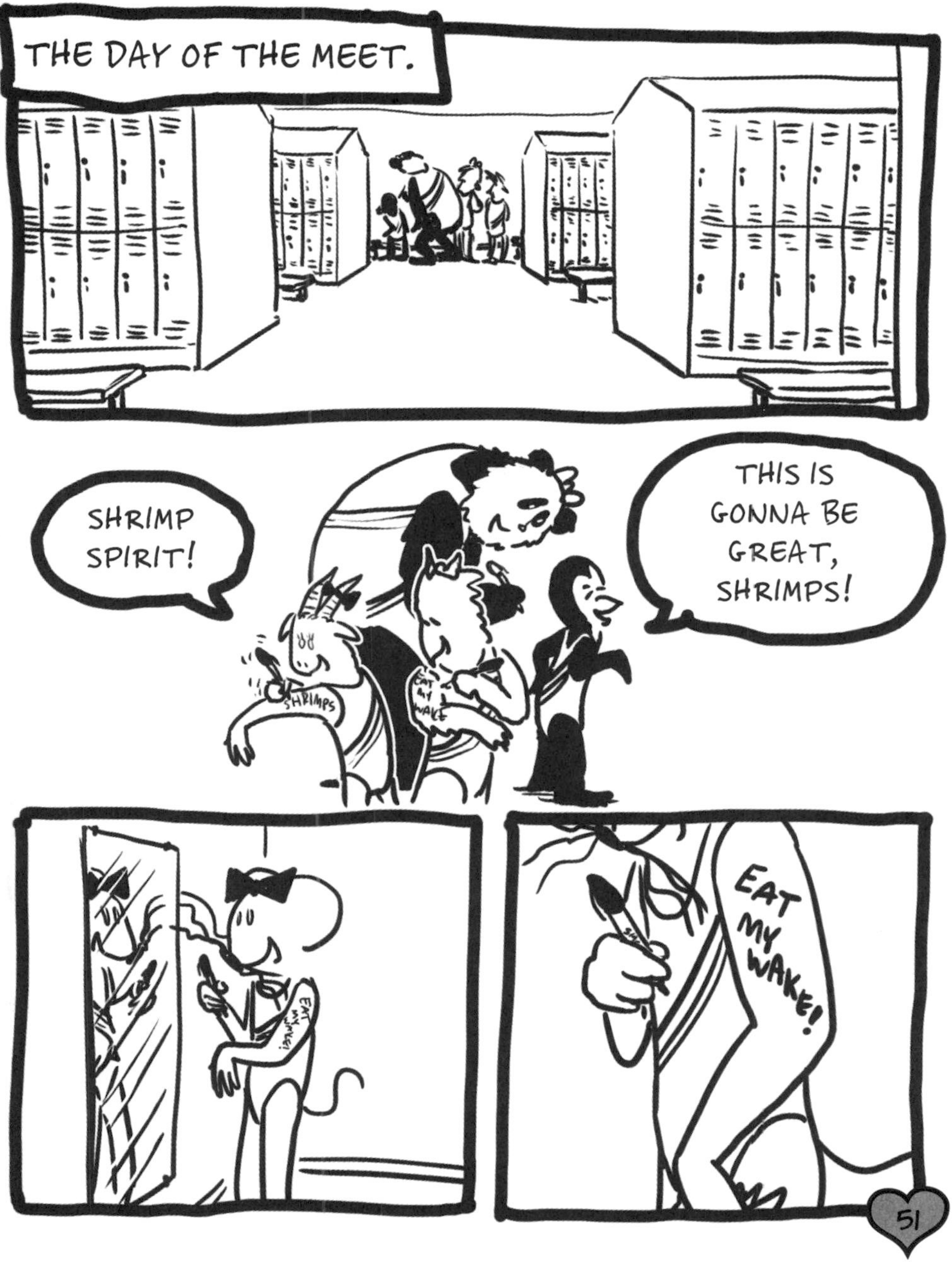
THE DAY OF THE MEET.
SHRIMP SPIRIT!
THIS IS GONNA BE GREAT, SHRIMPS!
SHRIMPS
EAT MY WAKE
EAT MY WAKE!
EAT MY WAKE!

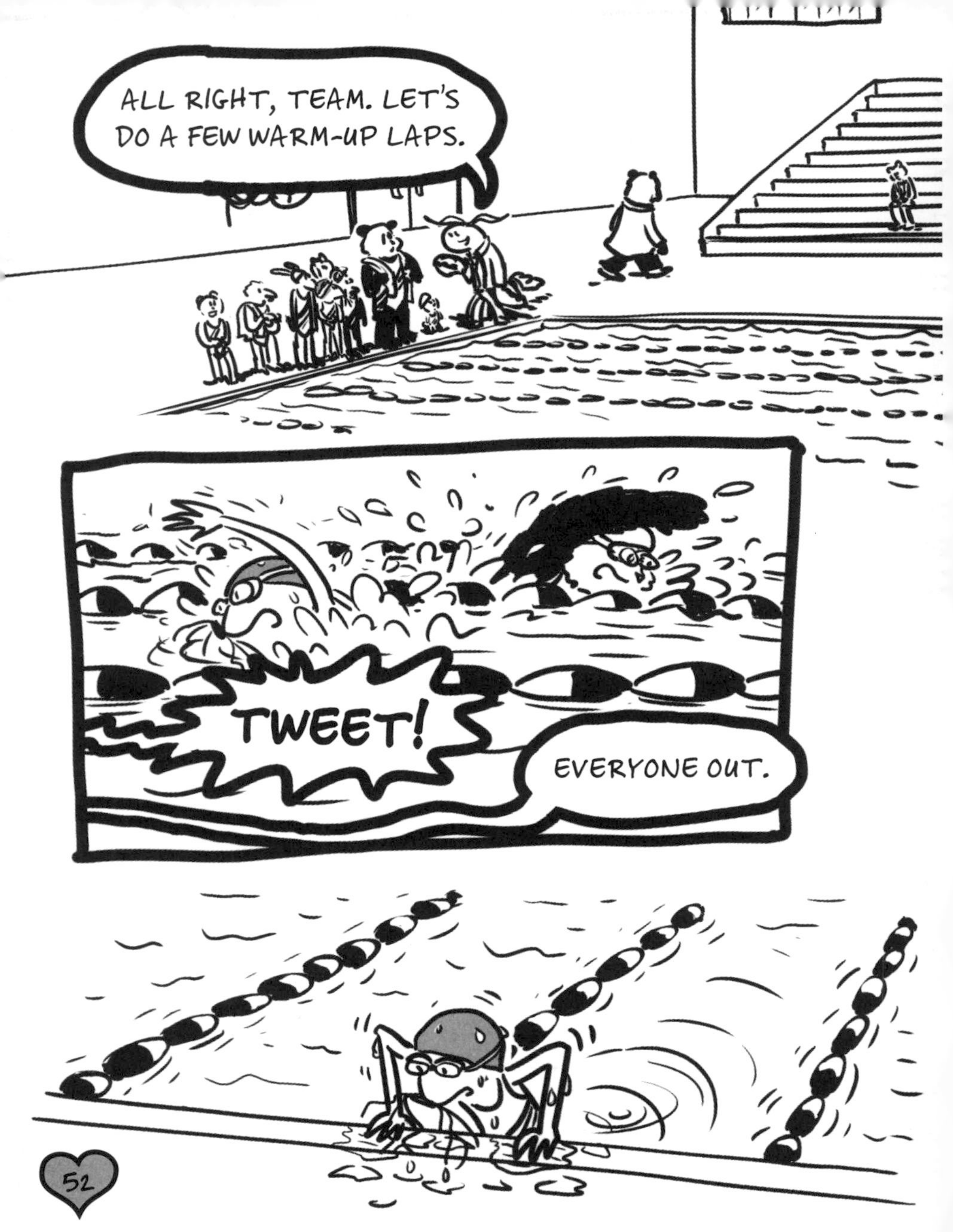
ALL RIGHT, TEAM. LET'S DO A FEW WARM-UP LAPS.
TWEET!
EVERYONE OUT.

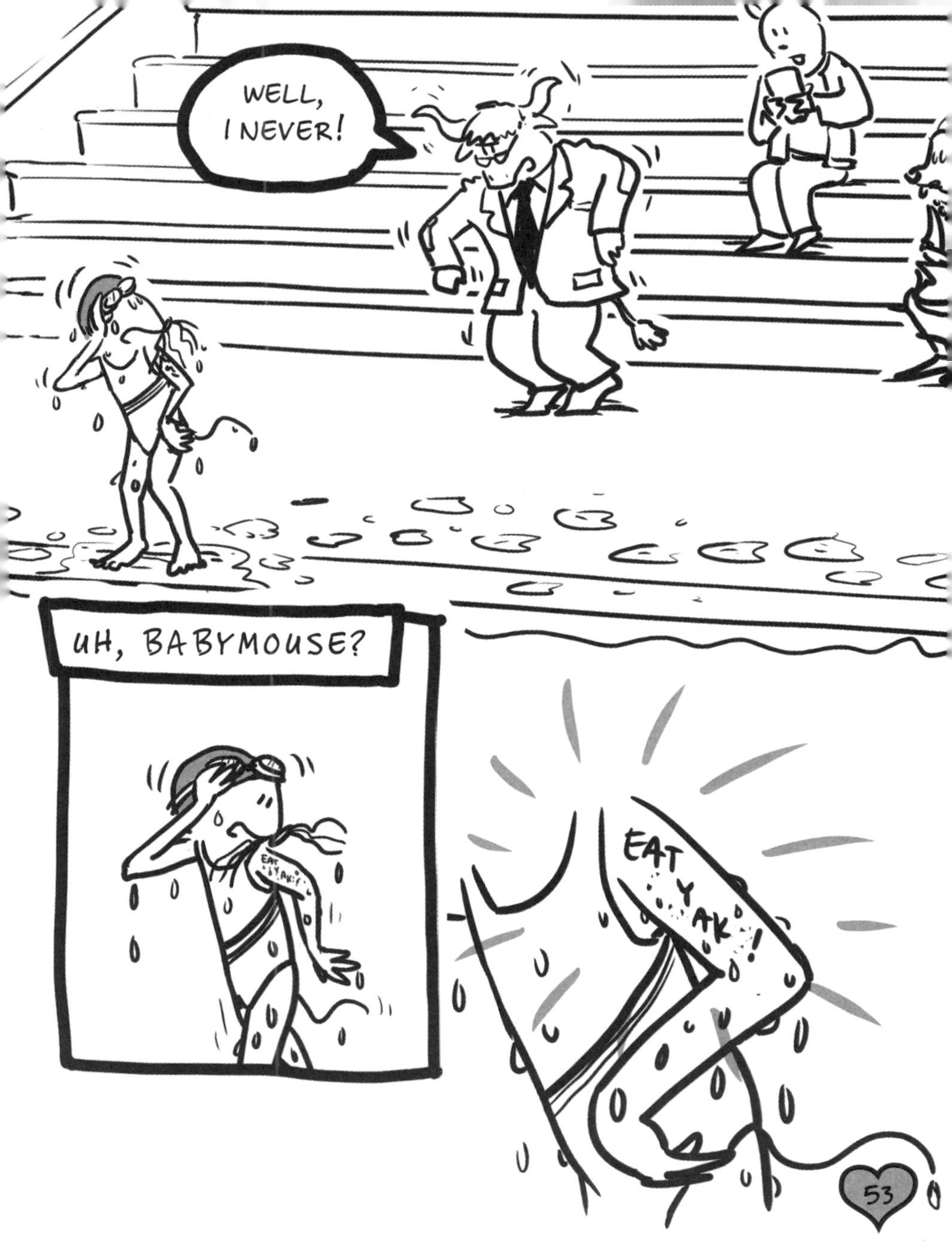
WELL, I NEVER!
UH, BABYMOUSE?
EAT YAK!

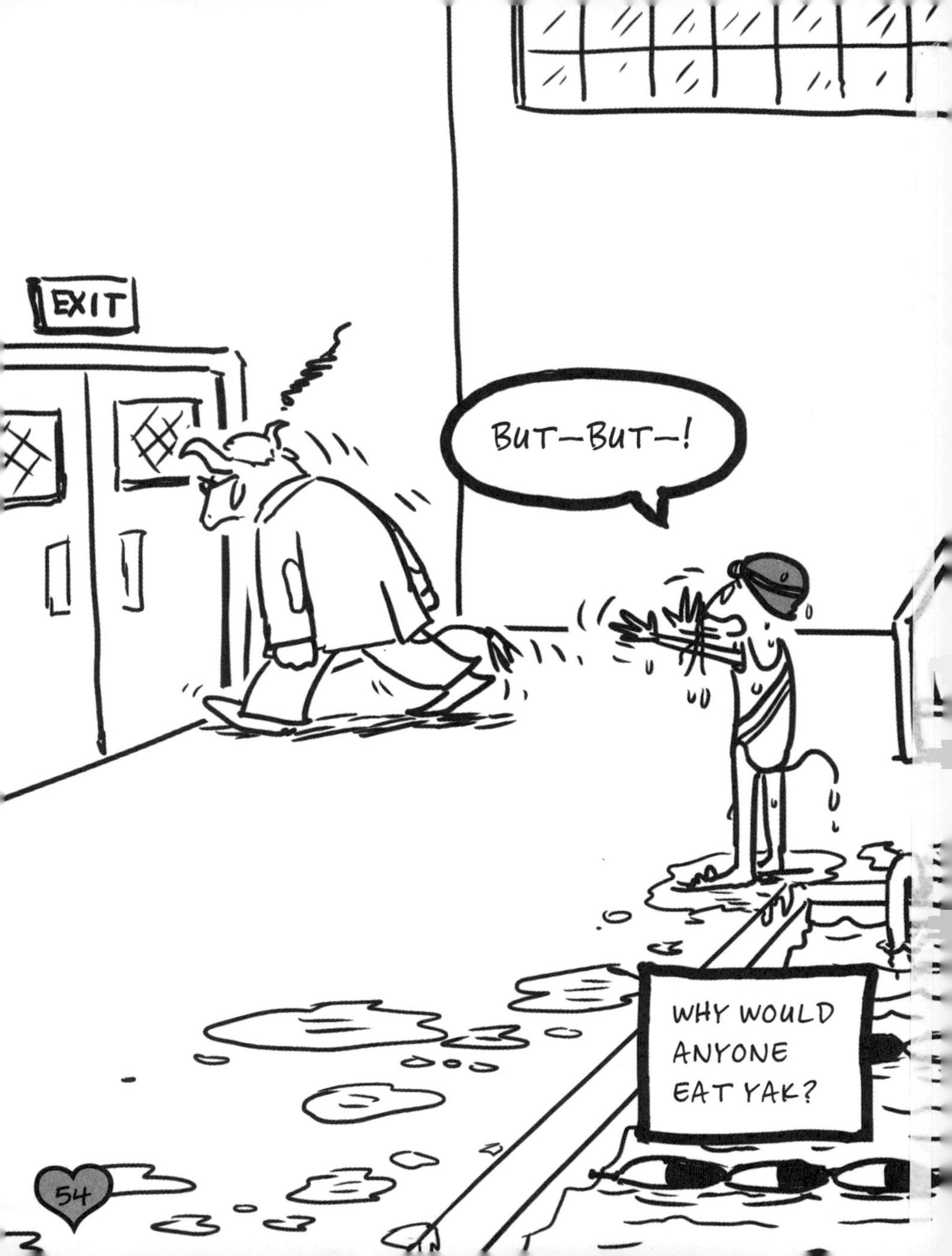
EXIT
BUT—BUT—!
WHY WOULD ANYONE EAT YAK?

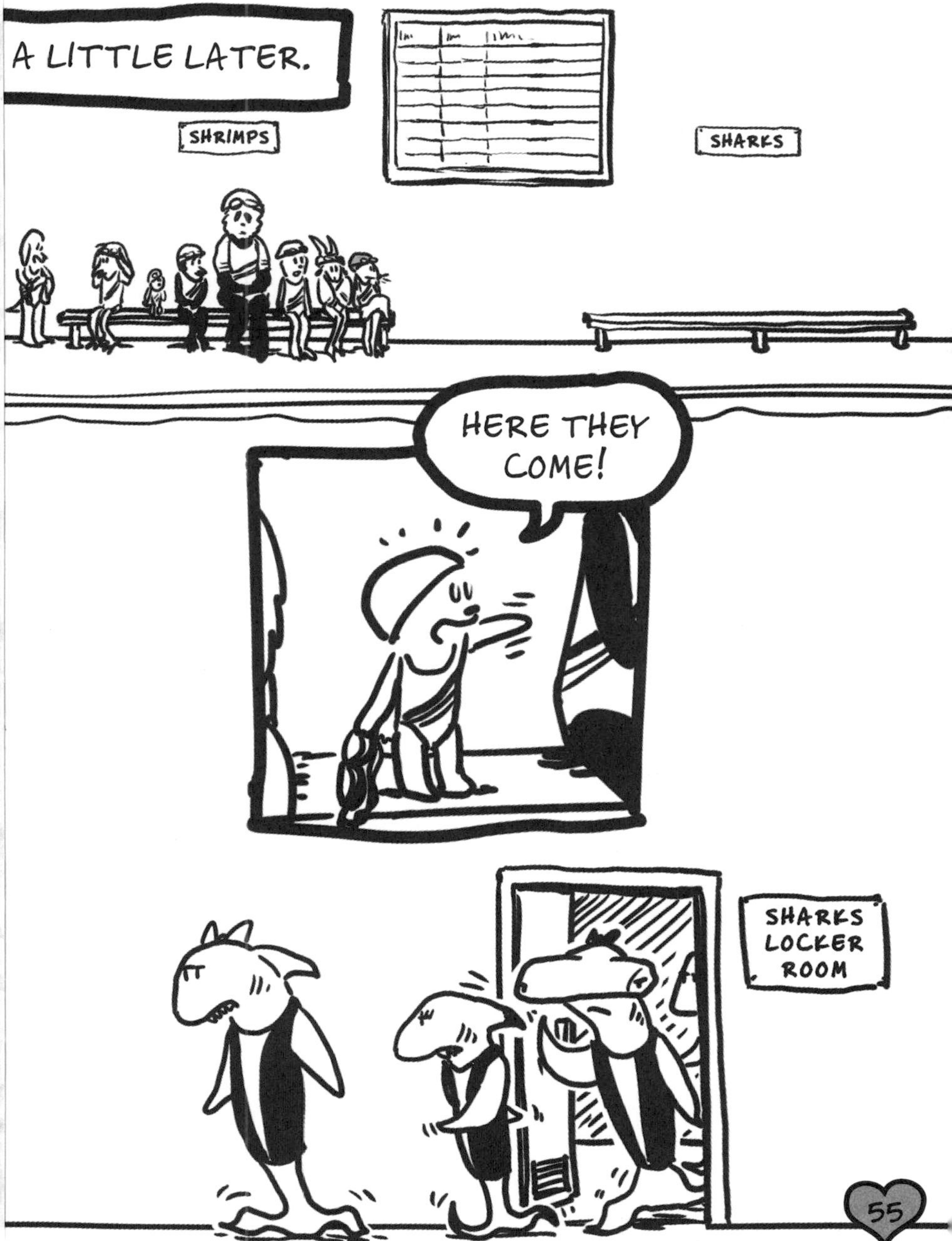
A LITTLE LATER.
SHRIMPS
SHARKS
HERE THEY COME!
SHARKS LOCKER ROOM

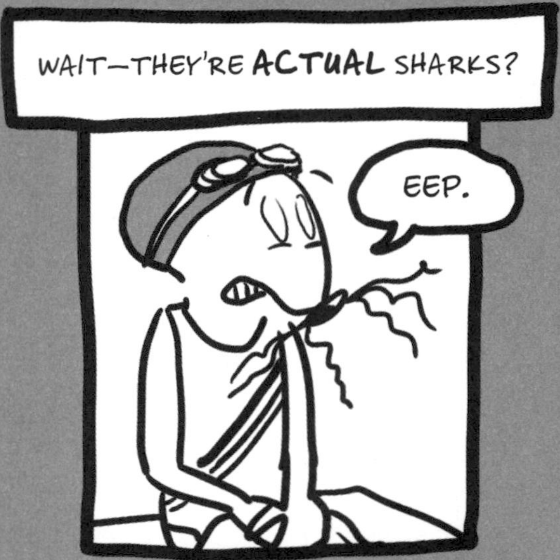
WAIT—THEY'RE **ACTUAL** SHARKS?
EEP.

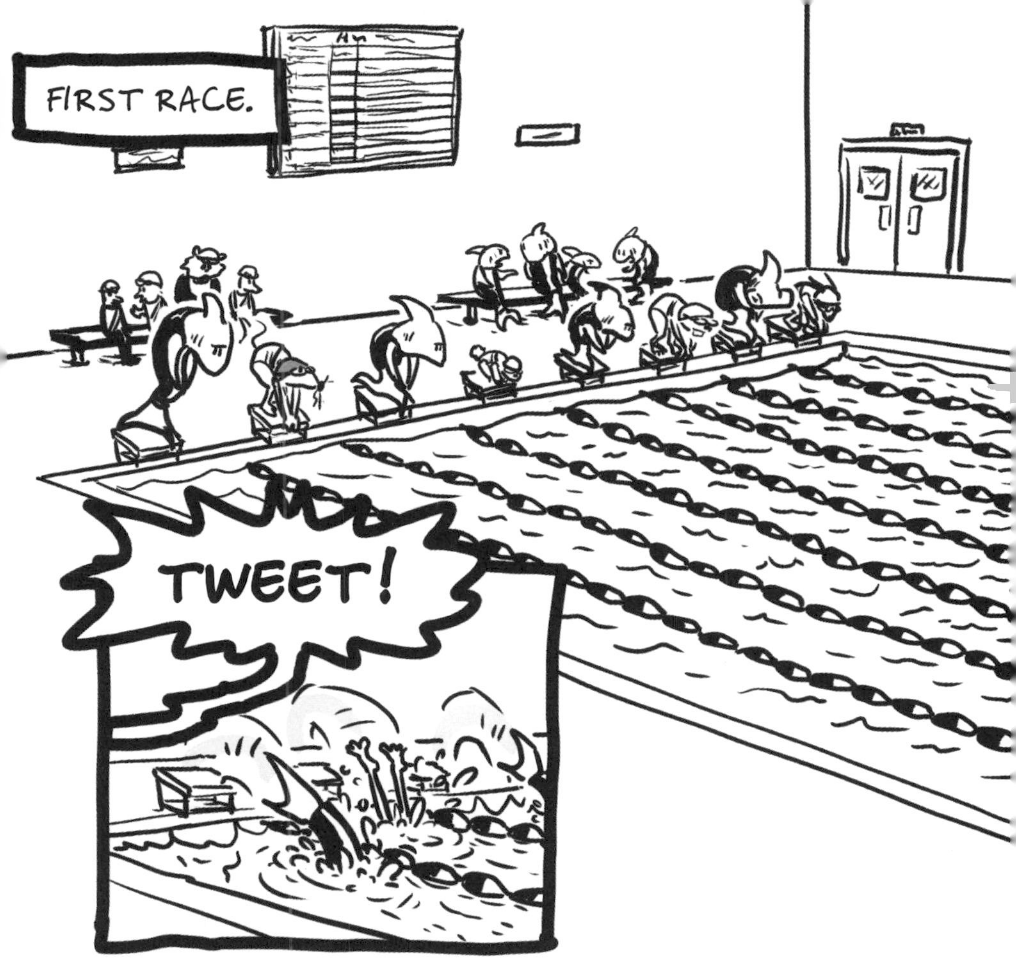
FIRST RACE.
TWEET!

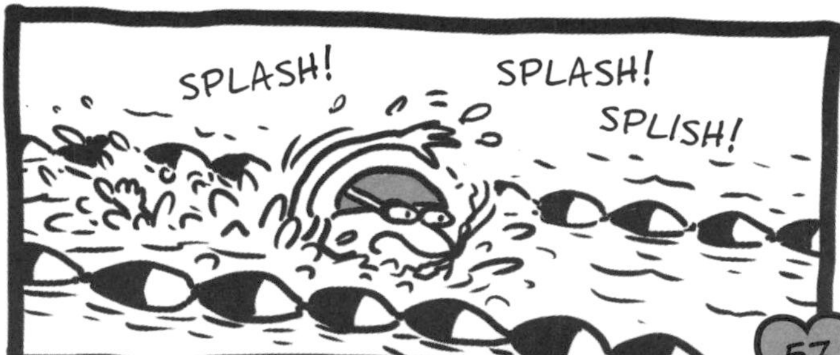
SPLASH!
SPLASH!
SPLISH!

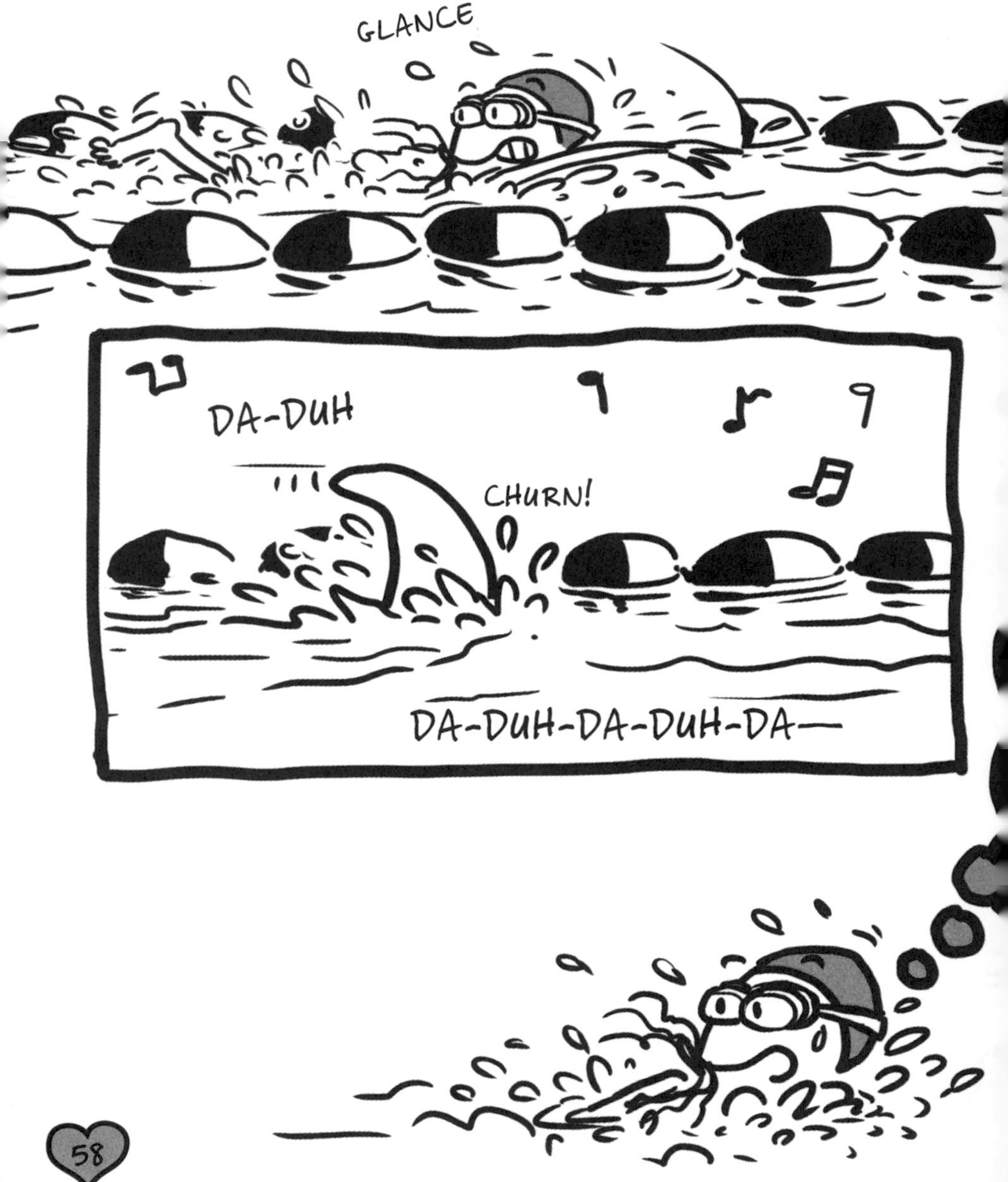
GLANCE
DA-DUH
CHURN!
DA-DUH-DA-DUH-DA—

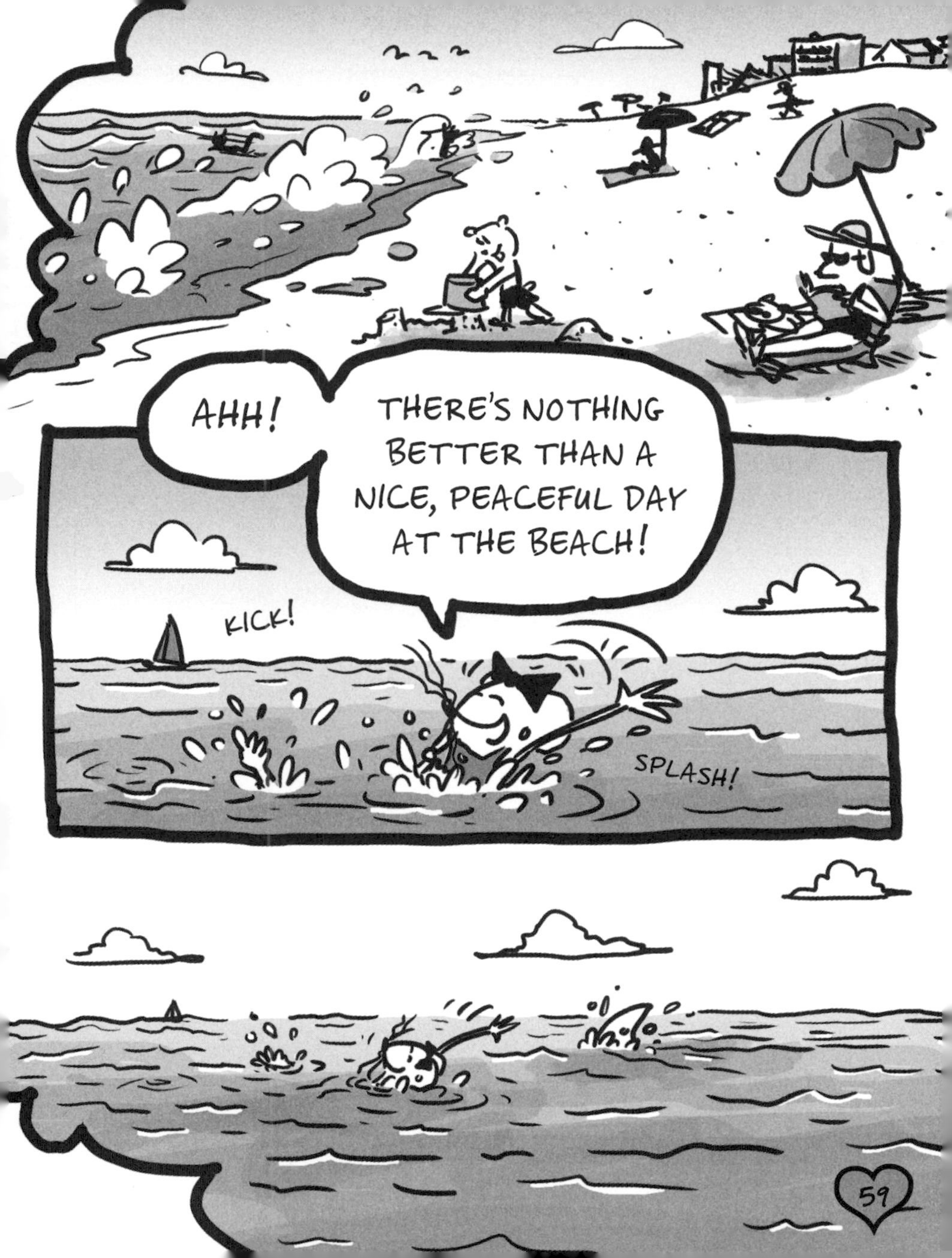
AHH!
THERE'S NOTHING BETTER THAN A NICE, PEACEFUL DAY AT THE BEACH!
KICK!
SPLASH!

TUG!

BLOOP!

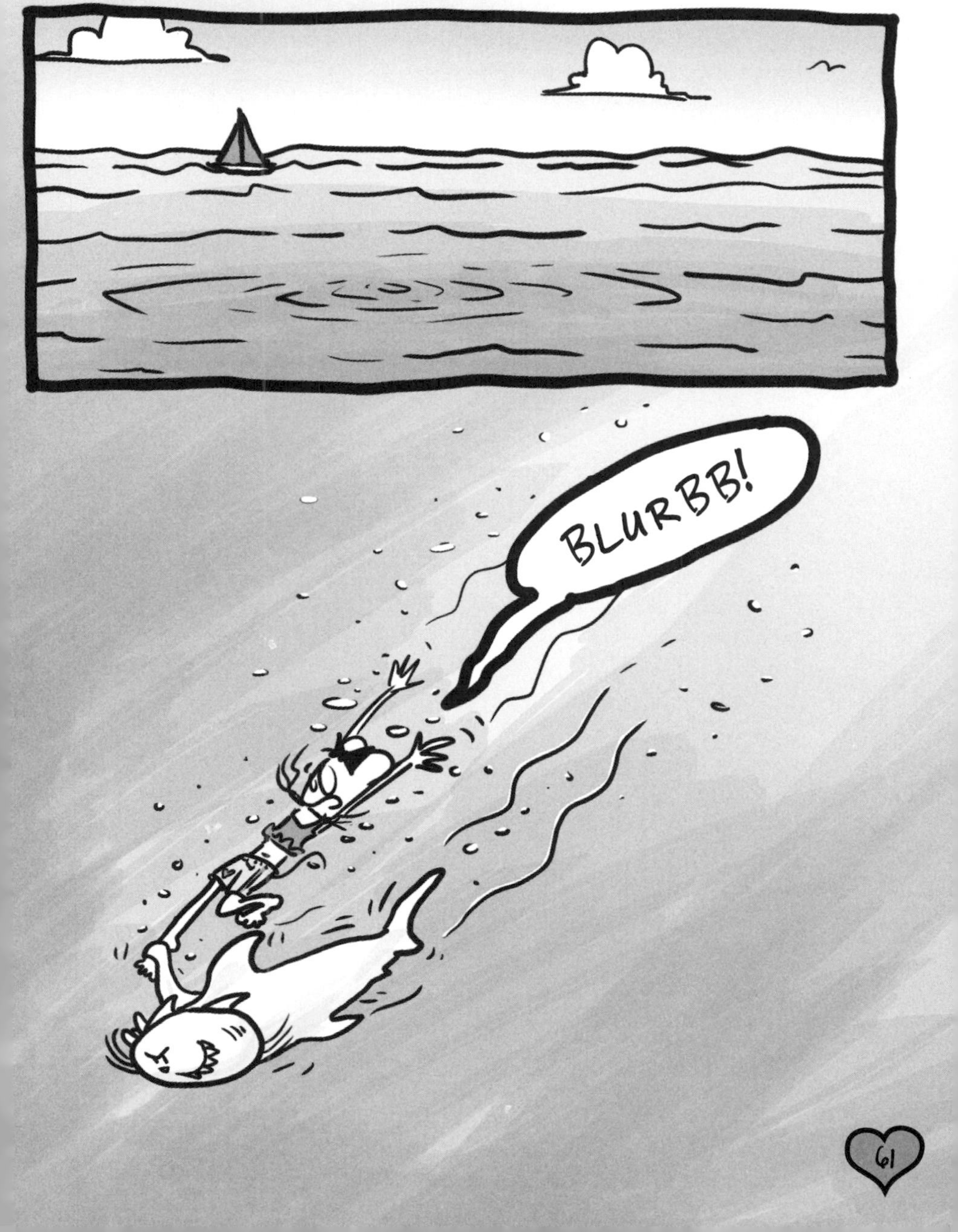
BLURBB!

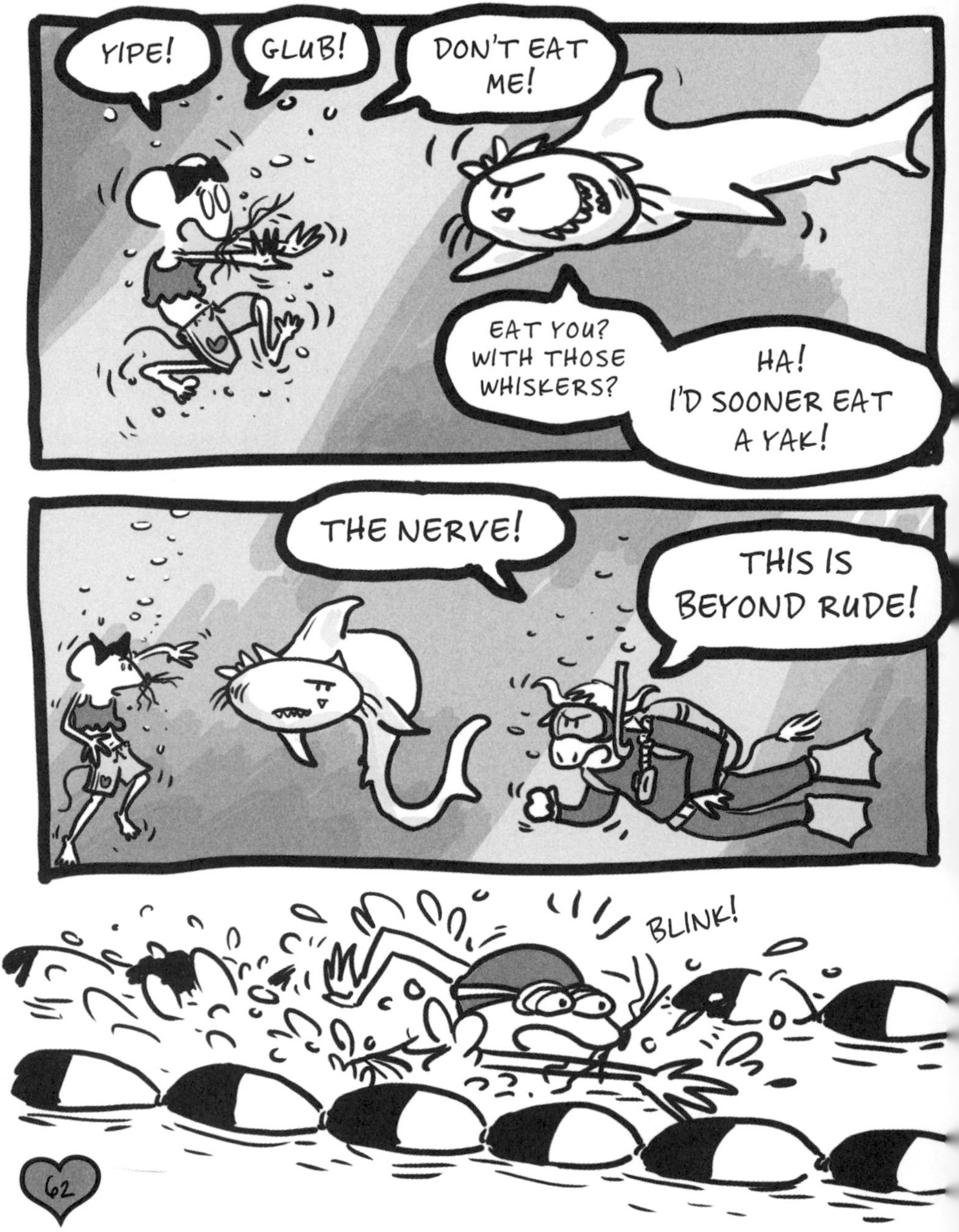
YIPE!
GLUB!
DON'T EAT ME!
EAT YOU? WITH THOSE WHISKERS?
HA! I'D SOONER EAT A YAK!
THE NERVE!
THIS IS BEYOND RUDE!
BLINK!

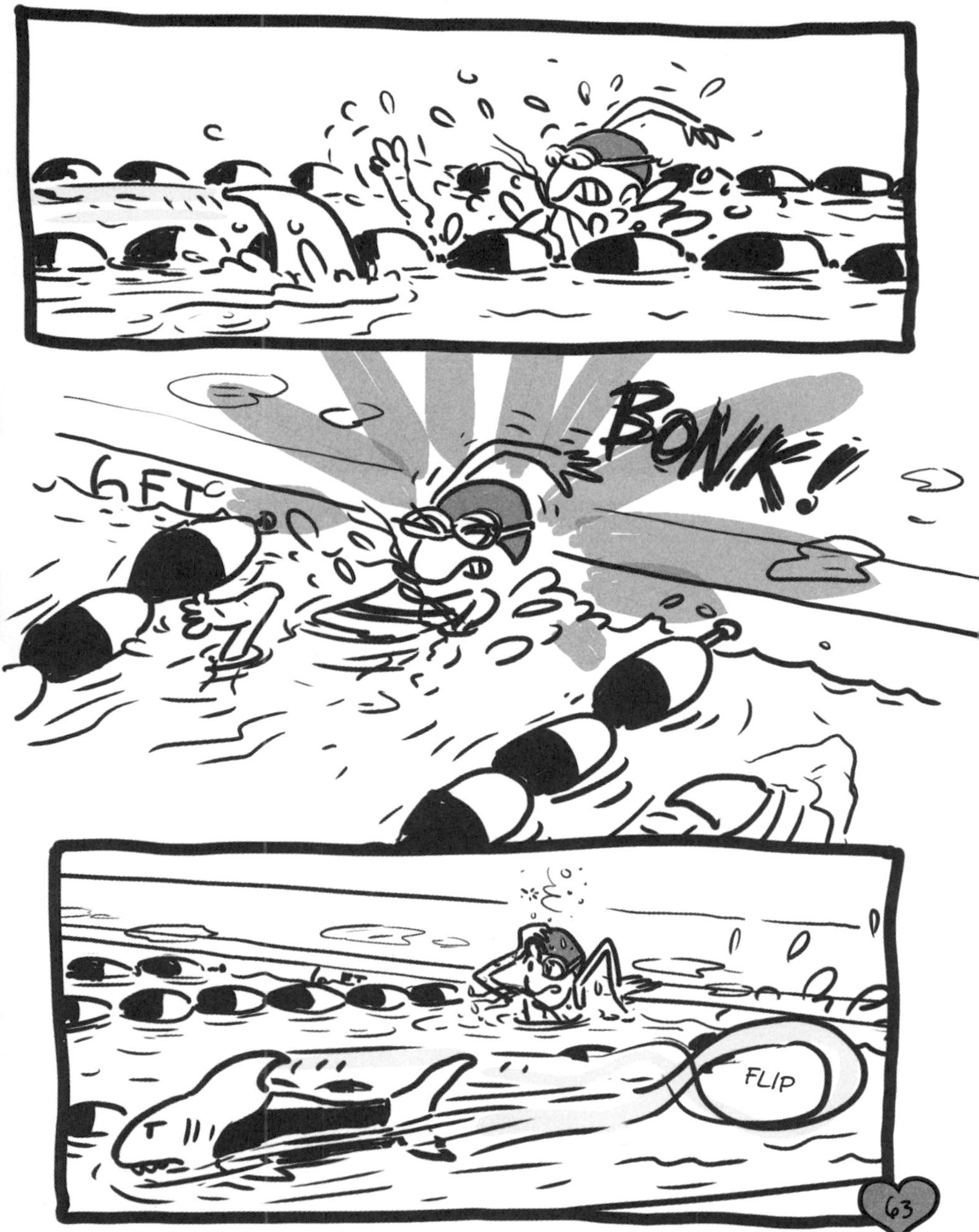
BONK!!
FLIP

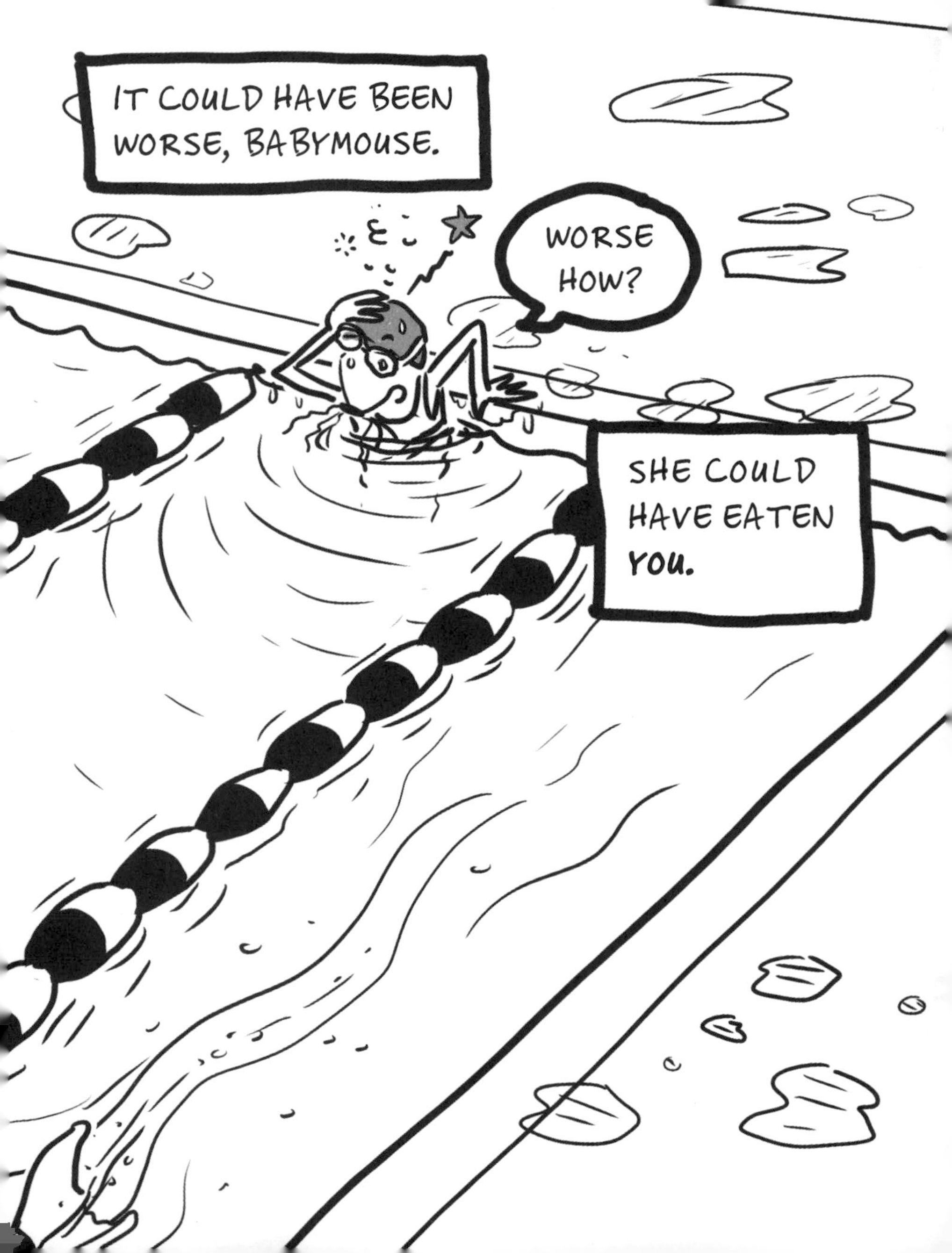
IT COULD HAVE BEEN WORSE, BABYMOUSE.
WORSE HOW?
SHE COULD HAVE EATEN YOU.

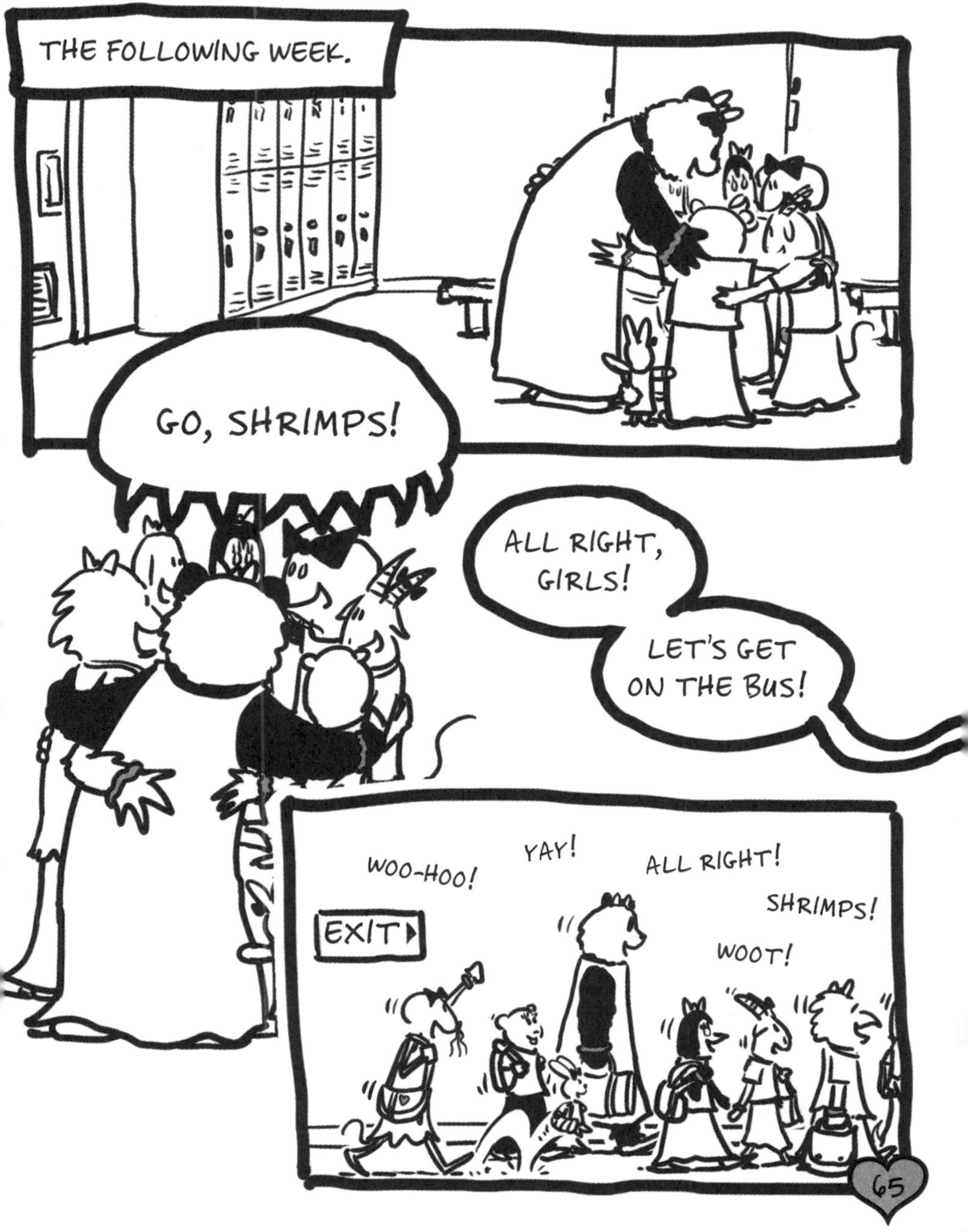
THE FOLLOWING WEEK.
GO, SHRIMPS!
ALL RIGHT, GIRLS!
LET'S GET ON THE BUS!
WOO-HOO!
YAY!
ALL RIGHT!
EXIT
SHRIMPS!
WOOT!

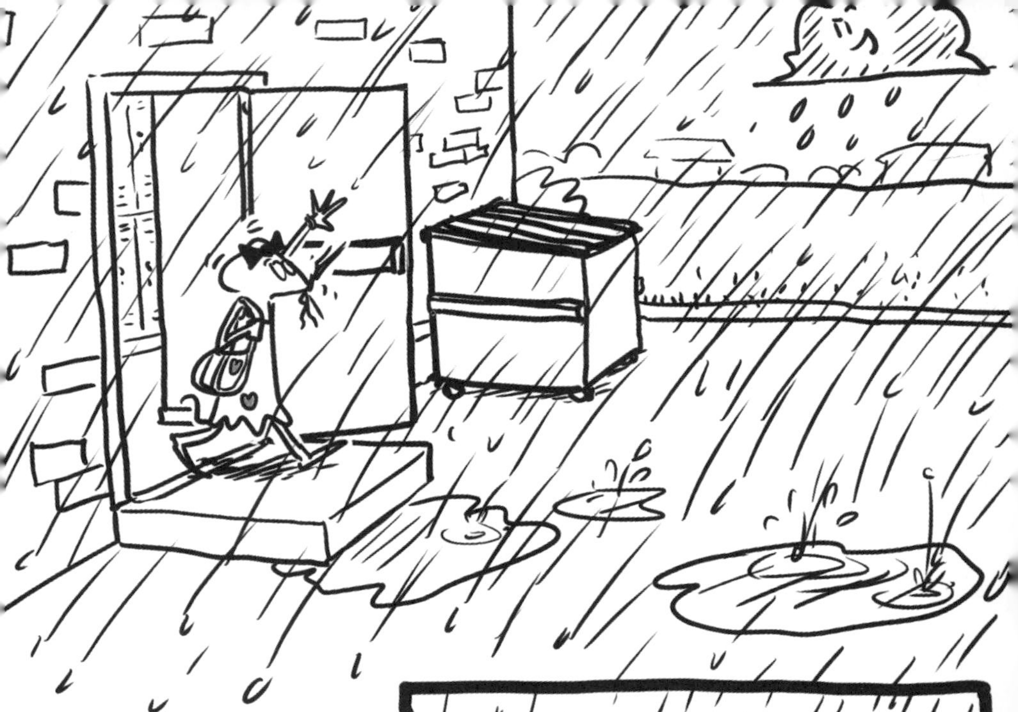

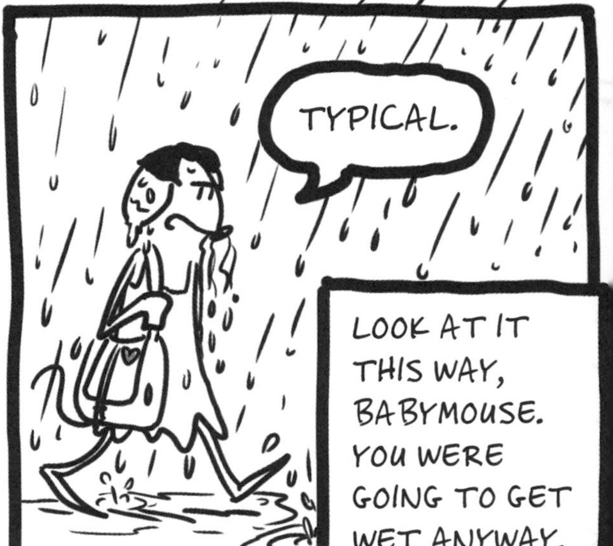
TYPICAL.
LOOK AT IT THIS WAY, BABYMOUSE. YOU WERE GOING TO GET WET ANYWAY.

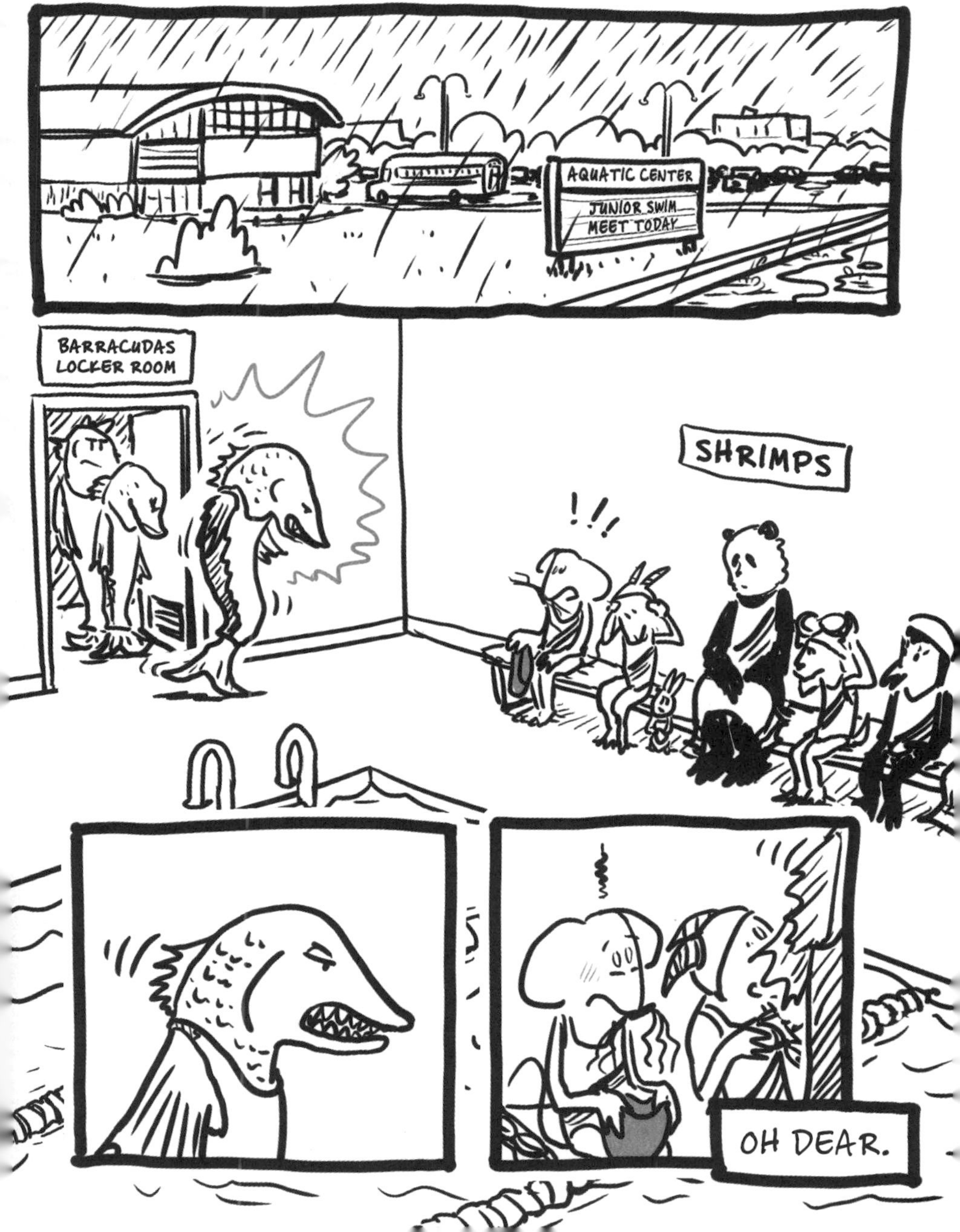
AQUATIC CENTER
JUNIOR SWIM MEET TODAY
BARRACUDAS LOCKER ROOM
SHRIMPS
!!!
OH DEAR.

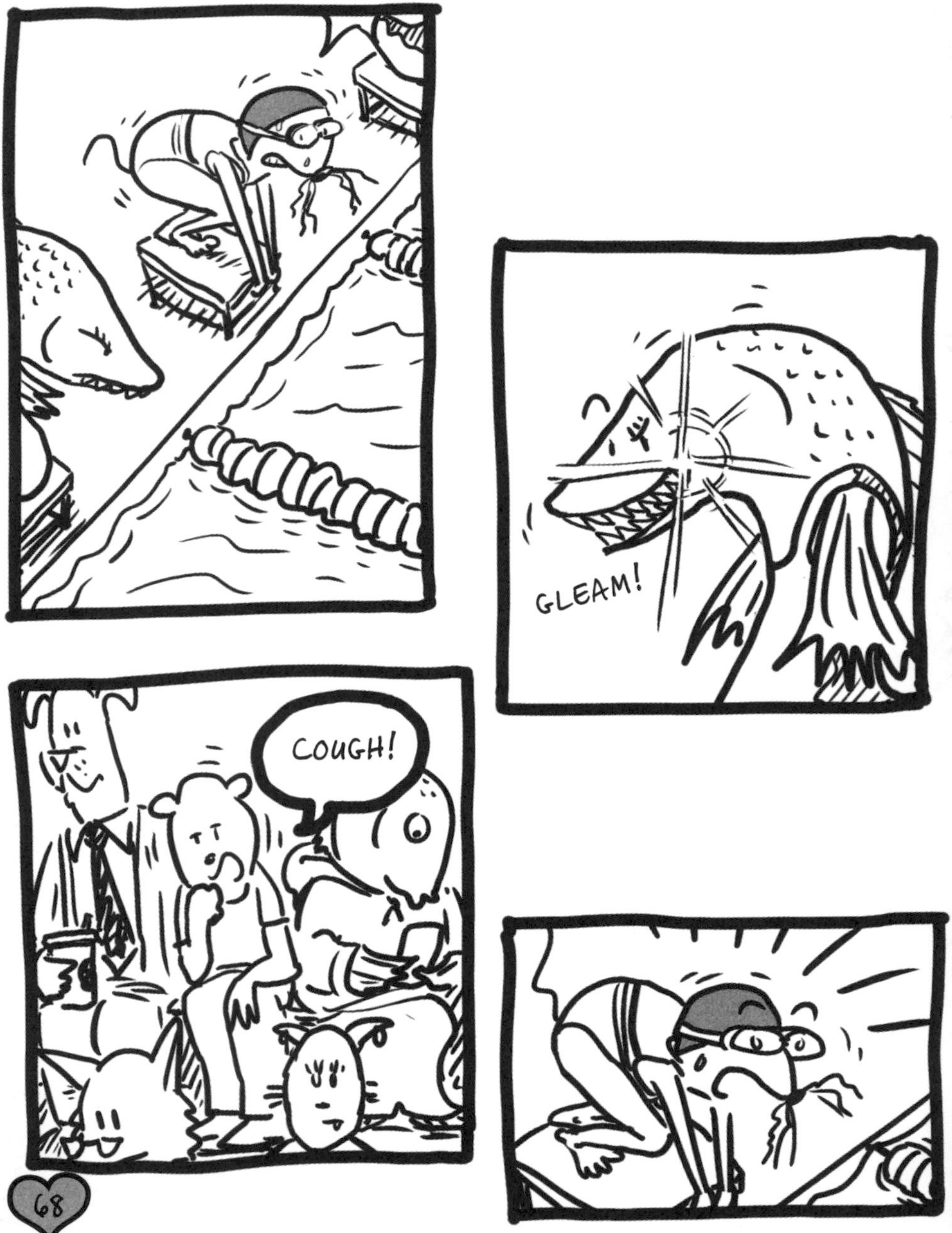
GLEAM!
COUGH!

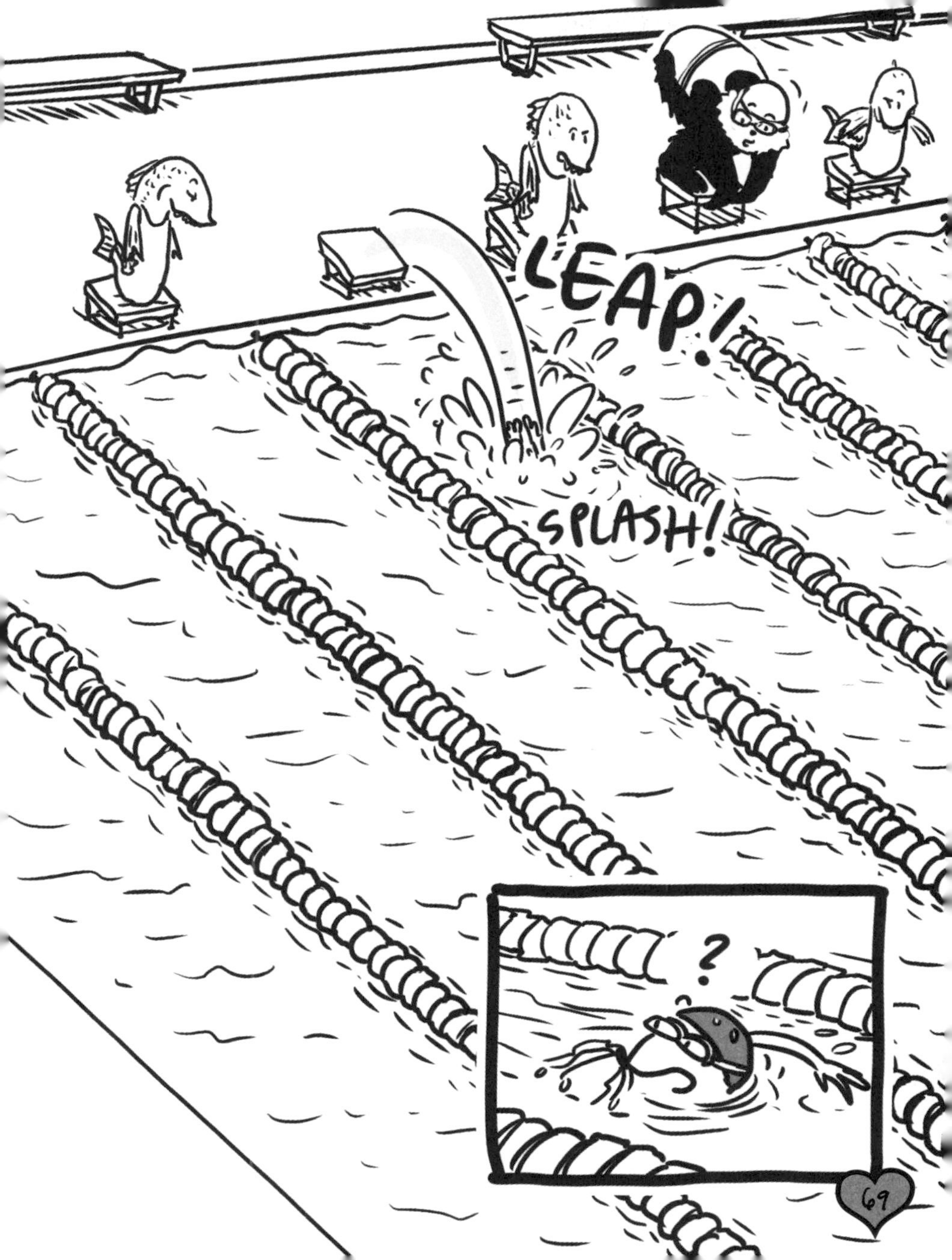
LEAP!
SPLASH!
?

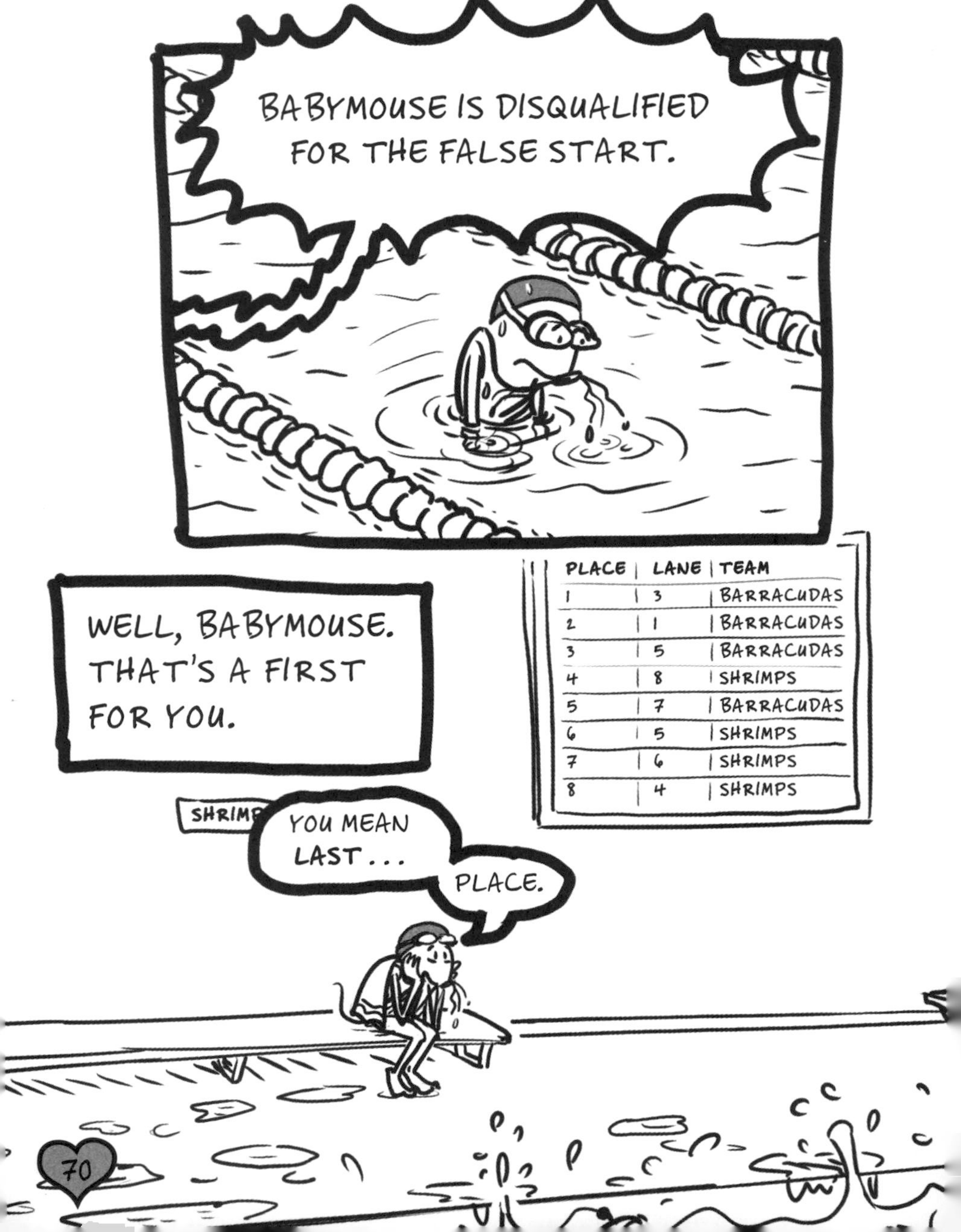
BABYMOUSE IS DISQUALIFIED FOR THE FALSE START.
WELL, BABYMOUSE. THAT'S A FIRST FOR YOU.
PLACE | LANE | TEAM
1 | 3 | BARRACUDAS
2 | 1 | BARRACUDAS
3 | 5 | BARRACUDAS
4 | 8 | SHRIMPS
5 | 7 | BARRACUDAS
6 | 5 | SHRIMPS
7 | 6 | SHRIMPS
8 | 4 | SHRIMPS
SHRIM
YOU MEAN LAST . . .
PLACE.

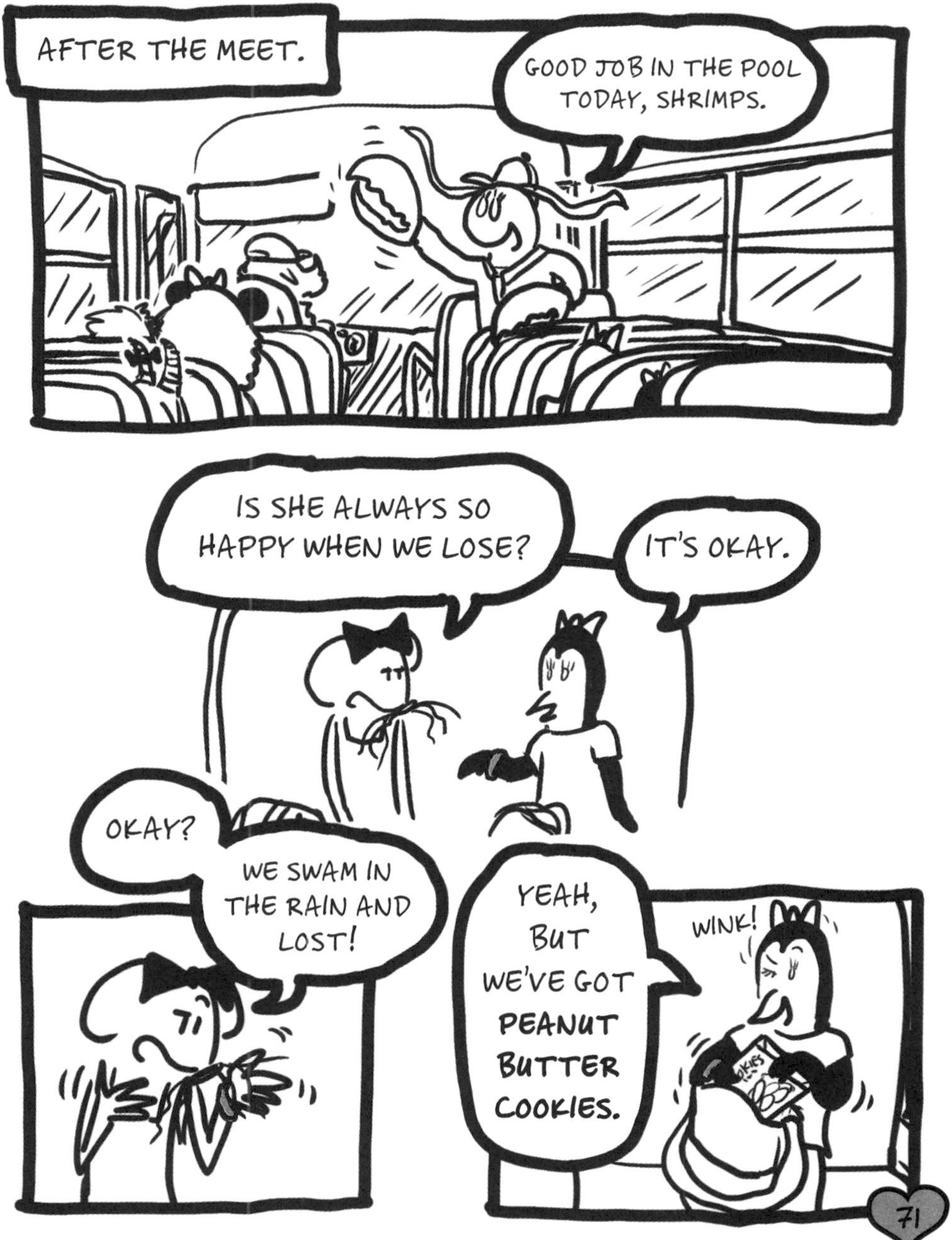
AFTER THE MEET.
GOOD JOB IN THE POOL TODAY, SHRIMPS.
IS SHE ALWAYS SO HAPPY WHEN WE LOSE?
IT'S OKAY.
OKAY?
WE SWAM IN THE RAIN AND LOST!
YEAH, BUT WE'VE GOT **PEANUT BUTTER COOKIES.**
WINK!

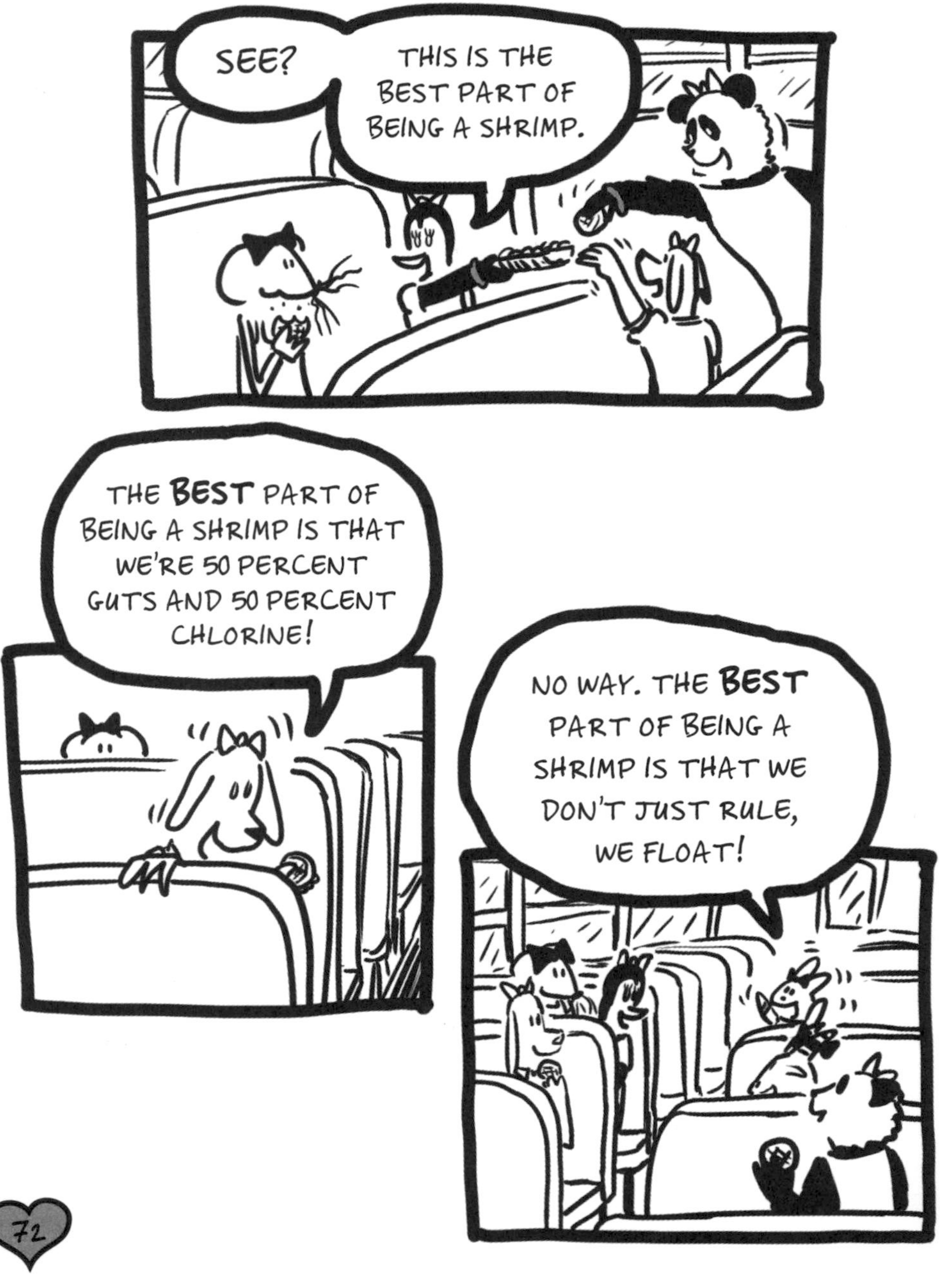
SEE?
THIS IS THE BEST PART OF BEING A SHRIMP.
THE **BEST** PART OF BEING A SHRIMP IS THAT WE'RE 50 PERCENT GUTS AND 50 PERCENT CHLORINE!
NO WAY. THE **BEST** PART OF BEING A SHRIMP IS THAT WE DON'T JUST RULE, WE FLOAT!

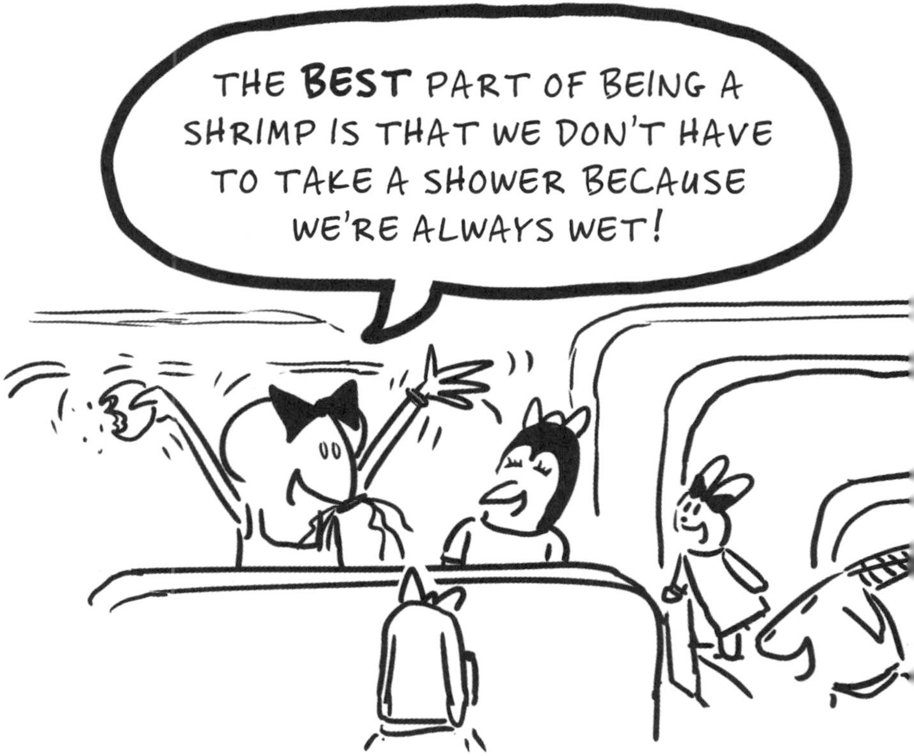
THE **BEST** PART OF BEING A SHRIMP IS THAT WE DON'T HAVE TO TAKE A SHOWER BECAUSE WE'RE ALWAYS WET!

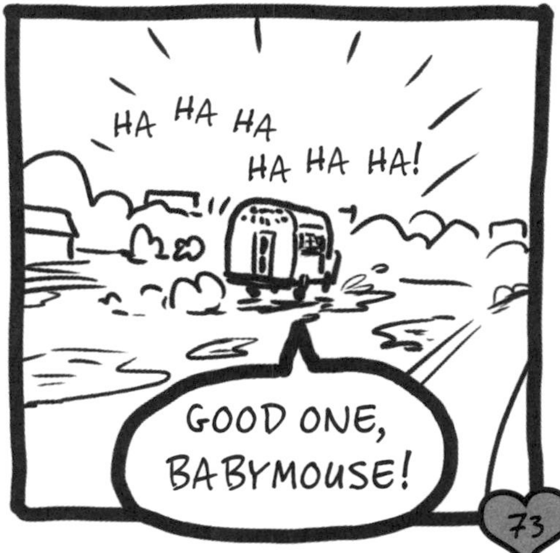
HA HA HA
HA HA HA!
GOOD ONE, BABYMOUSE!

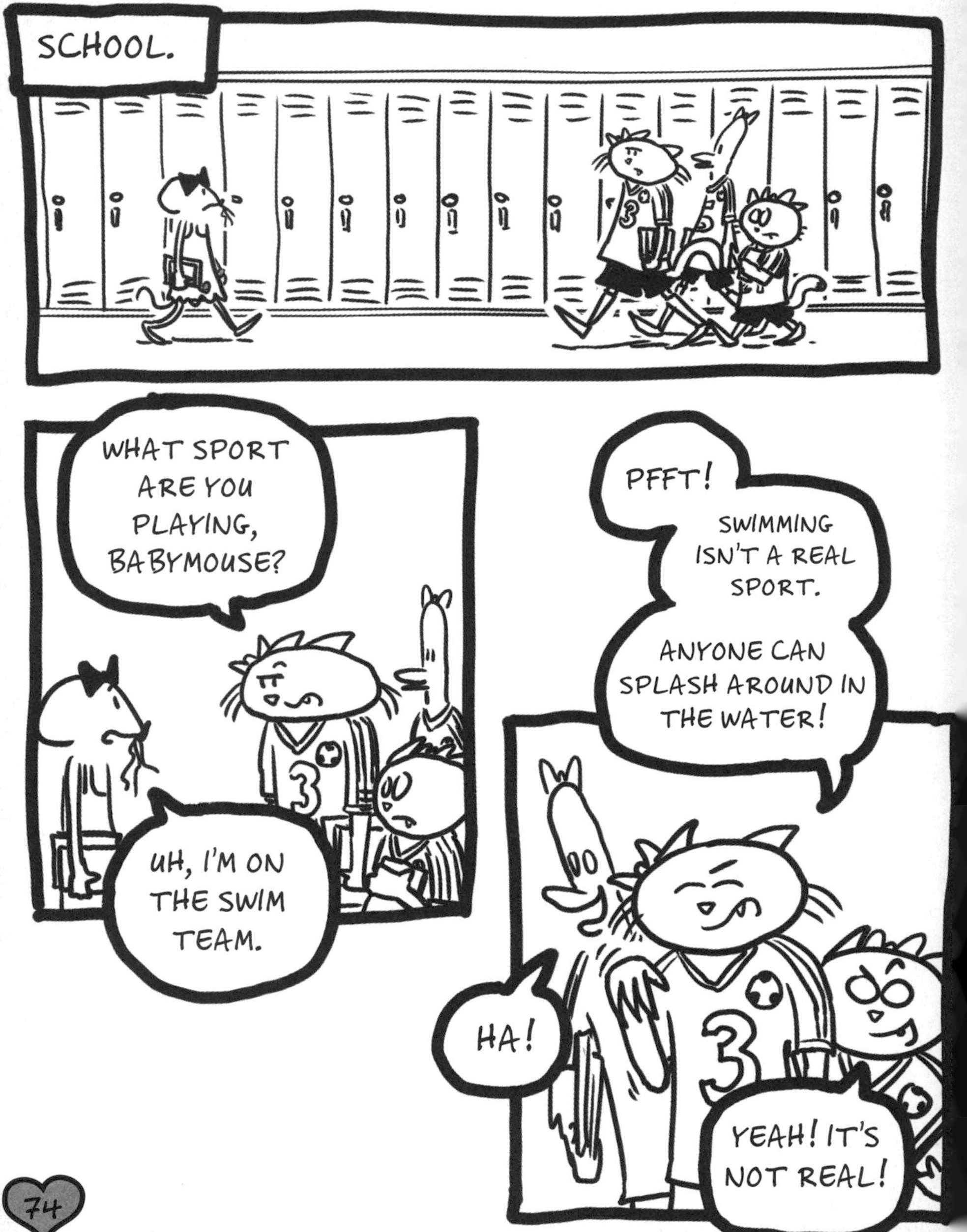
SCHOOL.
WHAT SPORT ARE YOU PLAYING, BABYMOUSE?
UH, I'M ON THE SWIM TEAM.
PFFT!
SWIMMING ISN'T A REAL SPORT.
ANYONE CAN SPLASH AROUND IN THE WATER!
HA!
YEAH! IT'S NOT REAL!

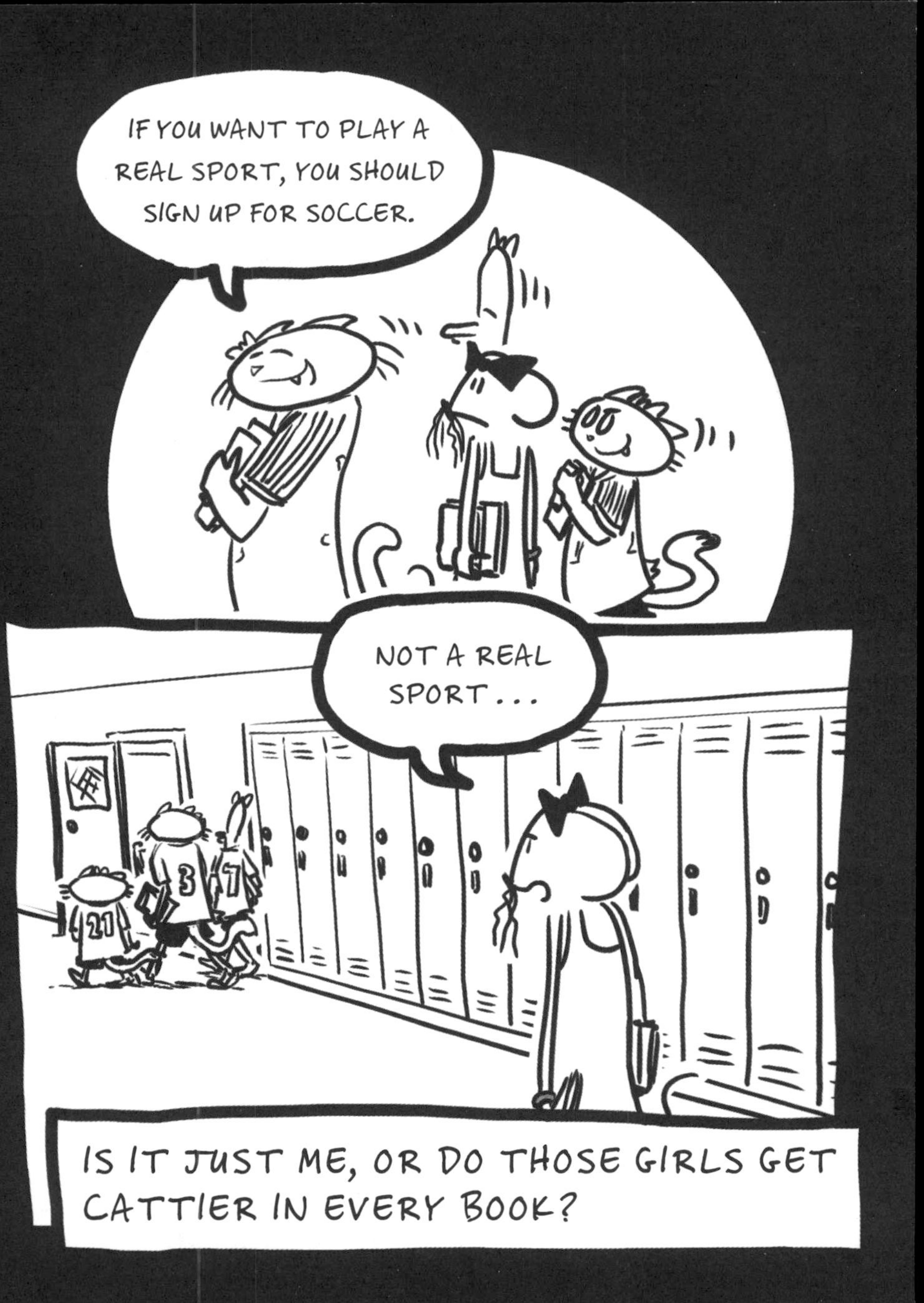
IF YOU WANT TO PLAY A REAL SPORT, YOU SHOULD SIGN UP FOR SOCCER.
NOT A REAL SPORT . . .
21
3
7
IS IT JUST ME, OR DO THOSE GIRLS GET CATTIER IN EVERY BOOK?

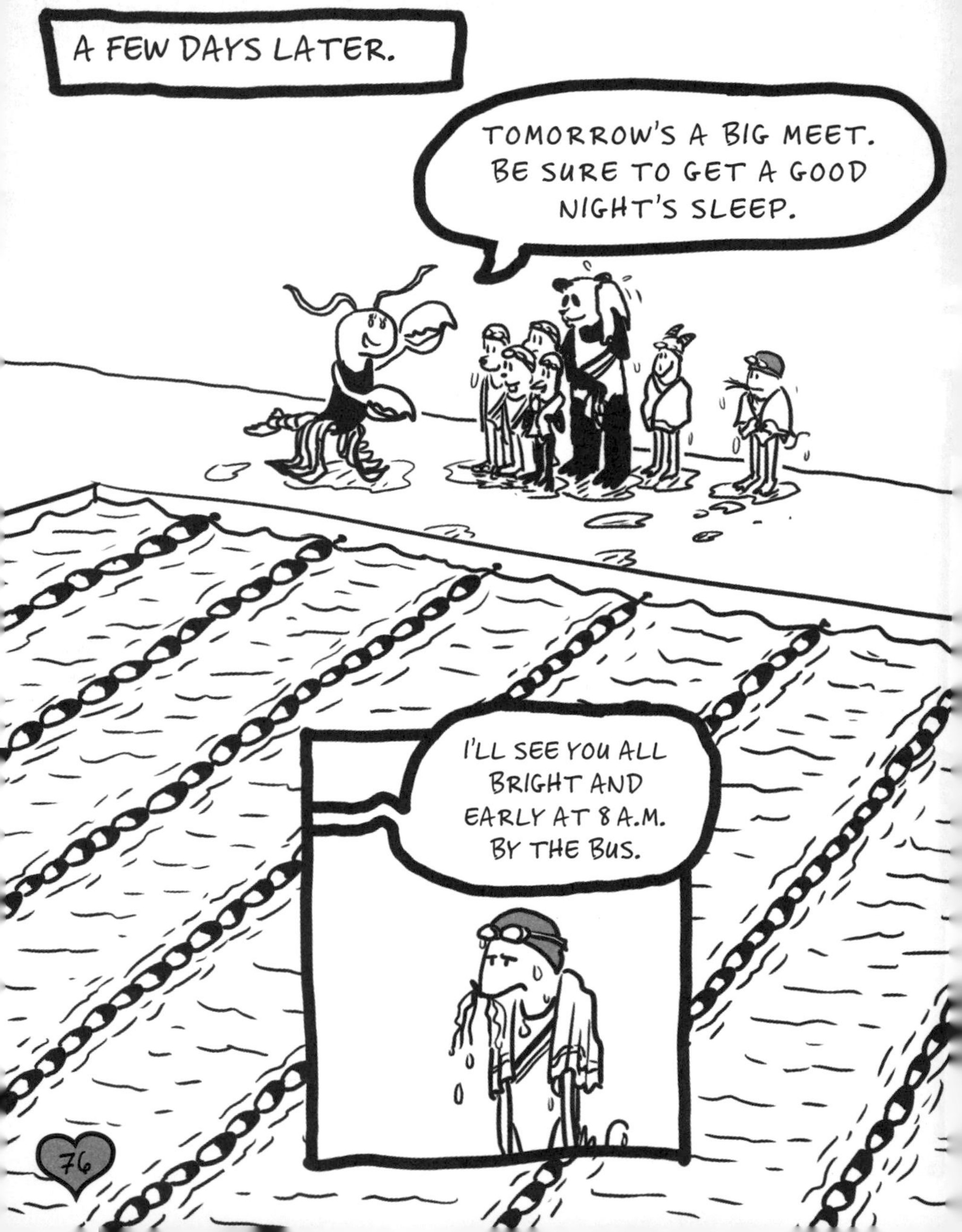
A FEW DAYS LATER.
TOMORROW'S A BIG MEET. BE SURE TO GET A GOOD NIGHT'S SLEEP.
I'LL SEE YOU ALL BRIGHT AND EARLY AT 8 A.M. BY THE BUS.

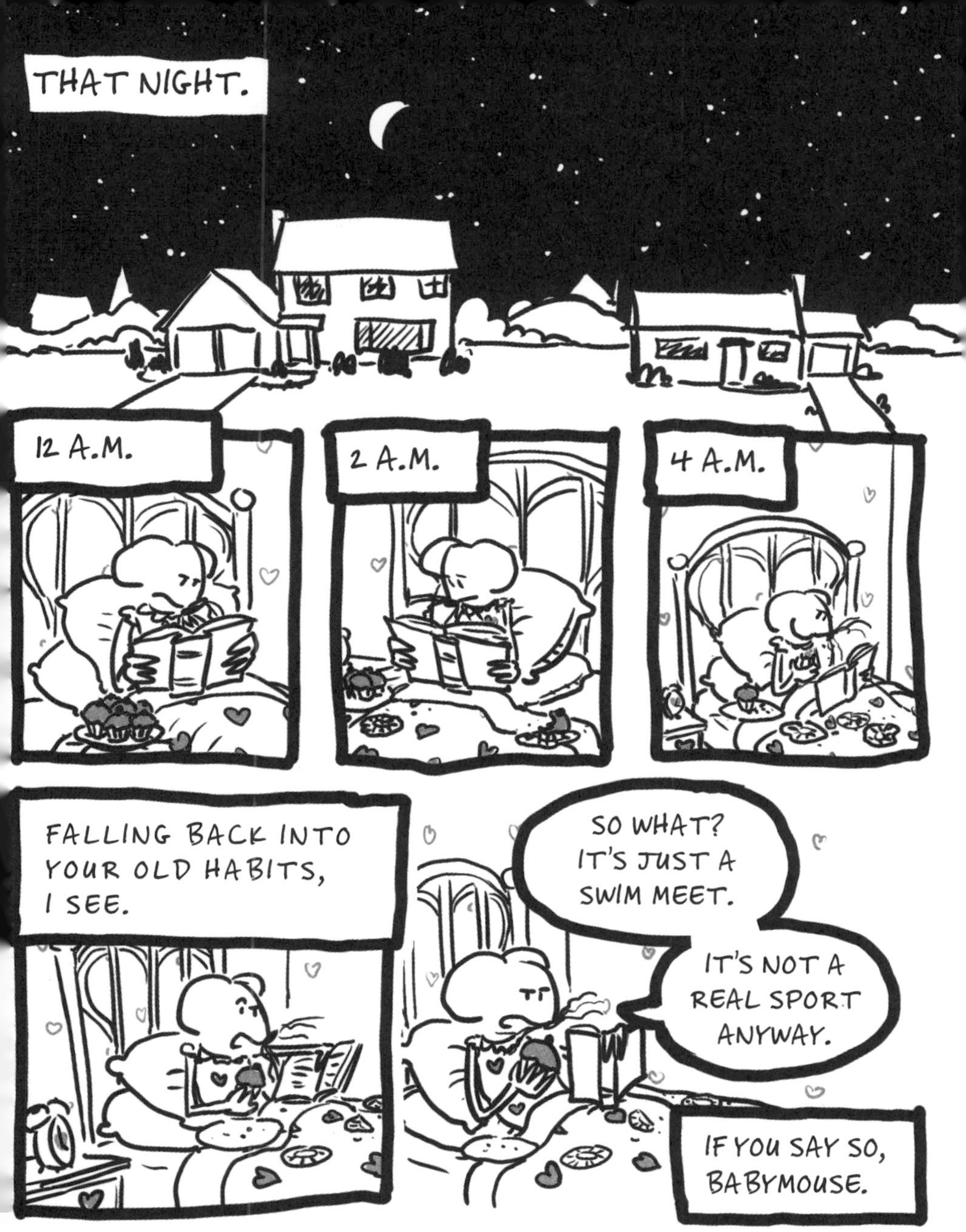
THAT NIGHT.
12 A.M.
2 A.M.
4 A.M.
FALLING BACK INTO YOUR OLD HABITS, I SEE.
SO WHAT? IT'S JUST A SWIM MEET.
IT'S NOT A REAL SPORT ANYWAY.
IF YOU SAY SO, BABYMOUSE.

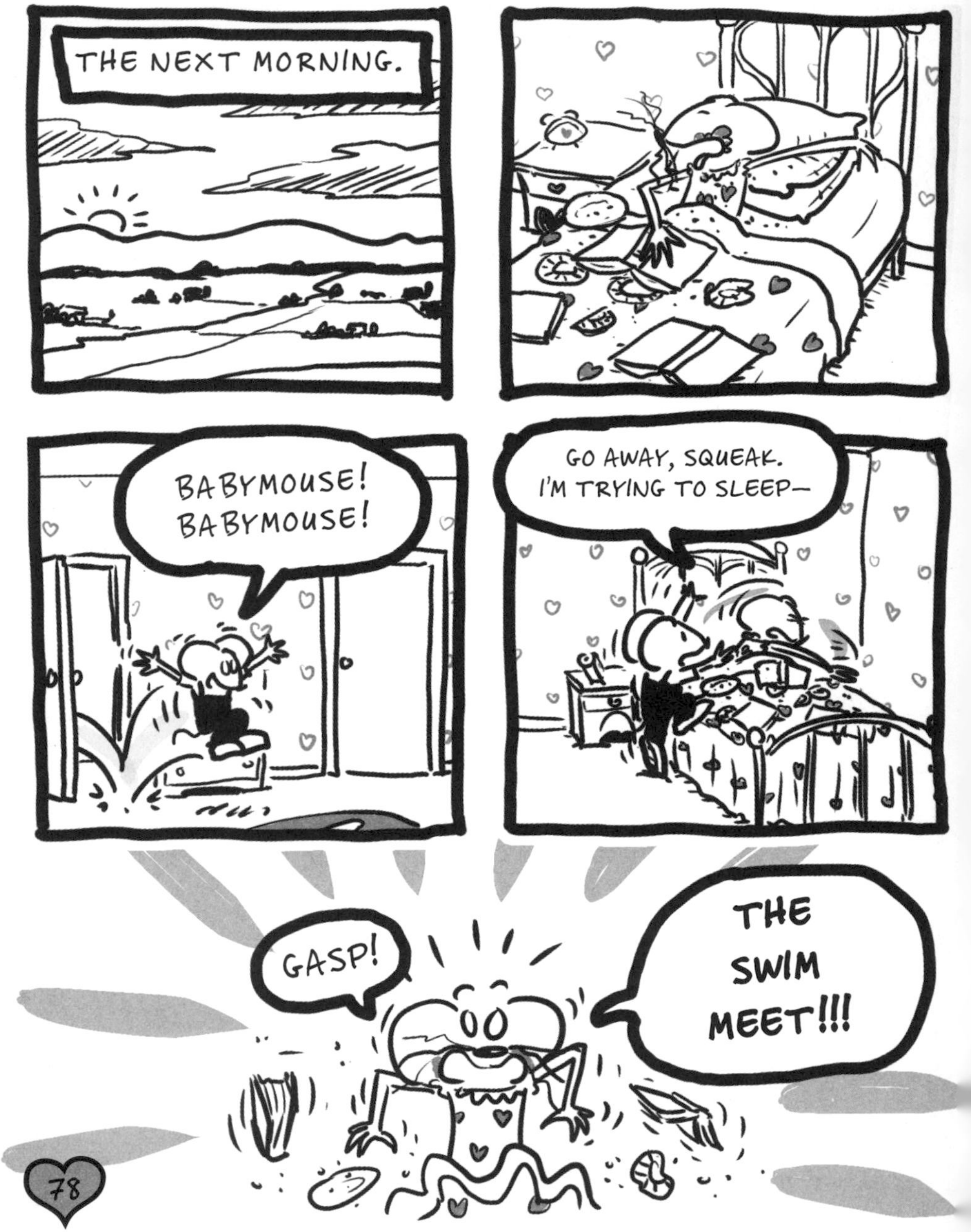
THE NEXT MORNING.
BABYMOUSE! BABYMOUSE!
GO AWAY, SQUEAK. I'M TRYING TO SLEEP—
GASP!
THE SWIM MEET!!!

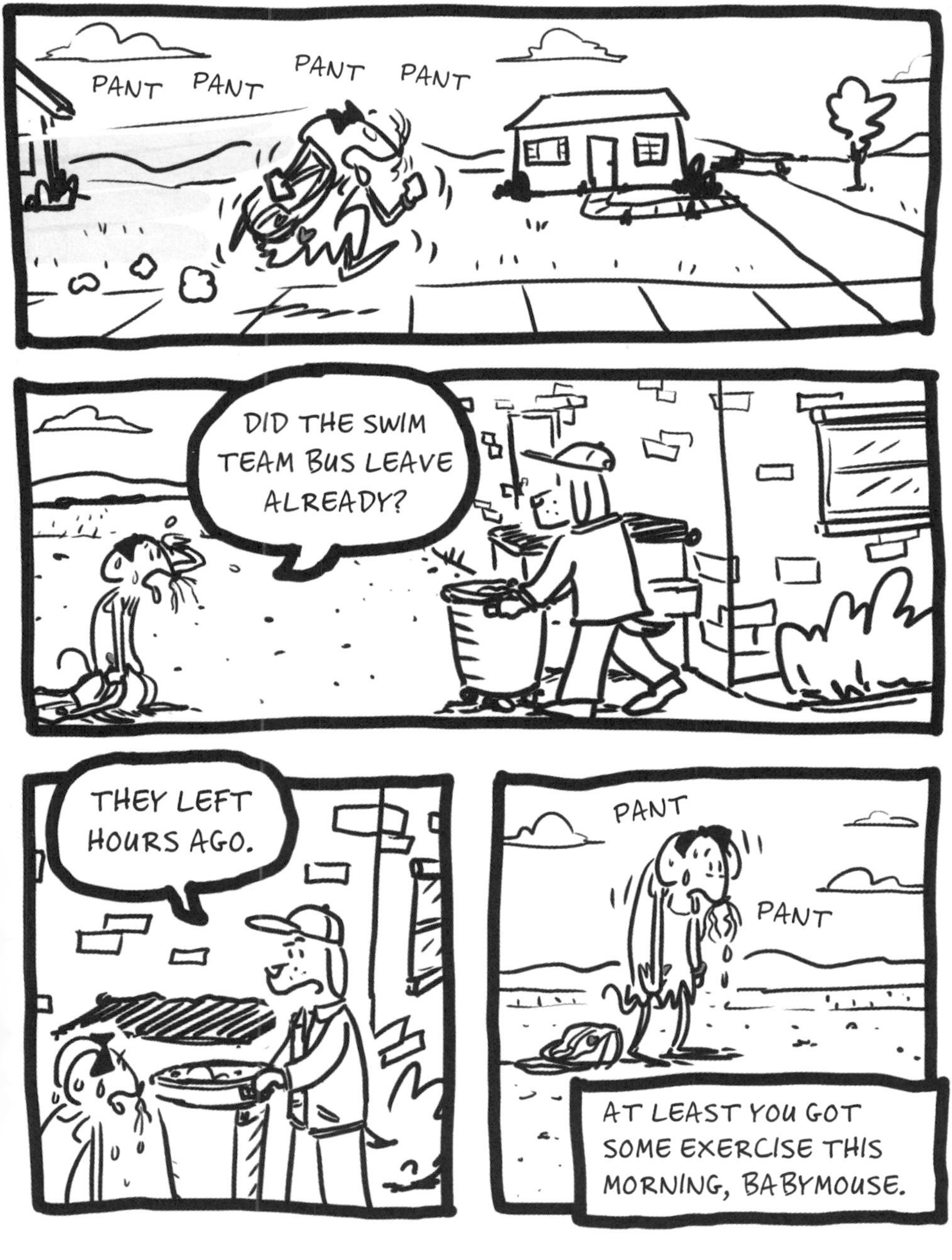
PANT PANT
PANT PANT
DID THE SWIM TEAM BUS LEAVE ALREADY?
THEY LEFT HOURS AGO.
PANT
PANT
AT LEAST YOU GOT SOME EXERCISE THIS MORNING, BABYMOUSE.

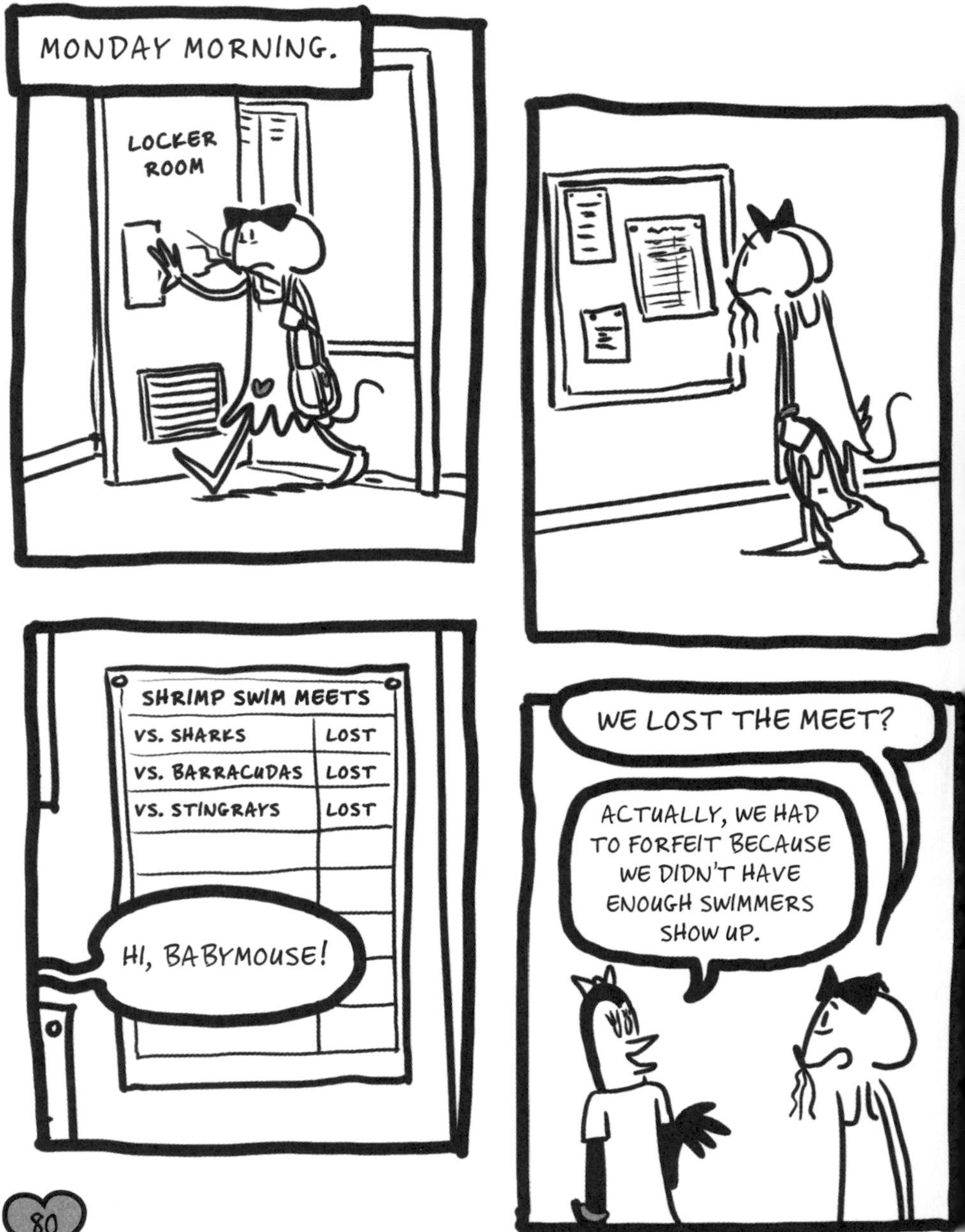
MONDAY MORNING.
LOCKER ROOM
SHRIMP SWIM MEETS
VS. SHARKS LOST
VS. BARRACUDAS LOST
VS. STINGRAYS LOST
HI, BABYMOUSE!
WE LOST THE MEET?
ACTUALLY, WE HAD TO FORFEIT BECAUSE WE DIDN'T HAVE ENOUGH SWIMMERS SHOW UP.

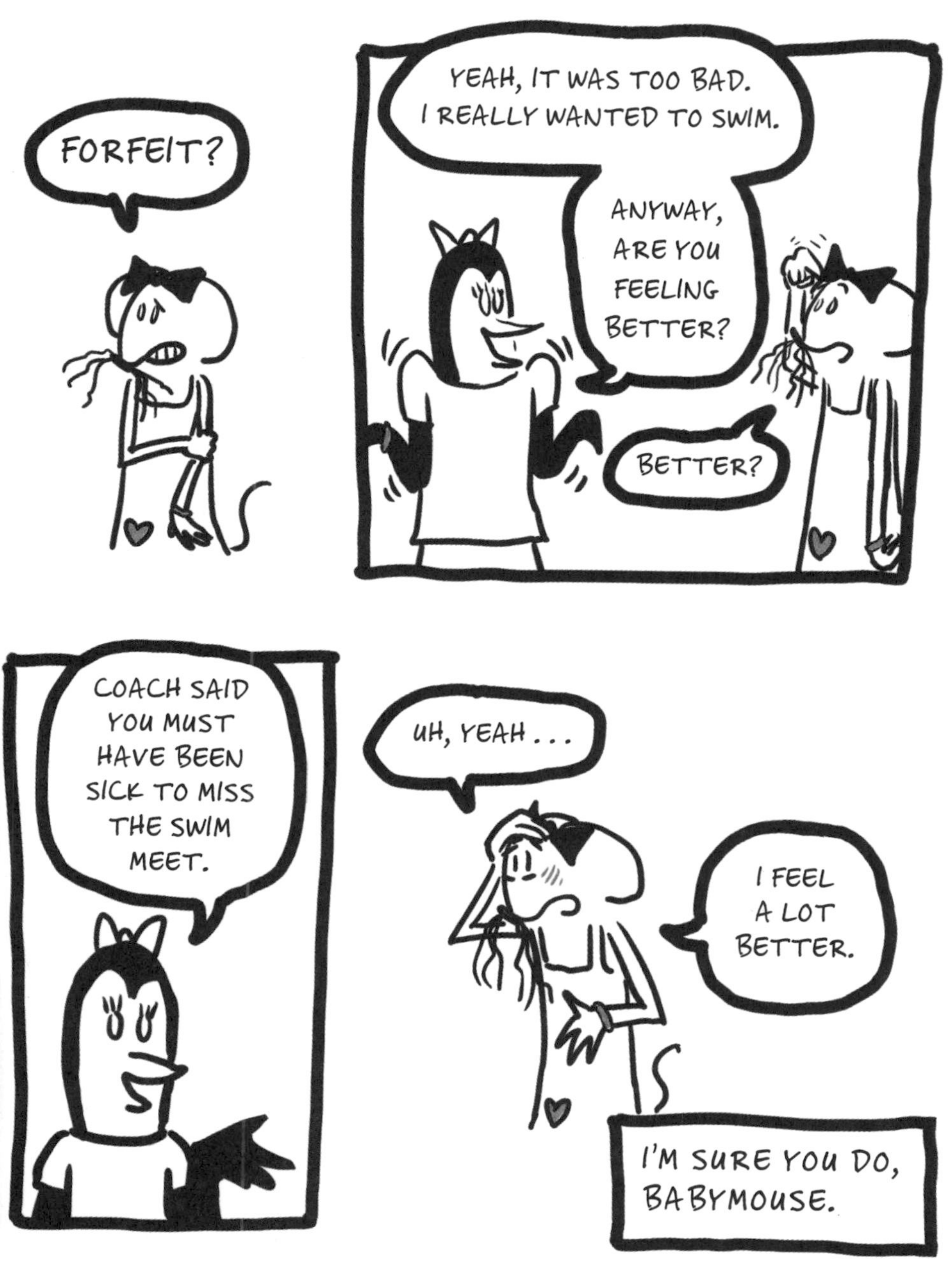
FORFEIT?
YEAH, IT WAS TOO BAD. I REALLY WANTED TO SWIM.
ANYWAY, ARE YOU FEELING BETTER?
BETTER?
COACH SAID YOU MUST HAVE BEEN SICK TO MISS THE SWIM MEET.
UH, YEAH . . .
I FEEL A LOT BETTER.
I'M SURE YOU DO, BABYMOUSE.

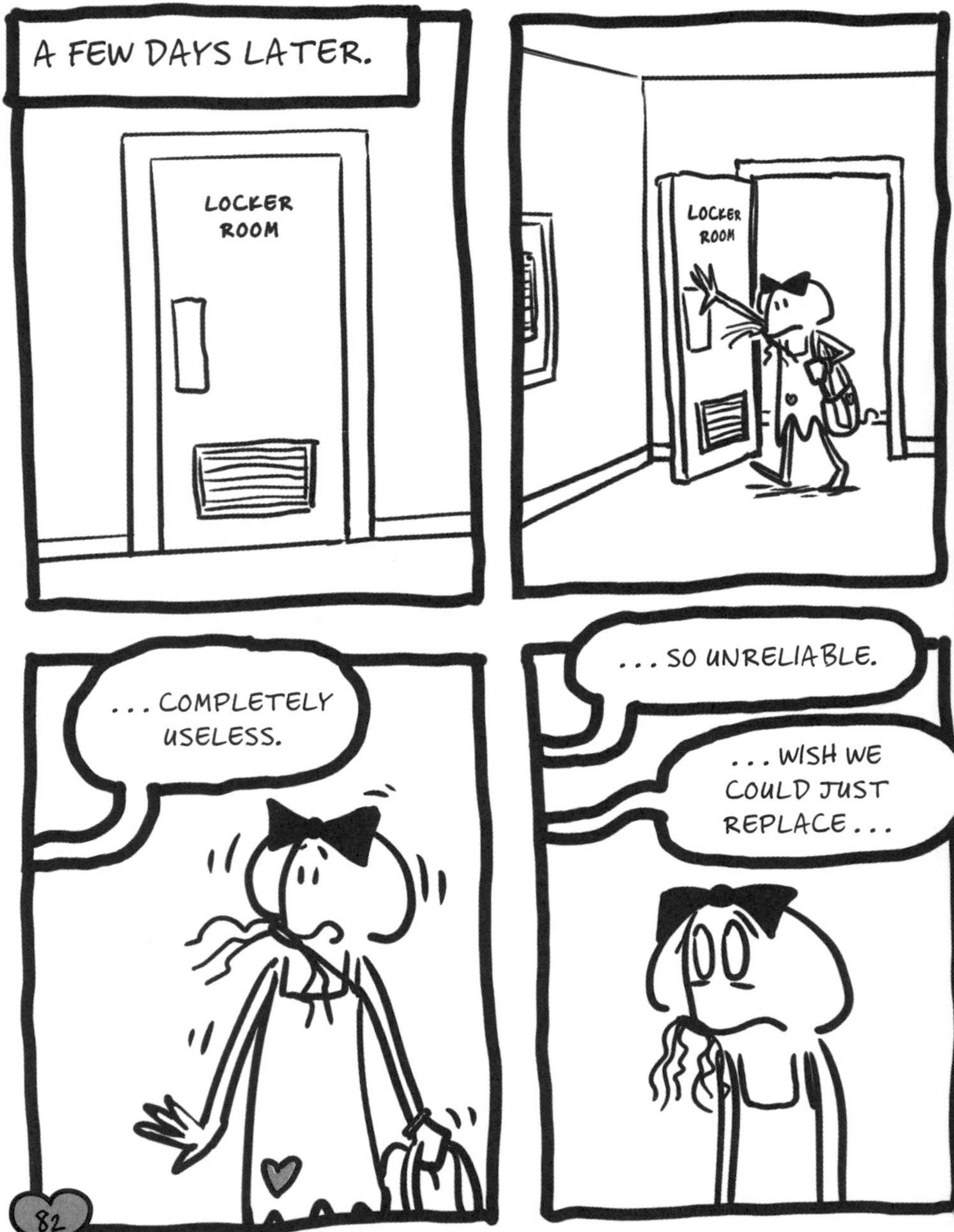
A FEW DAYS LATER.
LOCKER ROOM
LOCKER ROOM
. . . COMPLETELY USELESS.
. . . SO UNRELIABLE.
. . . WISH WE COULD JUST REPLACE . . .

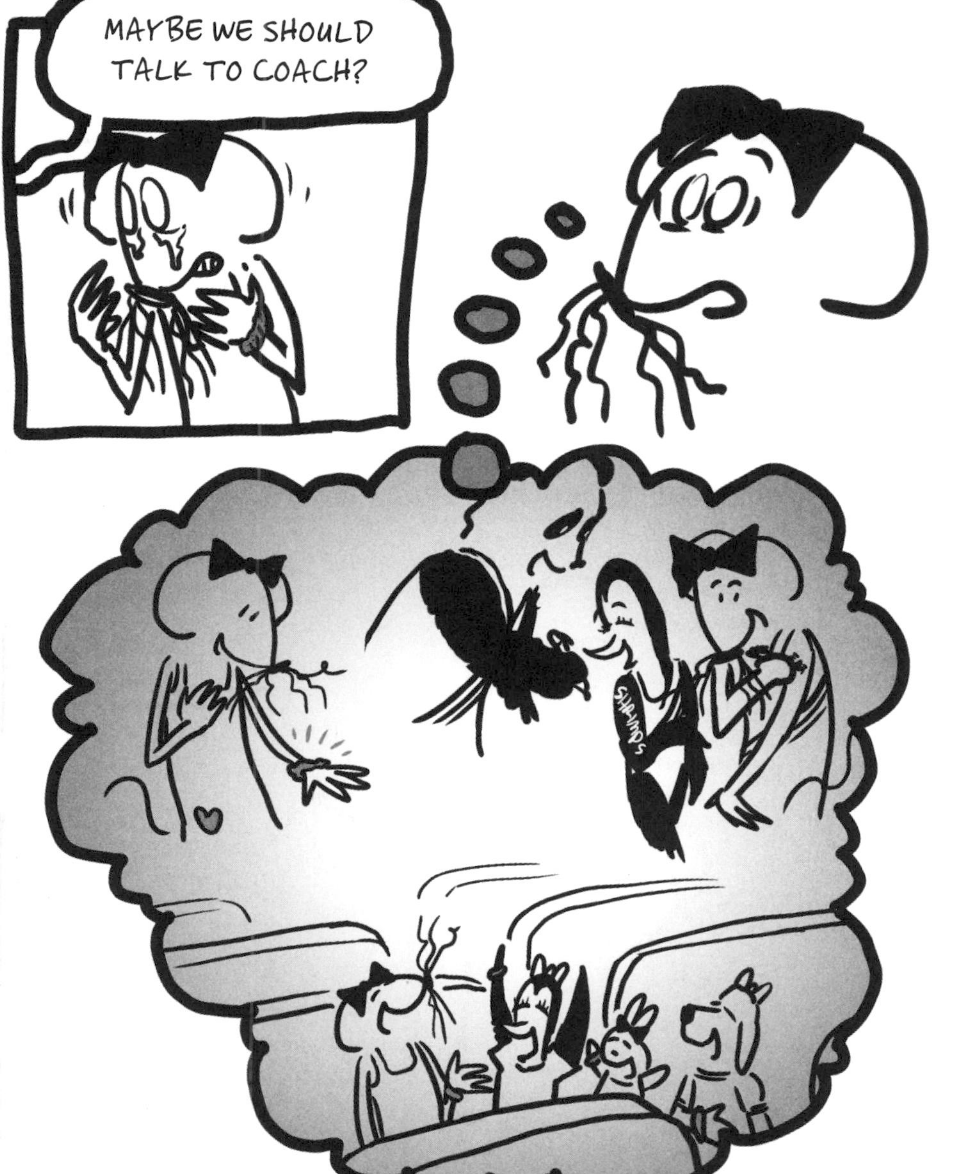
MAYBE WE SHOULD TALK TO COACH?
SHRIMPS

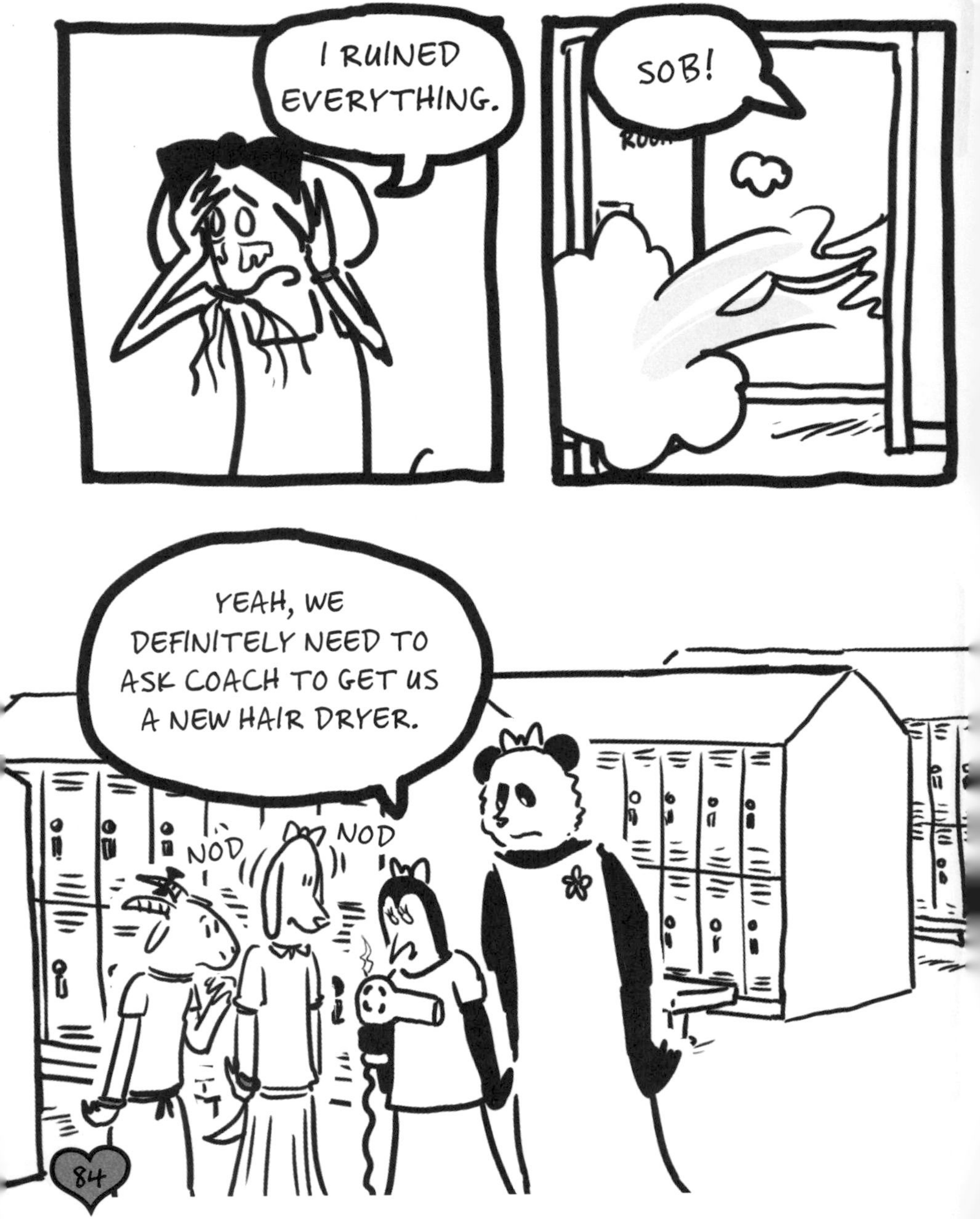
I RUINED EVERYTHING.
SOB!
YEAH, WE DEFINITELY NEED TO ASK COACH TO GET US A NEW HAIR DRYER.
NOD
NOD

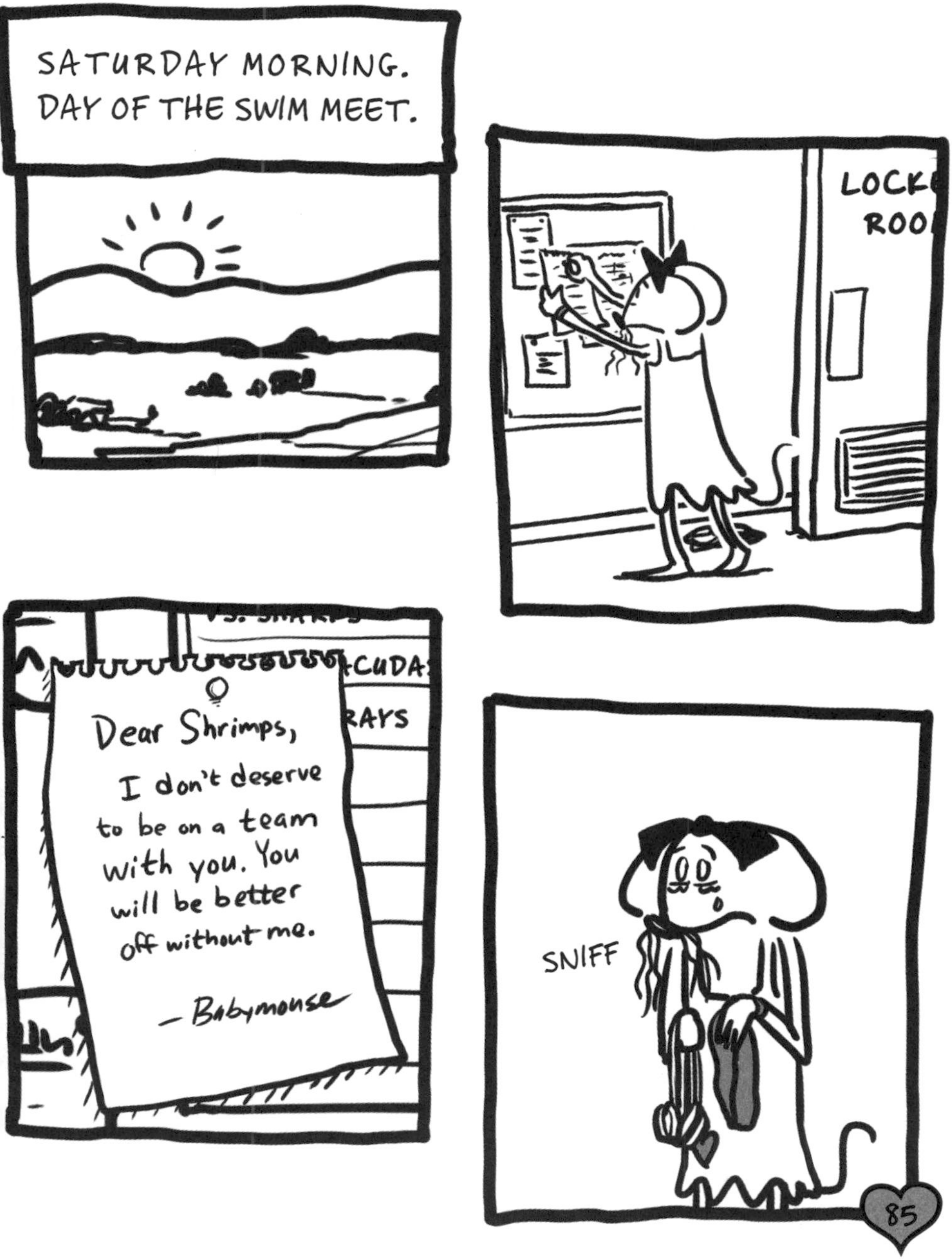
SATURDAY MORNING.
DAY OF THE SWIM MEET.
LOCK
ROO
CUDA
RAYS
Dear Shrimps,
I don't deserve to be on a team with you. You will be better off without me.
— Babymouse
SNIFF

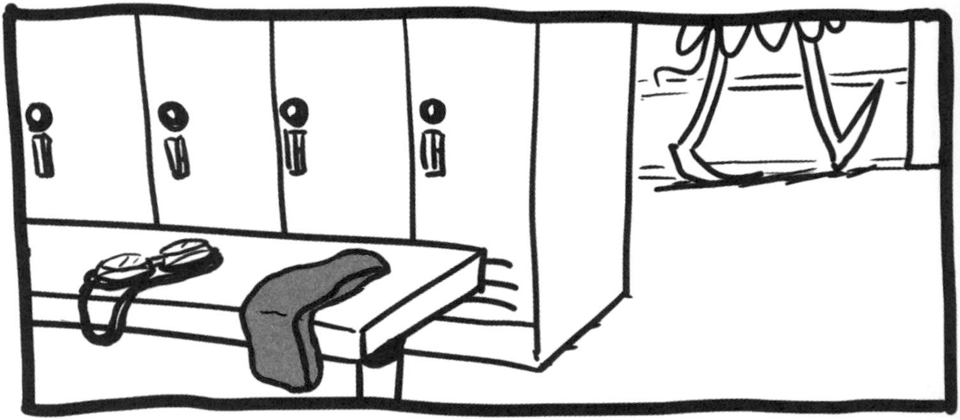

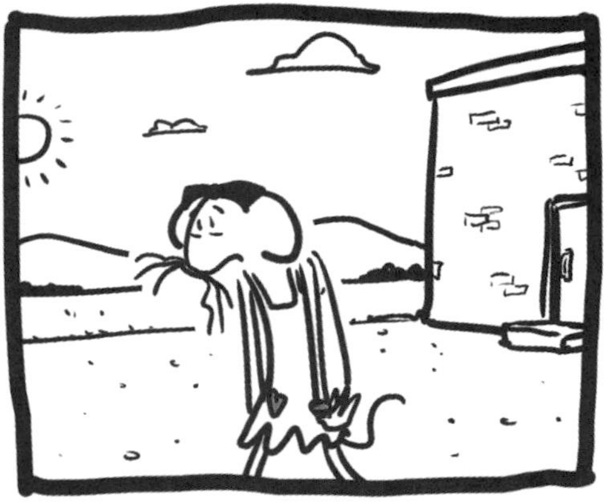

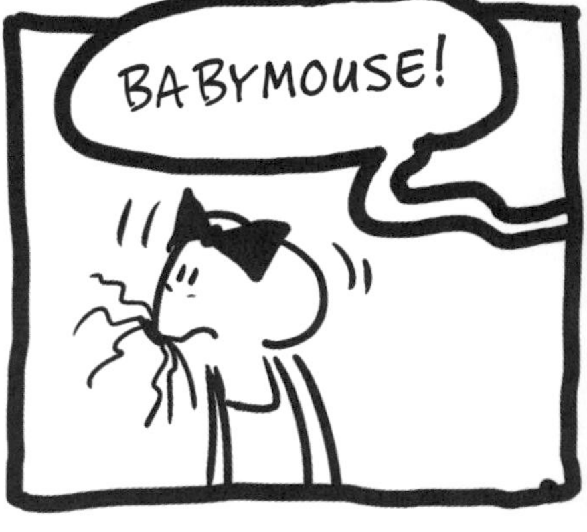
BABYMOUSE!

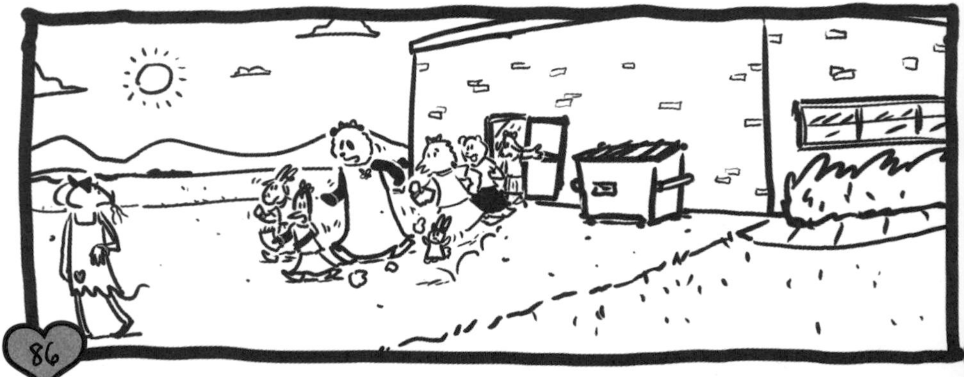

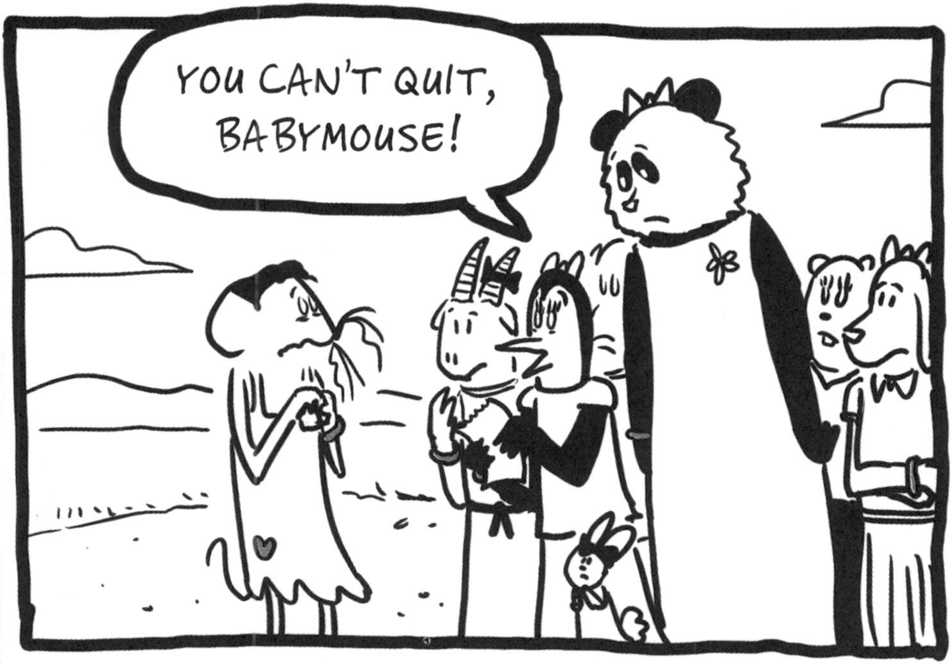
YOU CAN'T QUIT, BABYMOUSE!

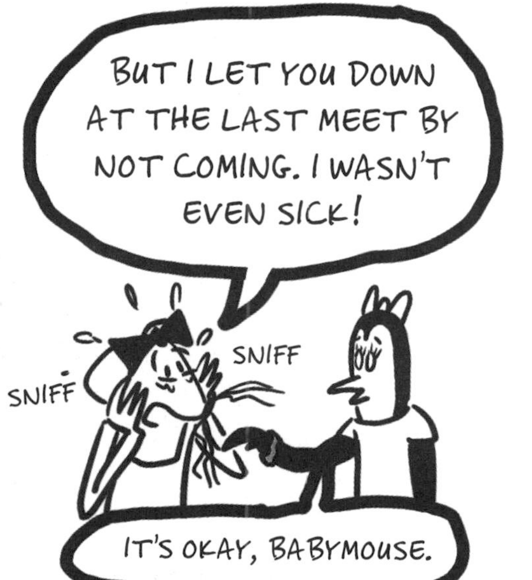
BUT I LET YOU DOWN AT THE LAST MEET BY NOT COMING. I WASN'T EVEN SICK!
SNIFF
SNIFF
IT'S OKAY, BABYMOUSE.

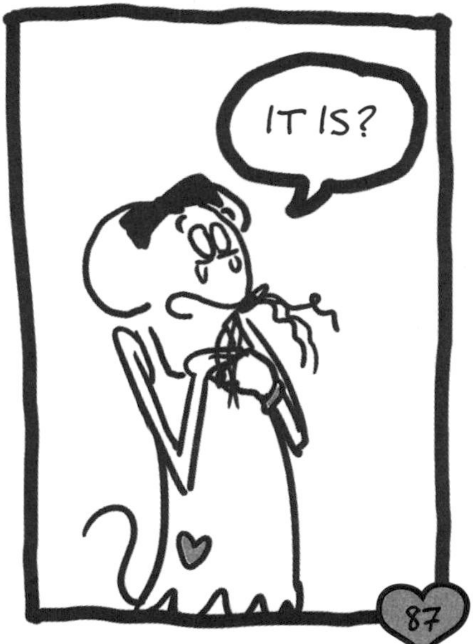
IT IS?

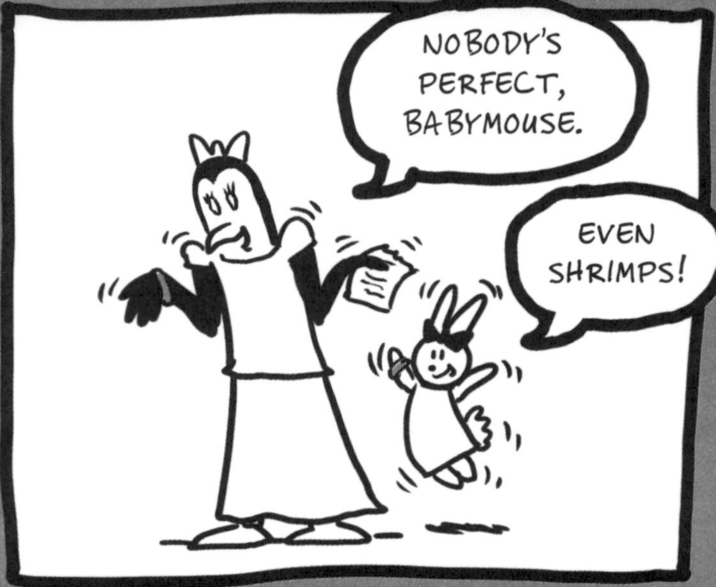
NOBODY'S PERFECT, BABYMOUSE.
EVEN SHRIMPS!

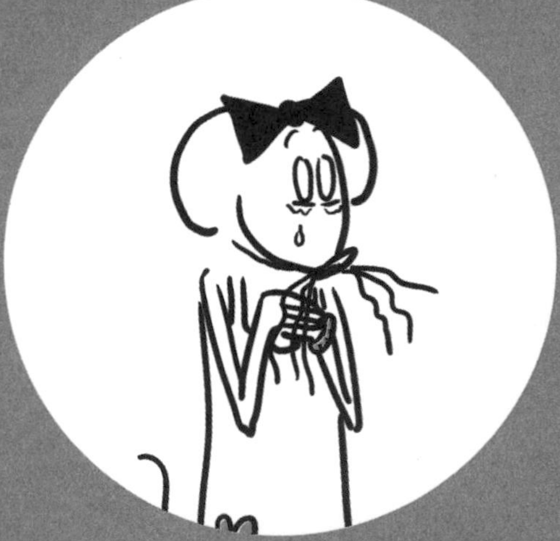

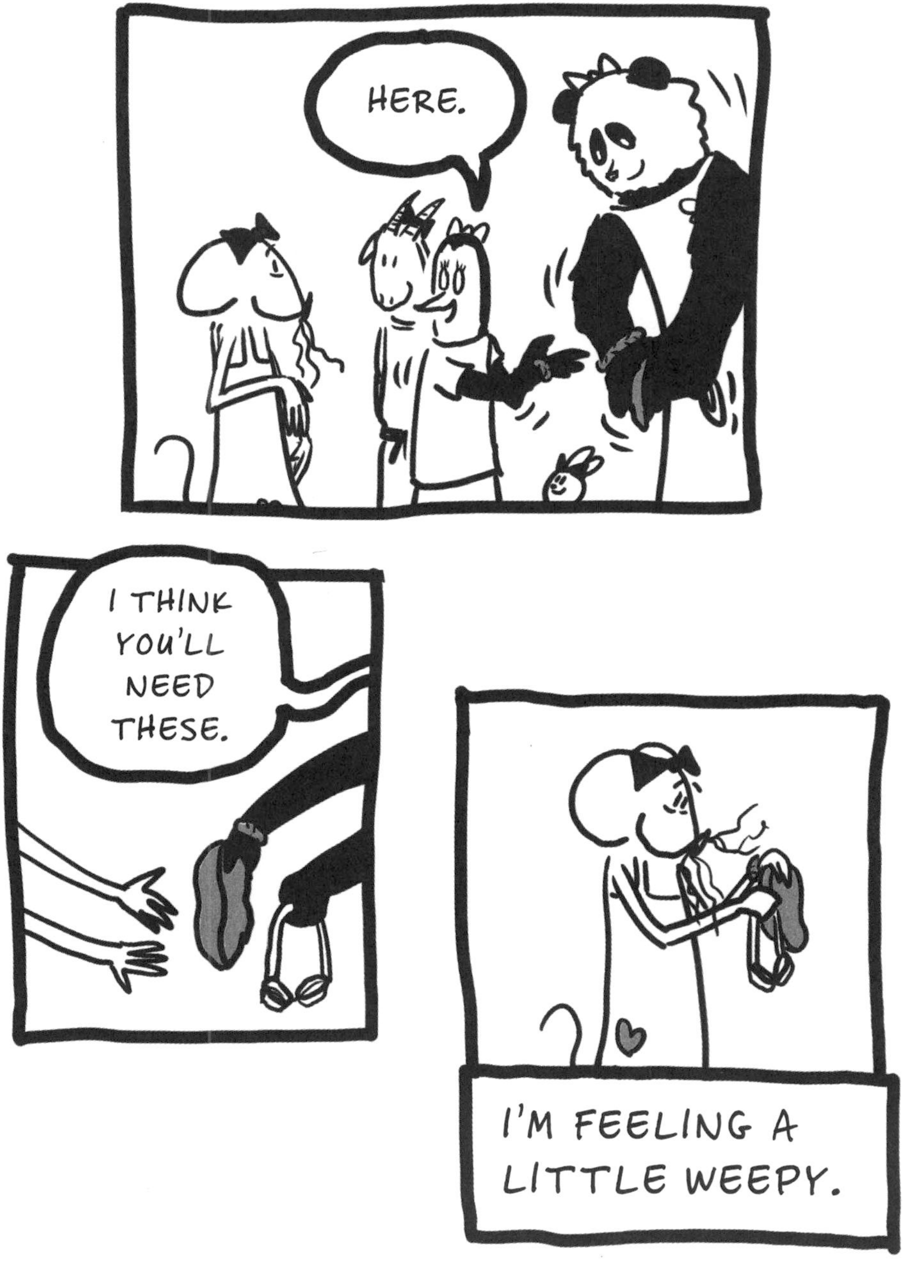
HERE.
I THINK YOU'LL NEED THESE.
I'M FEELING A LITTLE WEEPY.

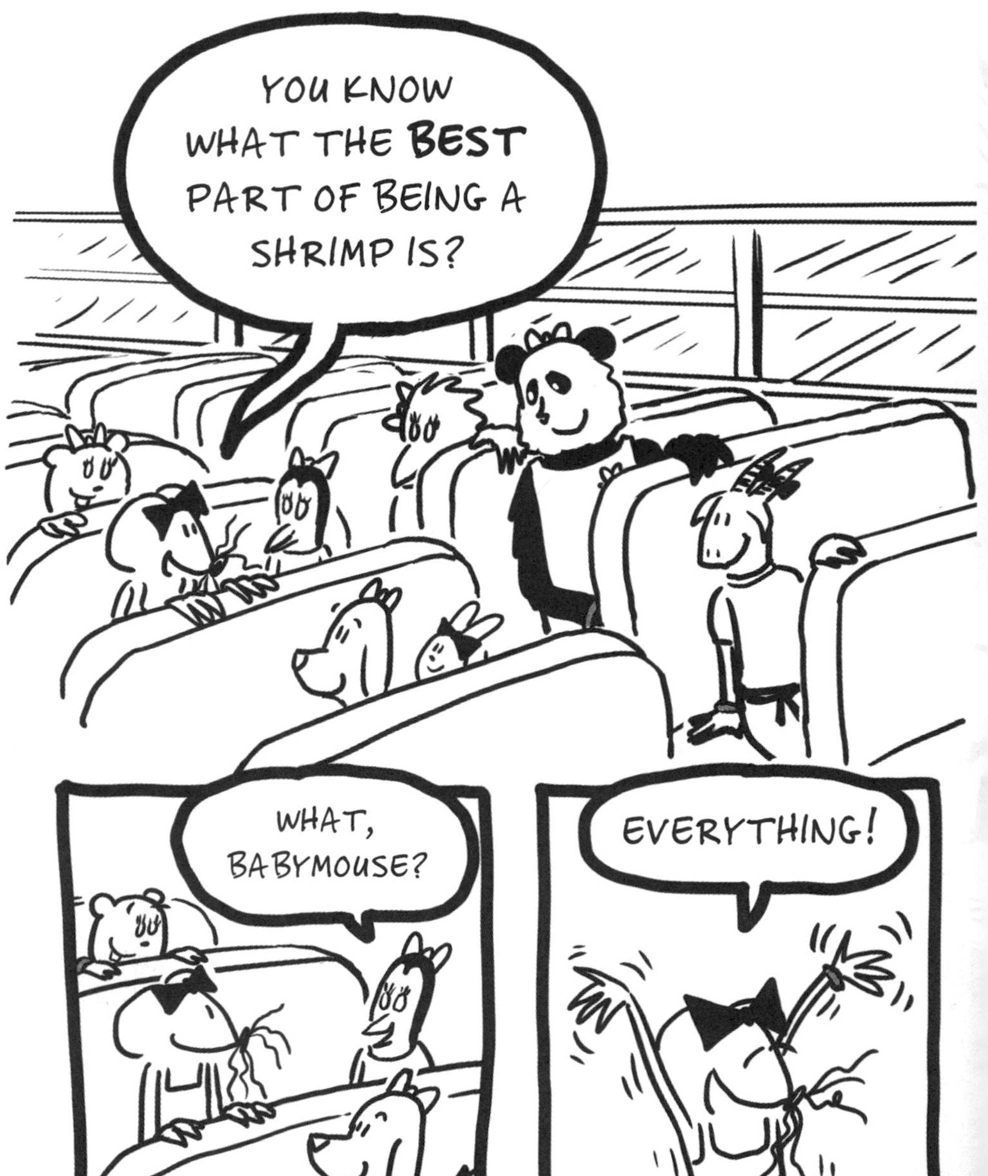
YOU KNOW WHAT THE **BEST** PART OF BEING A SHRIMP IS?
WHAT, BABYMOUSE?
EVERYTHING!

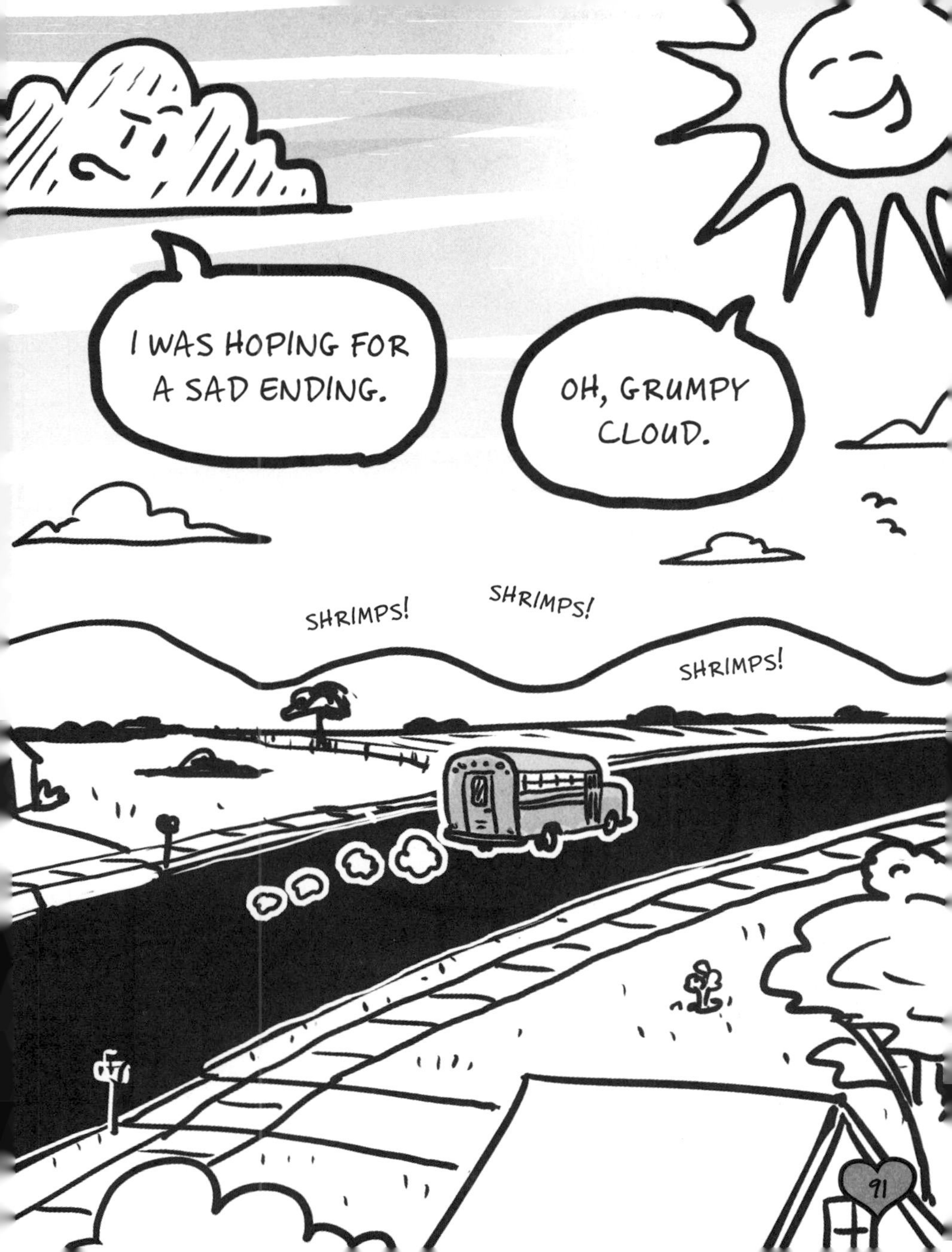
I WAS HOPING FOR A SAD ENDING.
OH, GRUMPY CLOUD.
SHRIMPS!
SHRIMPS!
SHRIMPS!

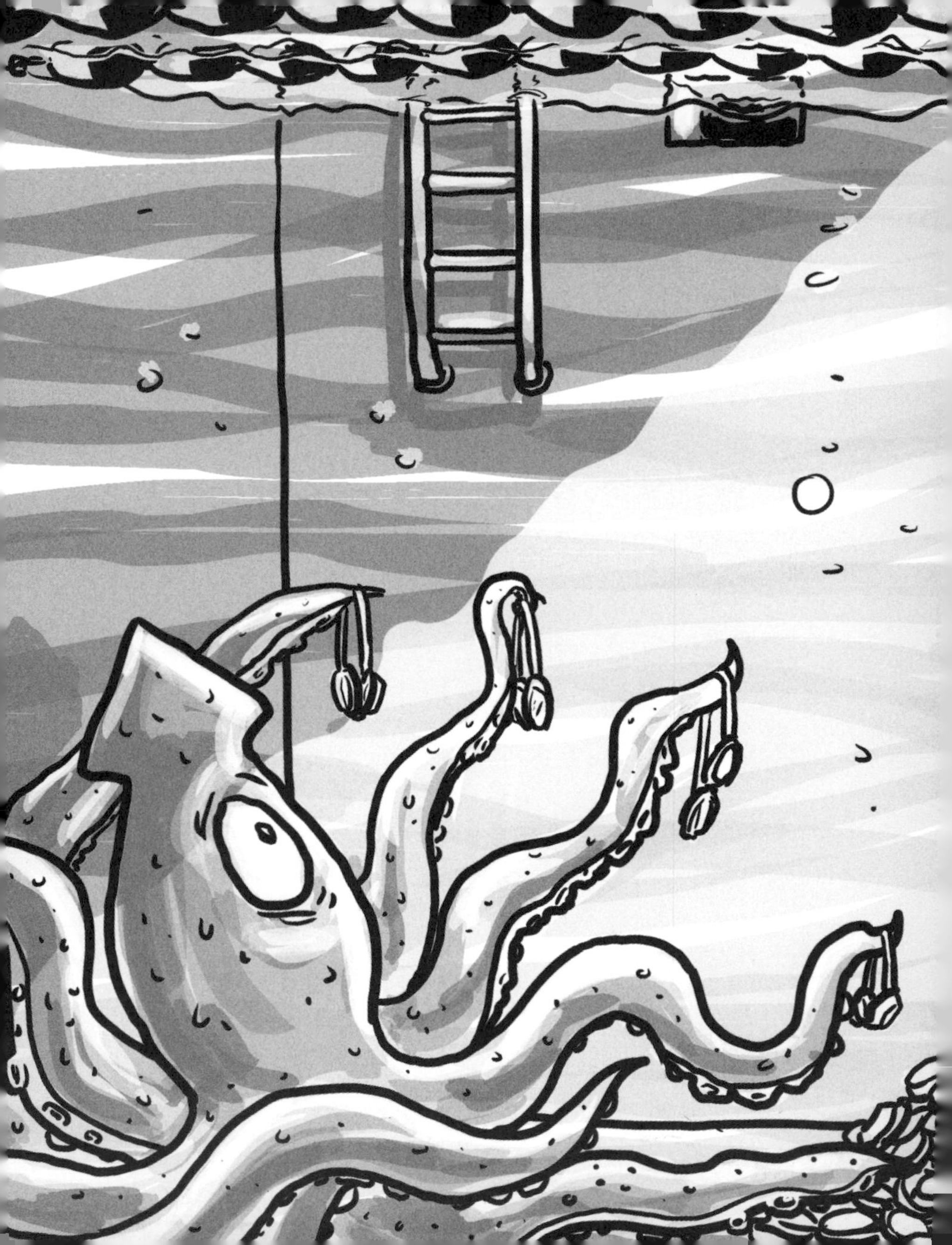

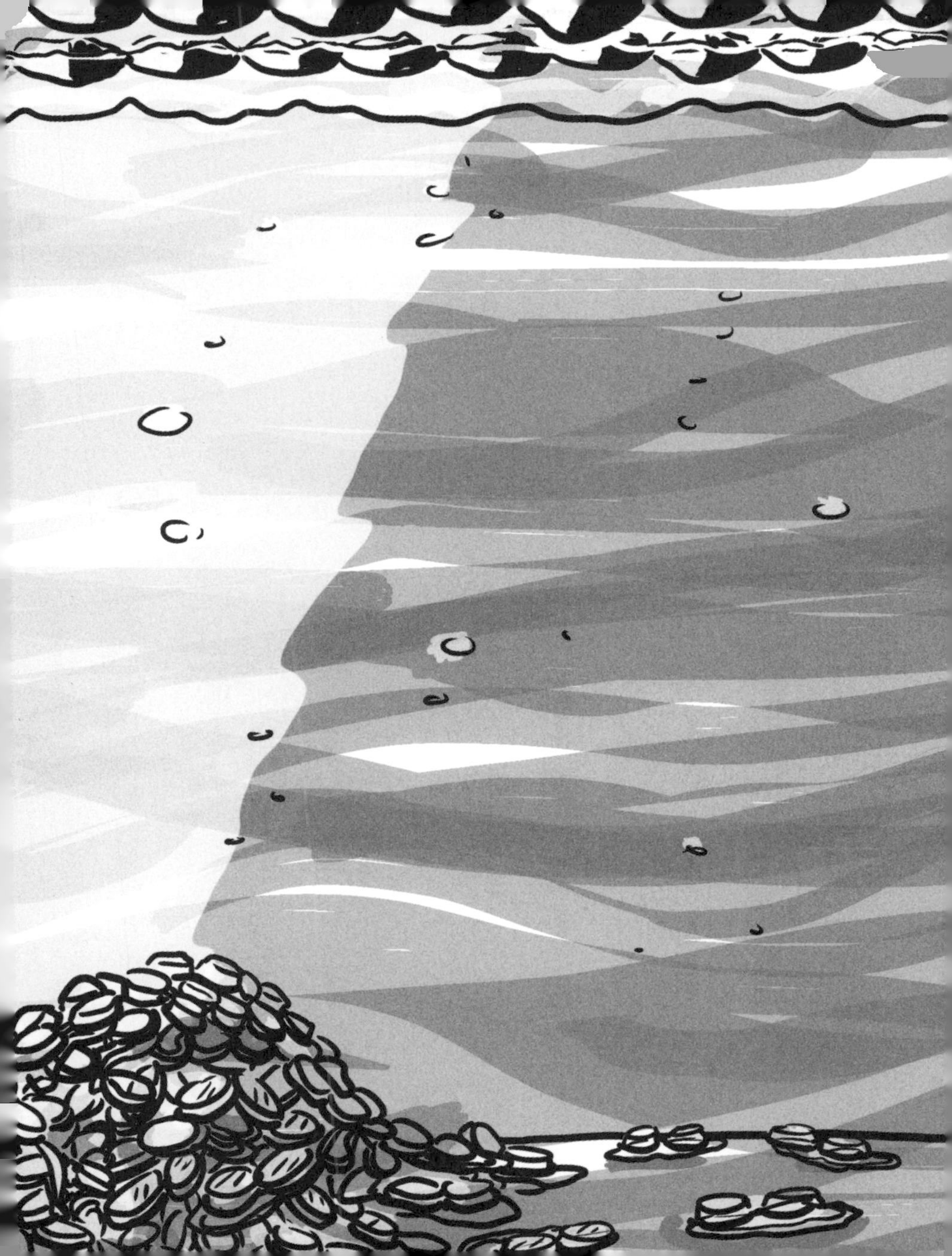

YOU DRAW IT!

CHARACTER: THE SQUID

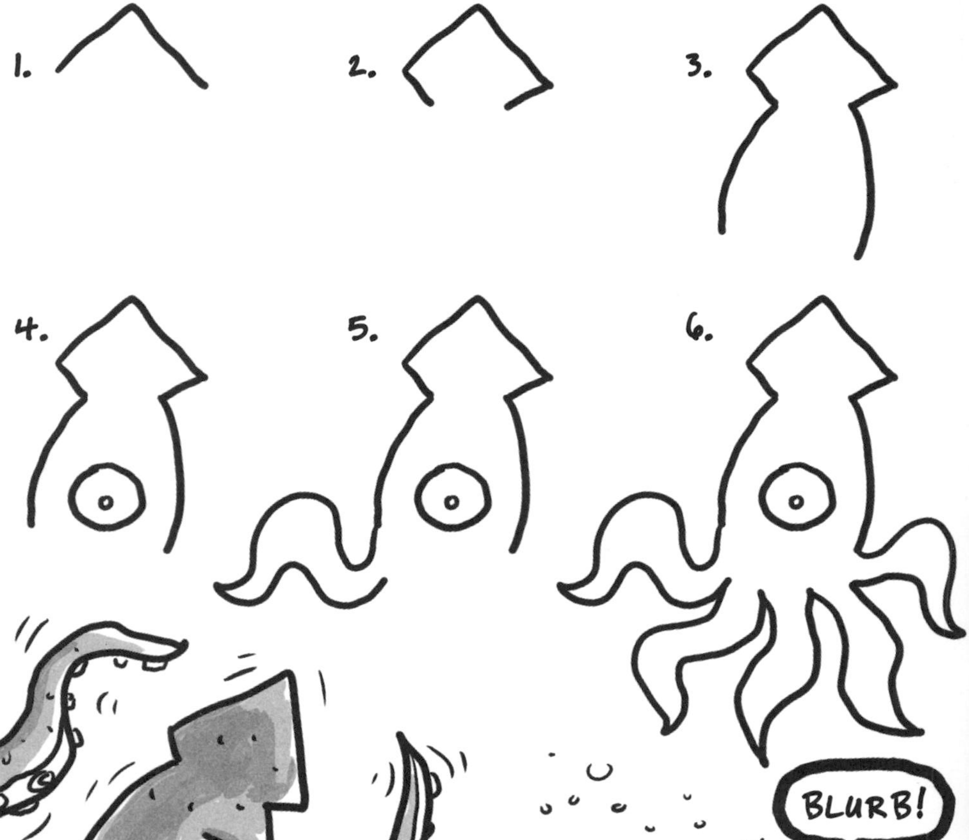
1.
2.
3.
4.
5.
6.

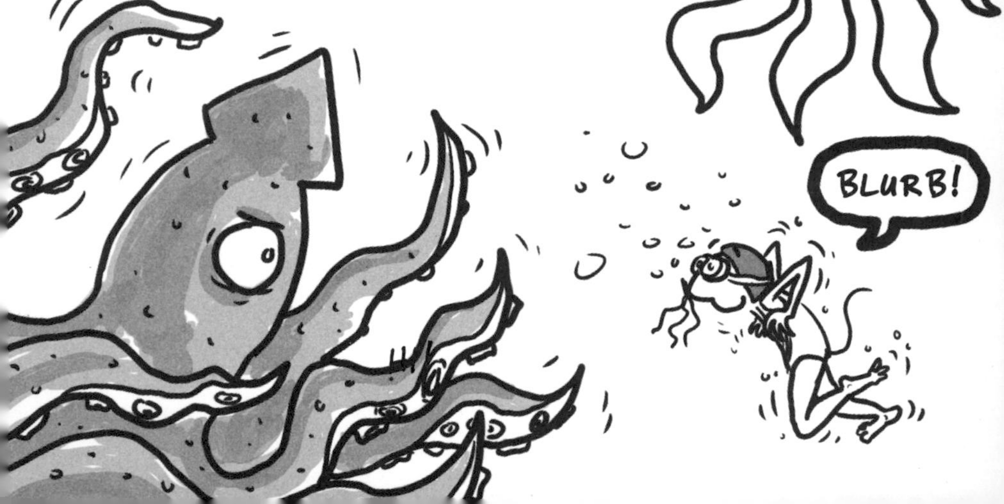
BLURB!

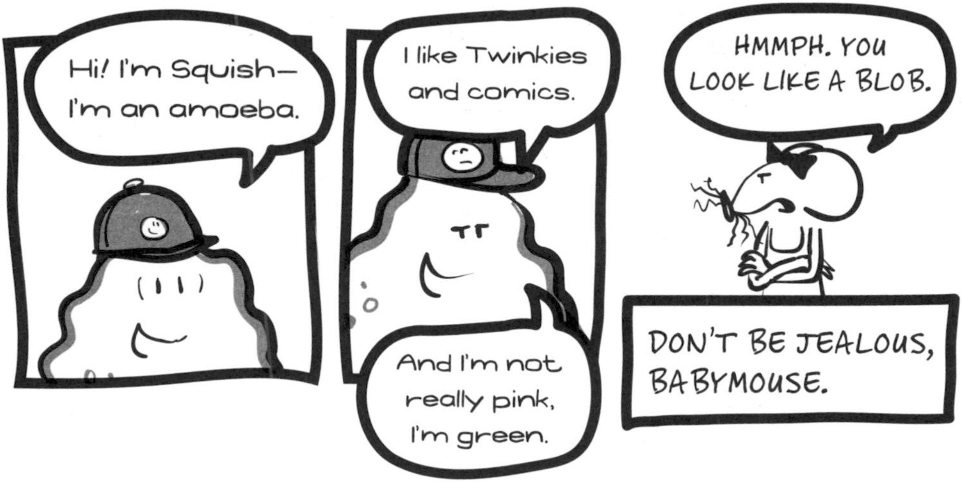
Hi! I'm Squish—
I'm an amoeba.
I like Twinkies
and comics.
And I'm not
really pink,
I'm green.
HMMPH. YOU
LOOK LIKE A BLOB.
DON'T BE JEALOUS,
BABYMOUSE.

READ ABOUT
SQUISH'S AMAZING ADVENTURES IN:

#1 SQUISH: Super Amoeba

#2 SQUISH: Brave New Pond

#3 SQUISH: The Power of the Parasite

#4 SQUISH: Captain Disaster

#5 SQUISH: Game On!

#6 SQUISH: Fear the Amoeba

#7 SQUISH: Deadly Disease of Doom

DO YOU LIKE COMICS? DO YOU LIKE LAUGHING TILL MILK COMES OUT OF YOUR NOSE?

JENNIFER L. HOLM & MATTHEW HOLM
Edited by the creators of BABYMOUSE & LUNCH LADY
GENE LUEN YANG
ERIC WIGHT
URSULA VERNON
LEAP!
COMICS SQUAD
RECESS!
JARRETT J. KROSOCZKA

JARRETT J. KROSOCZKA ★ PEANUTS
Edited by the creators of BABYMOUSE & LUNCH LADY
CECIL CASTELLUCCI & SARA VARON
JASON SHIGA
JEFFREY BROWN
CECE BELL
NATHAN HALE
COMICS SQUAD
LUNCH!
GRRRRRRRRRR
JENNIFER L. HOLM & MATTHEW HOLM

AVAILABLE NOW!

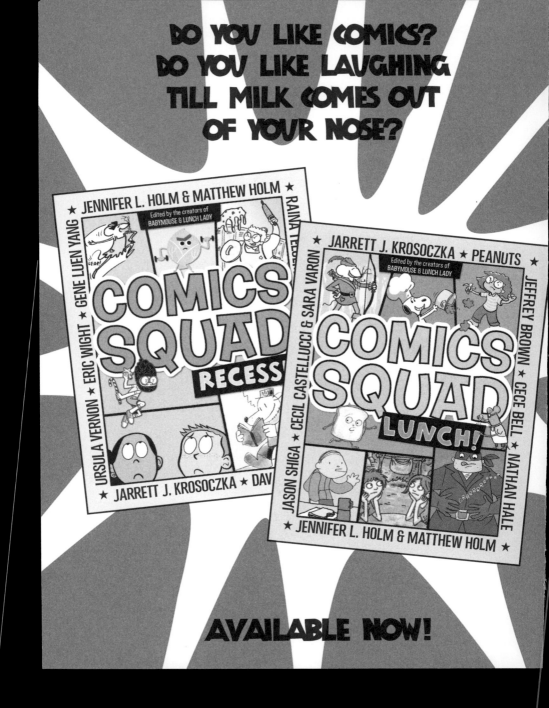